YOUNG BARBARIANS

"What's your name?" (*p* 44).

YOUNG BARBARIANS

Ian Maclaren

CANONGATE · KELPIES

First published 1907 by Hodder and Stoughton, London
First published in Kelpies 1985

Cover illustration by Jill Downie

Printed in Great Britain
by Redwood Burn Ltd, Trowbridge, Wiltshire

ISBN 0 86241 076 2

*The publishers acknowledge the financial assistance
of the Scottish Arts Council in the
publication of this volume*

To
G.A.M. and R.W.R.M.
my friends since the days of boyhood

CANONGATE PUBLISHING LTD
17 JEFFREY STREET, EDINBURGH EH1 1DR

I

" SPEUG "

MUIRTOWN SEMINARY was an imposing
building of the classical order, facing the
north meadow and commanding from its upper
windows a fine view of the River Tay running
rapidly and cleanly upon its gravel bed. Behind the
front building was the paved court where the boys
played casual games in the breaks of five minutes
between the hours of study, and this court had an
entrance from a narrow back street along which, in
snow time, a detachment of the enemy from the
other schools might steal any hour and take us by
disastrous surprise. There were those who wished
that we had been completely walled up at the back,
for then we had met the attack at a greater advantage
from the front. But the braver souls of our commonwealth considered that this back way, affording
opportunities for ambushes, sallies, subtle tactics, and
endless vicissitudes, lent a peculiar flavour to the war
we waged the whole winter through and most of the
summer, and brought it nearer to the condition of
Red Indian fighting, which was our favourite reading

1

and our example of heroism. Again and again we studied the adventures of Bill Biddon, the Indian spy, not only on account of his hairbreadth escapes when he eluded the Indians after a miraculous fashion and detected the presence of the red var-mint by the turning of a leaf on the ground, but also in order to find out new methods of deceit by which we could allure our Indians into narrow places, or daring methods of attack by which we could success-fully outflank them on the broader street and drive them into their own retreats with public ignominy.

Within the building the glory of the Seminary was a massive stone stair, circular in shape, and having a "well" surrounded on the ground floor by a wall some three feet high. Down this stair the masters descended at nine o'clock for the opening of the school, with Bulldog, who was the mathematical master and the awful pride of the school, at their head, and it was strictly forbidden that any boy should be found within the "well." As it was the most tempting of places for the deposit of anything in the shape of rubbish, from Highland bonnets to little boys, and especially as any boy found in the well was sure to be caned, there was an obvious and irresistible opportunity for enterprise. Peter McGuffie, commonly called the Sparrow, or in Scotch tongue "Speug," and one of the two heads of our commonwealth, used to wait with an expres-sion of such demureness that it ought to have been a danger signal till Bulldog was halfway down the stair, and a row of boys were standing in expectation with their backs to the forbidden place. Then, passing swiftly along, he swept off half a dozen caps and threw them over, and suddenly seizing a tempting urchin landed him on the bed of caps which had been duly prepared. Without turning his head one-eighth of an inch, far less condescending to look over, Bulldog as he passed made a mental note of the prisoner's name, and identified the various bonnetless boys, and then, dividing his duty over the hours of the day, attended to each culprit separately and carefully. If any person, from the standpoint of this modern and philanthropic day, should ask why some innocent victim did not state his case and lay the blame upon the guilty, then it is enough to say that that person had never been a scholar at Muirtown Seminary, and has not the slightest knowledge of the character and methods of Peter McGuffie. Had any boy of our time given information to a master, or, in the Scotch tongue, " had clyped," he would have had the coldest reception at the hands of Bulldog, and when his conduct was known to the school he might be assured of such constant and ingenious attention at the hands of Speug that he would have been ready to drown himself in the Tay rather than continue his studies at Muirtown Seminary.

Speug's father was the leading horsedealer of the

Scots Midlands, and a sporting man of established repute, a short, thick-set, red-faced, loud-voiced, clean-shaven man, with hair cut close to his head, whose calves and whose manner were the secret admiration of Muirtown. Quiet citizens of irreproachable respectability and religious orthodoxy regarded him with a pride which they would never confess ; not because they would have spoken or acted as he did for a king's ransom, and not because they would have liked to stand in his shoes when he came to die—considering, as they did, that the future of a horsedealer and an owner of racing horses was dark in the extreme—but because he was a perfect specimen of his kind and had made the town of Muirtown to be known far and wide in sporting circles. Bailie McCallum, for instance, could have no dealings with McGuffie senior, and would have been scandalised had he attended the Bailie's kirk ; but sitting in his shop and watching Muirtown life as it passed, the Bailie used to chuckle after an appreciative fashion at the sight of McGuffie, and to meditate with much inward satisfaction on stories of McGuffie's exploits—how he had encountered southern horsedealers and sent them home humbled with defeat, and had won hopeless races over the length and breadth of the land. " It's an awfu' trade," McCallum used to remark, " and McGuffie is no' the man for an elder ; but sall, naebody ever got the better o' him at a bargain." Among the lads of the Seminary he was a local hero, and on their way home from school they loitered to study him, standing in the gateway of his stables, straddling his legs, chewing a straw, and shouting his views on the Muirtown races to friends at the distance of half a street. When he was in good humour he would nod to the lads and wink to them with such acuteness and drollery that they attempted to perform the same feat all the way home and were filled with despair. It did not matter that we were fed, by careful parents, with books containing the history of good men who began life with 2s. 11d., and died leaving a quarter of a million, made by selling soft goods and attending church, and with other books relating pathetic anecdotes of boys who died young and, before they died, delighted society with observations of the most edifying character on the shortness of life. We had rather have been a horse-dealer and kept a stable.

Most of us regarded McGuffie senior as a model of all the virtues that were worthy of a boy's imitation, and his son with undisguised envy, because he had a father of such undeniable notoriety, because he had the run of the stables, because he was on terms of easy familiarity with his father's grooms, and because he was encouraged to do those things which we were not allowed to do, and never exhorted to do those things which he hated to do. All the good advice we ever got, and all the examples of those two excellent young gentlemen.

the sons of the Rev. Dr. Dowbiggin, were blown
to the winds when we saw Speug pass, sitting
in the high dogcart beside his father, while that
talented man was showing off to Muirtown a newly
broken horse. Speug's position on that seat of
unique dignity was more than human, and none
of us would have dared to recognise him, but it
is only just to add that Peter was quite unspoiled
by his privileges, and would wink to his humble
friends upon the street after his most roguish
fashion and with a skill which proved him his
father's son. Social pride and the love of exclusive
society were not failings either of Mr. McGuffie
senior or of his hopeful son. Both were willing
to fight any person of their own size (or, indeed,
much bigger), as well as to bargain with anybody,
and at any time, about anything, from horses to
marbles.

Mrs. McGuffie had been long dead, and during
her lifetime was a woman of decided character,
whom the grooms regarded with more terror than
they did her husband, and whom her husband
himself treated with great respect, a respect which
grew into unaffected reverence when he was returning from a distant horse-race and was detained,
by professional duties, to a late hour in the evening.
As her afflicted husband refused to marry again,
in decided terms, Peter, their only child, had been
brought up from an early age among grooms and

other people devoted to the care and study of
horses. In this school he received an education
which was perhaps more practical and varied than
finished and polite. It was not to be wondered,
therefore, that his manners were simple and natural
to a degree, and that he was never the prey in
any ordinary circumstances either of timidity or of
modesty. Although a motherless lad, he was never
helpless, and from the first was able to hold his own
and to make his hands keep his head.

His orphan condition excited the compassion of
respectable matrons, but their efforts to tend him
in his loneliness were not always successful, nor
even appreciated to the full by the young McGuffie.
When Mrs. Dowbiggin, who had a deep interest
in what was called the " work among children," and
who got her cabs from McGuffie's stable, took pity
on Peter's unprotected childhood, and invited him
to play with her boys, who were a head taller and
paragons of excellence, the result was unfortunate,
and afforded Mrs. Dowbiggin the text for many
an exhortation. Peter was brought back to the
parental mansion by Dr. Dowbiggin's beadle within
an hour, and received a cordial welcome from a
congregation of grooms, to whom he related his
experiences at the Manse with much detail and
agreeable humour. During the brief space at his
disposal he had put every toy of the Dowbiggins'
in a thorough state of repair, and had blacked their

innocent faces with burnt cork so that their mother
did not recognise her children. He had also taught
them a negro melody of a very taking description,
and had reinforced their vocabulary with the very
cream of the stable. From that day Mrs. Dowbiggin
warned the mothers of Muirtown against allowing
their boys to associate with Speug, and Speug could
never see her pass on the street without an expression
of open delight.

When Mr. McGuffie senior brought his son, being
then ten years old, to the Seminary for admittance,
it was a chance that he was not refused and that
we did not miss our future champion.   Mr. McGuffie's
profession and reputation were a stumbling-block
to the rector, who was a man of austere countenance
and strict habits of life, and Peter himself was a
very odd-looking piece of humanity and had already
established his own record.   He was undersized
and of exceptional breadth, almost flat in countenance, and with beady black eyes which on occasion
lit up his face as when one illuminates the front
of a house, but the occasions were rarely those
which would commend themselves to the headmaster
of a public school.   How the dealer in horses
removed the rector's difficulties was never accurately
known, but boys passing the door of the rector's
retiring-room when he was closeted with Mr. McGuffie
overheard scraps of the conversation, and Muirtown
was able to understand the situation.   It was under-

stood that in a conflict of words the rector, an
absent-minded scholar of shrinking manner, was not
likely to come off best, and it is certain that the
head of the school ever afterwards referred to Mr.
McGuffie as "a man of great resolution of character
and endowed with the gift of forcible speech."
As regards the son, his affectionate father gave
him some brief directions before leaving, and in
the presence of his fellow-scholars, of which this
only was overheard, and seemed, indeed, to be the
sum and substance : " Never give in, ye de'il's
buckie." With these inspiriting words Mr. McGuffie
senior departed through the front door amid a hush
of admiration, leaving Peter to his fate not far
from that " well " which was to be the scene of
many of his future waggeries.

With the progress of civilization school life in
Scotland has taken on a high degree of refinement,
and rumour has it—but what will people not say ?
—that a new boy will come in a cab to the Seminary
and will receive a respectful welcome from the
generation following Peter, and that the whole
school will devote itself to his comfort for days
—showing him where to hang his cap, initiating him
into games, assisting him with his lessons, and treating his feelings with delicate respect. It has been
my own proud satisfaction, as a relic of a former
barbarian age, to read the rules which, I believe,
are now printed in black letters with red capitals

and hung in the rooms of Muirtown Seminary. My feelings will not allow me to give them all, but the following have moved me almost to tears :—

Rule 1.—That every boy attending this school is expected to behave himself in speech and deed as a gentleman.

Rule 2.—That any one writing upon a wall, or in any way marking the school furniture, will be considered to have committed an offence, and will be punished.

Rule 3.—That every boy is exhorted to treat every other with courtesy, and any one guilty of rudeness to a fellow-scholar is to be reported to the headmaster.

Rule 4.—That it is expected of every boy to cultivate neatness of appearance, and especially to see that his clothes, collars, cuffs, and other articles of clothing be not soiled.

These admirable rules suggest a new atmosphere and one very different from that in which we passed our stormy youth, for no sentiment of this kind softened life in earlier days or affected our Spartan simplicity. The very sight of a newcomer in a speckless suit, with an irreproachable tie and both tails on his glengarry bonnet, excited a profound emotion in the school and carried it beyond self-control. What could be expected of a fellow so bedecked and preserved as if he had just stepped out of a bandbox or a tailor's shop? Left alone

in his pride and perfection—the very beginning of
a Pharisee—he would only go from bad to worse
and come at last to a sad end. We hardly claimed
to be philanthropists, but we did feel it was our
duty to rescue this lad. It might be, of course, that
we could not finally save him, but he ought at
least to have a chance, and Speug had a quite
peculiar satisfaction in at once removing the two
offensive tails by one vigorous pull, while the rump-
ling of a collar was a work of missionary zeal. No
system of philanthropy is successful with all cases,
and we had our failures, which we think about
unto this day, and which have only justified our
sad predictions. Boys like the two Dowbiggins never
improved, and were at last given up in despair
even by Speug, their tails being renewed day by
day and their faces remaining in all circumstances
quite unmoved ; but within a month the average boy
had laid aside the last remnant of conventionality,
and was only outdone by Peter himself in studied
negligence of attire.

Peter's own course of discipline was sharp, but it
did not last long, for certain practical reasons.

"What business have you here, ye son of a horse-
couper ? " was the encouraging salutation offered by
a solicitor's son to the stumpy little figure bereft of
its father and left to fight its battles alone.

"Mair business than you, spindleshanks, ye son o'
a thievin' lawyer," and although Peter was four years

younger and small for his age, he showed that he
had not learned boxing from his father's grooms
without profit, and his opponent attended no more
classes that day. This encounter excited the deepest
interest and revived the whole life of the school.
One lad after another experimented on Peter and
made as much of it as drawing a badger. He was
often hurt, but he never uttered any cry. He gave
rather more than he got, and lads going home in the
afternoon could see him giving an account of the
studies of the day to an admiring audience in the
stableyard. By-and-by he was left severely alone,
and for the impudence of him, and his courage, and
his endurance, and his general cockiness, and his
extraordinary ingenuity in mischief, he was called
"Speug," which is Scotch for a sparrow, and figura-
tively expressed the admiration of the school.

It would be brazen falsehood to say that Peter
was a scholar, or, indeed, gave any voluntary attention to the course of learning laid down by the
authorities of Muirtown Seminary. He sat unashamed
at the foot of every class, maintaining a certain
impenetrable front when a question came his length,
and with the instinct of a chieftain never risking
his position in the school by exposing himself to
contempt. When Thomas John Dowbiggin was dis-
tinguishing himself after an unholy fashion by trans-
lating Cæsar into English like unto Macaulay's
History, Speug used to watch him with keen interest,

and employ his leisure time in arranging some little surprise to enliven the even tenor of Thomas John's life. So curious a being, however, is a boy, and so inconsistent, that as often as Duncan Robertson answered more promptly than Thomas John, and obtained the first place, Speug's face lit up with unaffected delight, and he was even known to smack his lips audibly. When the rector's back was turned he would convey his satisfaction over Thomas John's discomfiture with such delightful pantomine that the united class did him homage, and even Thomas John was shaken out of his equanimity ; but then Duncan Robertson's father was colonel of a Highland regiment, and Duncan himself was a royal fighter, and had not in his Highland body the faintest trace of a prig, while Thomas John's face was a standing reproof of everything that was said and done outside of lesson time in Muirtown School.

Peter, however, had his own genius, and for captivating adventures none was to be compared with him. Was it not Speug who floated down the tunnel through which a swift running stream of clean water reached the Tay, and allured six others to follow him, none of whom, happily, were drowned ? and did not the whole school with the exception of the Dowbiggins, await his exit at the black mouth of the tunnel and reward his success with a cheer ? Was it not Speug, with Duncan Robertson's military assistance, who constructed a large earthwork in a pit at the top of the Meadow, which was called the Redan and was blown up with gunpowder one Saturday afternoon, seven boys being temporarily buried beneath the ruins, and Peter himself losing both eyebrows? And when an old lady living next the school laid a vicious complaint against Speug and some other genial spirits for having broken one of her windows in a snowball fight, he made no sign and uttered no threat, but in the following autumn he was in a position to afford a ripe pear to each boy in the four upper forms—except the Dowbiggins, who declined politely—and to distribute a handful for a scramble among the little boys. There was much curiosity about the source of Peter's generosity, and it certainly was remarkable that the pear was of the same kind as the old lady cultivated with much pride, and that her fruit was gathered for her in the course of one dark night. Speug was capable of anything except telling a lie. He could swim the Tay at its broadest and almost at its swiftest, could ride any horse in his father's stable, could climb any tree in the meadows, and hold his own in every game, from marbles and "catch the keggie," a game based on smuggling, to football, where he was a very dangerous forward, and cricket, where his batting was fearsome for its force and obstinacy. There was nothing he could not do with his hands, and no one whom he was not ready to face.

Speug was a very vigorous barbarian indeed, and

the exact type of a turbulent Lowland Scot, without whom the Seminary had missed its life and colour, and who by sheer force of courage and strength asserted himself as our chief captain. After many years have passed, Speug stands out a figure of size and reality from among the Dowbiggins and other poor fleeting shadows. Thomas John, no doubt, carried off medals, prizes, certificates of merit, and everything else which could be obtained in Muirtown Seminary by a lad who played no games and swatted all evening at next day's work. The town was weary of seeing Thomas John and his brother—each wearing the same smug expression, and each in faultlessly neat attire—processing up in turn to receive their honours from the hands of the Lord Provost, and the town would cheer with enthusiasm when Duncan Robertson made an occasional appearance, being glad to escape from the oppression of the Dowbiggin *régime*. Nor was the town altogether wrong in refusing to appreciate the Dowbiggins at their own value, and declining to believe that the strength of the country was after their fashion. When Thomas John reached the University he did not altogether fulfil the expectations of his family, and by the time he reached the pulpit no one could endure his unredeemed dulness. When last I heard of him he was secretary to a blameless society which has for its object the discovery of the lost Ten Tribes, and it occurs to me that it would have been a good thing for Thomas John to have been blown up in the destruction of the Redan : he might have become a man.

After the Seminary had done its best for Speug he retired upon his laurels and went to assist his father in the business of horsedealing, to which he brought an invincible courage and a large experience in bargaining. For years his old fellow-scholars saw him breaking in young horses on the roads round Muirtown, and he covered himself with glory in a steeplechase open to all the riders of Scotland. When Mr. McGuffie senior was killed by an Irish mare, Peter sold the establishment and went into foreign parts in search of adventure, reappearing at intervals of five years from Australia, Texas, the Plate, Cape of Good Hope, assured and reckless as ever, but always straightforward, masterful, openhanded, and gallant. His exploits are over now, and all England read his last, how he sent on in safety a settler's household through a narrow pass in Matabele Land, and with a handful of troopers held the savages in check until pursuit was vain.

"From the account of prisoners we learn," wrote the war correspondent, "that Captain McGuffie, of the Volunteer Horse, fought on after his men had been all killed and his last cartridge fired. With his back to a rock in a narrow place he defended himself with such skill and courage that the Matabele declared him the best fighting man they had ever met, and he was found with a mound of dead at his feet." Only last week two Seminary men were reading that account together and recalling Peter, and such is the inherent wickedness of human nature, that the death (from apoplexy) of Thomas John Dowbiggin would have been much less lamented. "That is just how Speug would have liked to die, for he dearly loved a fight and knew not fear." They revived the ancient memories of Peter's boyhood, and read the despatch of the commanding officer, with his reference to the gallant service of Captain McGuffie, and then they looked at Peter's likeness in the illustrated papers, the eyes as bold and mischievous as ever. "Well done, Speug!" said a doctor of divinity—may he be forgiven!—"well done, Speug, a terrier of the old Scots breed."

Peter's one rival in the idolatry of the school was Duncan Ronald Stewart Robertson, commonly known as Dunc, and Dunc was in everything except honesty, generosity, and courage, the exact opposite of Peter McGuffie. Robertson's ancestors had been lairds of Tomnahurich, a moor in Rannoch, with half a dozen farms, since the Deluge, as they believed, and certainly since history began. For hundreds of years they had been warriors, fighting other clans, fighting among themselves, fighting for Prince Charlie, and for more than a century fighting for England as officers in the Highland regiments. The present laird had been in the Crimean war and

the Mutiny, besides occasional expeditions, and was
colonel of the Perthshire Buffs. When he came to
our examination in full uniform, having first inspected
the local garrison on the meadow, it was the greatest
day in our time. We cheered him when he came in,
counting the medals on his breast, amidst which we
failed not to notice the Victoria Cross. We cheered
him in the class-rooms, we cheered him when he
mounted his horse outside and rode along the
terrace, and Peter led a detachment by the back way
up to Breadalbane Street to give him one cheer more.
Robertson was a tall, well-knit, athletic lad, with red
hair, blue eyes, and a freckled face, not handsome,
but carrying himself with much dignity and grace.
Speug always appeared in tight-fitting trousers,
as became Mr. McGuffie's son, but Robertson
wore the kilt and never looked anything else but a
gentleman, yet his kilt was ever of the shabbiest, and
neither had his bonnet any tails. His manners were
those of his blood, but a freer and heartier and more
harum-scarum fellow never lived. It is a pleasant
remembrance, after many years, to see again a group
of lads round the big fire in the winter time, and
to hear Duncan Robertson read the stirring ballad,
" How Horatius kept the bridge in the brave days of
old," till Peter can contain himself no longer, and
proposes that a select band shall go instantly to
McIntyre's Academy and simply compel a conflict.
Dunc went into his father's regiment and fell at

Tel-el-Kebir, and there is one Seminary man at least who keeps the portraits of the two captains— Peter McGuffie, the Scot, the horsedealer's son, and a very vulgar varlet indeed, and Duncan Robertson, the Celt, a well-born man's son, and a gentleman himself from head to foot—in remembrance of a school which was rough and old-fashioned, where, indeed, softness and luxury were impossible, but where men were made who had the heart in them to live and die for their country.

II

BULLDOG

THE headmaster of a certain great English school is accustomed to enlarge in private on the secret of boy management, and this is the sum of his wisdom—Be kind to the boy, and he will despise you ; put your foot on his neck, and he will worship you. This deliverance must, of course, as its eminent author intends, be read with sense, and with any modification it must be disappointing to philanthropists, but it is confirmed by life. Let a master, not very strong in character and scholarship, lay himself out to be a boy's friend—using affectionate language, overseeing his health, letting him off impositions, sparing the rod, and inciting him to general benevolence—and the boy will respond, without any doubt, but it will be after his own fashion. The boy will take that master's measure with extraordinary rapidity ; he will call him by some disparaging nickname, with an unholy approximation to truth ; he will concoct tricky questions to detect his ignorance ; he will fling back his benefits with contempt ; he will make his life a misery, and will despise him as long as he lives. Let a man of masculine character and evident ability set himself to rule and drill boys, holding no unnecessary converse with them, working them to the height of their powers, insisting on the work being done, not fearing to punish with severity using terrible language on occasion, dealing with every boy alike without favour or partiality, giving rare praise with enthusiasm, and refraining always from mocking sarcasm—which boys hate and never forgive—and he will have his reward. They will rage against him in groups on the playing-fields and as they go home in companies, but ever with an intense appreciation of his masterliness; they will recall with keen enjoyment his detection of sneaks and his severity on prigs; they will invent a name for him to enshrine his achievements, and pass it down to the generation following; they will dog his steps on the street with admiration, all the truer because mingled with awe. And the very thrashings of such a man will be worth the having, and become the subject of boasting in after years.

There was a master once in Muirtown Seminary whose career was short and inglorious, as well as very disappointing to those who believed in the goodness of the boy. Mr. Byles explained to Mrs. Dowbiggin his idea of a schoolmaster's duty, and won the heart of that estimable person, although the Doctor maintained an instructive silence, and afterwards hinted to his spouse that Mr. Byles had not quite grasped the boy nature, at least in Muirtown.

"Yes, Mrs. Dowbiggin, I have always had a love for boys—for I was the youngest of our family, and the rest were girls—seven dear girls, gentle and sweet. They taught me sympathy. And don't you think that boys, as well as older people, are ruled by kindness and not by force? When I remember how I was treated, I feel this is how other boys would wish to be treated. Muffins? Buttered, if you please. I dote on muffins! So I am a school-master."

"You are needed at the Seminary, Mr. Byles, I can tell you, for the place is just a den of savages! Will you believe me, that a boy rolled James on the ground till he was like a clay cat yesterday—and James is so particular about being neat!—and when I complained to Mr. MacKinnon, he laughed in my face and told me that it would do the laddie good? There's a master for you! Thomas John tells me that he is called 'Bulldog,' and although I don't approve of disrespect, I must say it is an excellent name for Mr. MacKinnon. And I've often said to the Doctor, 'If the masters are like that, what can you expect of the boys?'"

"Let us hope, Mrs. Dowbiggin, that there will soon be some improvement; and it will not be my fault if there isn't. What I want to be is not a master, but the boys' friend, to whom the boys will feel as to a mother, to whom they will confide their difficulties and trials," and Mr. Byles' face had a soft, tender, far-away look.

It was only for one winter that he carried on his mission, but it remains a green and delectable memory with old boys of the Seminary. How he would not use the cane, because it brutalized boys, as he explained, but kept Peter McGuffie in for an hour, during which time he remonstrated with Peter for his rude treatment of James Dowbiggin, whom he had capsized over a form, and how Peter's delighted compatriots climbed up one by one to the window and viewed him under Mr. Byles' ministrations with keen delight, while Speug intimated to them by signs that they would have to pay handsomely for their treat. How he would come on Jock Howieson going home in a heavy rain, and ostentatiously refusing even to button his coat, and would insist on affording him the shelter of an umbrella, to Jock's intense humiliation, who knew that Peter was following with derisive criticism. How, by way of conciliation, Mr. Byles would carry sweets in his coat-tail pocket and offer them at unsuitable times to the leading anarchists, who regarded this imbecility as the last insult. It is now agreed that Mr. Byles' sudden resignation was largely due to an engineering feat of Peter's, who had many outrages to avenge, and succeeded in attaching no less than

three squibs to the good man's desk ; but it is likely
that an exhortation from Bulldog, overheard by the
delighted school, had its due effect.

" Humanity or no humanity, my man, it's no
peppermint drops nor pats on the head that'll rule
Muirtown birkies ; their fathers were brought up on
the stick, and the stick'll make the sons men. If
ye'll take my advice, Mr. Byles, adverteese for a
situation in a lassies' school. Ye're ower dainty for
Muirtown Seminary."

This was not a charge which his worst enemy
could bring against Mr. Dugald MacKinnon, and
because he was the very opposite—a most unflinch-
ing, resolute, iron man—he engraved himself on the
hearts of three generations of Muirtown men. They
were a dour, hard-headed, enterprising lot—a blend
from the upland braes of Drumtochty and the stiff
carse of Gowrie and the Celts of Loch Tay, with some
good south country stuff—and there are not many
big cities on either side of the Atlantic where two or
three Muirtown men cannot this day be found.
They always carry in their hearts the " Fair City "—
which lieth in a basin among the hills, beside the
clean, swift-running river, like a Scots Florence ; and
they grow almost eloquent when they start upon
their home, but the terminus of recollection is ever
the same. When they have dallied with the swimming in the Tay, and the climbing of the hill which
looks down on the fair plain as far as Dundee, and

the golf on the meadows, and the mighty snow fights in days where there were men (that is, boys) in the land, and memory is fairly awake, some one suddenly says, " Bulldog." " Ah !" cries another, with long-drawn pleasure, as one tasting a delicate liquor ; and " Bulldog," repeats the third, as if a world of joy lay in the word. They rest for a minute, bracing themselves, and then conversation really begins, and being excited, they drop into the Scots tongue.

" Man," hurries in the first, " a' see him stannin' at his desk in the mornin' watchin' the laddies comin' in ower the top o' his spectacles, an' juist considerin' wha wud be the better o' a bit thrashin' that day."

" Sax feet high gin he wes an inch," bursts in the second, " an' as straight as a rush, though a'm thinkin' he wes seventy, or maybe eighty, some threipit (insisted) he was near ninety ; an' the een o' him—div ye mind, lads, hoo they gied back an' forward in his head—oscillatin' like ?   Sall, they were fearsome."

" An' the rush to get in afore the last stroke o' nine "—the third man cannot be restrained—" an' the crack o' his cane on the desk an' 'Silence ' ; man, ye micht hae heard a moose cross the floor at the prayer."

" Div ye think he keekit oot atween his eyelids, Jock ? "

" Him ? nae fear o't," and Howieson is full of contempt. " Ae day I pit a peen into that smooth-faced wratch Dowbiggin, juist because I cudna bear

the look o' him ; an' if he didna squeal like a stuck
pig. Did Bulldog open his een an' look?"

The audience has no remembrance of such a
humiliating descent.

"Na, na," resumes Jock, "he didna need ; he juist
repeated the first sentence o' the prayer ower again
in an awfu' voice, an' aifter it wes dune, doon he comes
to me. 'Whatna prank wes that?'"

"Wes't nippy?" inquires Bauldie with relish, anticipating the sequel.

"Michty," replies Jock ; "an' next he taks Dowbiggin. 'Who asked you to join in the prayer?' an'
ye cud hae heard his yowls on the street. Bulldog
hed a fine stroke." And the three smoked in silent
admiration for a space.

"Sandie, div ye mind the sins in the prayer? 'Lord
deliver the laddies before Thee from lying——'"

"'Cheating,'" breaks in Bauldie.

"'Cowardice,'" adds Sandie.

"'And laziness, which are as the devil,'" completes
Jock.

"An' the laist petition, a' likit it fine, 'Be pleased
to put common sense in their heads, and Thy fear in
their hearts, and——'"

"'Give them grace to be honest men all the days
of their life,'" chant the other two together.

"It wes a purpose-like prayer, an' a' never heard a
better, lads ; he walkit up to his words, did Bulldog,
an' he did his wark well." And as they thought of

that iron age, the railway president and the big banker
and the corn merchant—for that is what the fellows
have come to—smack their lips with relish and
kindly regret.

It may be disappointing, but it remains a fact, that
the human history of the ages is repeated in the
individual, and the natural boy is a savage, with the
aboriginal love of sport, hardy indifference to circumstances, stoical concealment of feelings, irrepressible
passion for fighting, unfeigned admiration for strength,
and slavish respect for the strong man. By-and-by
he will be civilized and Christianized, and settle down,
will become considerate, merciful, peaceable—will be
concerned about his own boys having wet feet, and
will preside at meetings for the prevention of cruelty
to animals ; but he has to go through his process of
barbarism. During this Red Indian stage a philanthropist is not the ideal of the boy. His master must
have the qualities of a brigand chief, an autocratic
will, a fearless mien, and an iron hand. On the first
symptom of mutiny he must draw a pistol from his
belt (one of twenty), and shoot the audacious rebel
dead on the spot. So perfectly did Bulldog fulfil
this ideal that Bauldie, who had an unholy turn for
caricature, once drew him in the costume and arms
of Chipanwhackewa, an Indian chief of prodigious
valour and marvellous exploits. This likeness was
passed from hand to hand, to be arrested and confis-
cated by its subject when in Jock Howieson's posses-

sion, and although Jock paid the penalty, as was most due, yet it was believed that Bulldog was much pleased by the tribute, and that he kept the picture in his desk.

His achievements in his own field, which extended from the supervision of handwriting to instruction in mathematics, were sustained and marvellous. When a boy was committed to his care at or about the age of eight, before which age he attended a girls' school and fed his imagination on what was in store for him under Bulldog, the great man wrote at the head of his copybook, in full text and something better than copper-plate, " He that spareth his rod hateth his son." With this animating sentiment the neophyte made a fearful beginning, and his master assisted him to transcribe it for years to come through half text and small text, till he could accomplish it with such delicate up-strokes and massive down-strokes, such fine curves and calculated distances, that the writing could hardly be distinguished from the origi-nal, and might be exhibited to the Lord Provost and bailies at the annual examination. It is said now that no school of any name in the land would con-descend to teach writing, and that boys coming from such high places can compass their own signatures with difficulty, and are quite illegible after a gentle-manly fashion ; but it was otherwise in one old grammar school. So famous was the caligraphy pro-duced at the Seminary, that Muirtown bankers, lawyers, and other great personages used to drop in of an afternoon, and having snuffed with the master would go over the copybooks and pick out suitable lads for their offices. And it is a solemn fact that one enterprising Muirtown clerk went up to London without a single introduction, and obtained a situation in the great firm of Brancker, Copleston, Goldbeater & Co., on the strength of a letter and sheet of figures he sent to old Fyler, the manager, whose reason was giving way under the scrawling of the junior clerks. Bulldog considered that his pupils' handwriting steadily deteriorated from the day of their departure. When they came to see him at school from Glasgow, London, and beyond the sea, as they all did, on their visits to Muirtown, besides giving them an affectionate welcome, which began at the door and ended at the desk, he never failed to produce their letters and point out the decadence in careful detail, while the school rejoiced greatly.

Any lad who showed some aptitude, or whose father insisted on the higher education, was allured into geometry and raised to the dignity of the blackboard, where he did his work in face of the school with fear and trembling. This was public life, and carried extremes of honour and disgrace. When Willie Pirie appeared at the board—who is now a Cambridge don of such awful learning that his juniors, themselves distinguished persons, can only imagine where he is in pure mathematics—the school, by tacit permission, suspended operations to see the performance. As Willie progressed, throwing in an angle here and a circle there, and utilising half the alphabet for signs, while he maintained the reasoning from point to point in his high, shrill voice, Bulldog stood a pace aside, a pointer in one hand and in the other a cloth with which at a time he would wipe his forehead till it was white with chalk, and his visage was glorious to behold. When the end came, Bulldog would seize the word out of Pirie's mouth and shout, " Q.E.D., Q . . . E . . . D. Splendid. Did ye follow that, laddies?" taking snuff profusely, with the cloth under one arm and the pointer under the other. " William Pirie, ye'll be a wrangler if ye hae grace o' continuance. Splendid!"

It was otherwise when Jock Howieson tried to indicate the nature of an isosceles triangle and confused it with a square, supporting his artistic efforts with remarks which reduced all the axioms of Euclid to one general ruin. For a while the master explained and corrected, then he took refuge in an ominous silence, after which, at each new development, he played on Jock with the pointer, till Jock, seeing him make for the cane, modestly withdrew, but did not reach his place of retreat without assistance and much plain truth.

" It's a shame to take any fee from your father, Jock Howieson, and it's little use trying to give ye any education. Ye've the thickest head and the least sense in all the schule. Man, they should take you home and set ye on eggs to bring out chickens ; ye micht manage that wi' care. The first three propositions, Jock, before ye leave this room, without a slip, or *ma certes* !" and Jock understood that if he misused his time his instructor would make good use of his.

It was Bulldog's way to promenade the empty schoolroom for ten minutes before the reassembling at two, and it was rare indeed that a boy should be late. When one afternoon there were only nineteen present and forty-three absent, he could only look at Dowbiggin, and when that exemplary youth explained that the school had gone up to the top of the Meadow for a bathe, and suggested they were still enjoying themselves, Bulldog was much lifted.

"Bathing is a healthy exercise, and excellent for the mind, but it's necessary to bring a glow to the skin aifterwards, or there micht be a chill," and he searched out and felt a superior cane kept for the treatment of truants and other grievous offenders.

It was exactly 2.15 when the door opened and a procession of forty-two entered panting and breathless, headed by Dunc Robertson, who carried his head erect, with a light in his eye, and closed by Peter, whose hair was like unto that of a drowned rat, and whose unconcealed desire was for obscurity. The nineteen could only smack their lips with expectation and indicate by signs the treat awaiting their comrades.

"I've had chairge of the departments of writing. arithmetic, and mathematics in the Muirtown Seminary," began Bulldog, "for fifty-five years laist Martinmas, and near eighteen hundred laddies hae passed through my hands. Some o' them were gude and some were bad "—Mr. MacKinnon spoke with a judicial calmness that was awful—" some were yir grandfathers, some were yir fathers ; but such a set of impudent, brazen-faced little scoundrels——" Then his composure failed him as he looked at the benches. "What have ye got to say for yirselves for it will be three weeks afore I'm over ye all ? "

For a while no one moved, and then Dunc Robertson rose in his place and made speech for his fellows like a gentleman's son.

"We are sorry for being late, sir, but it was not our blame ; we had been bathing in the golfers' pool, and were dressing to run down to school in good time. Little Nestie—I mean Ernest Molyneux, sir— had stayed in a little longer, and some one cried, ' Nestie's drowning ! ' and there the little chap was, being carried away by the current."

" Is ' Nestie '—drowned ? " and they all noticed the break in Bulldog's voice, and remembered that if he showed indulgence to any one, it was to the little English lad that had appeared in Muirtown life as one out of due place.

" No, sir, Nestie's safe, and some women have taken him home ; but he was very nearly gone," and Dunc was plainly shaken. " He's a good wee man, and—and it would have been terrible to see him die before our eyes."

" Who saved Nestie ? " Bulldog's face was white, and Jock swore afterwards the tears were in his eyes, but that we did not believe.

" It was one of the boys, sir, "—Robertson's voice was very proud—" and it was a gallant deed ; but I can't give his name, because he made me promise not to tell."

The master looked round the school, and there was a flush on his cheek.

" John Howieson," with a voice that knew no refusal, and Jock stood in his place.

" Give me the laddie's name who savit Nestie."

" It was Speug, sir, an'—it wes michty ; but a' wudna hae telt had ye no askit, an'—it's no my blame," and Jock cast a deprecatory glance where Peter was striving to hide himself behind a slate.

" Peter McGuffie, come out this moment," and Peter, who had obeyed this order in other circumstances with an immovable countenance, now presented the face of one who had broken a till.

" Tell the story, Duncan Robertson, every word of it, that each laddie in this room may remember it as lang as he lives."

" We had nearly all dressed, and some of us

had started for school . . . and when I got back McGuffie had jumped and was out in the current waiting for Nestie to come up. We saw his face at last, white on the water, and shouted to Peter, and . . . he had him in a minute, and . . . made for shore; big swimming, sir; not one of us could have done it except himself. A salmon-fisher showed us how to rub Nestie till he came round, and . . . he smiled to us, and said, 'I'm all right; sorry to trouble you chaps.' Then we ran down as hard as we could lick, and . . . that's all, sir."

"Ye're a leear, Duncan Robertson," suddenly broke out Speug, goaded beyond endurance; "ye helpit oot Nestie yirsell, an' ye're . . . as muckle tae blame as me."

"All I did, sir"—and Robertson's face was burning red—"was to meet Peter and take Nestie off his hands quite near the bank; he had the danger; I . . . did nothing—was too late, in fact, to be of use."

Speug might have contested this barefaced attempt at exculpation, but Bulldog was himself again and gripped the reins of authority.

"Silence!" and his emotion found vent in thunder; "no arguing in my presence. You're an impudent fellow, Peter McGuffie, and have been all your days, the most troublesome, mischievous, upsetting laddie in Muirtown School," and the culprit's whole mien was that of a dog with a bad conscience.

"Ye've fought with your fists, and ye've fought

with snowballs ; ye've played truant times without
number ; and as for your tricks in school, they're
beyond knowledge.   And now ye must needs put the
capper on the concern wi' this business !

"There's no use denying it, Peter, for the evidence
is plain"—and now Bulldog began to speak with
great deliberation. "Ye saw a little laddie out of
his depth and likely to be drowned." (Peter dared
not lift his head this time ; it was going to be a bad
case.)

"Ye micht have given the alarm and got the
salmon-fishers, but, instead of acting like ony quiet,
decent, well-brought-up laddie, and walking down to
the school in time for the geometry" (the school believed that the master's eye rested on William Dowbiggin), "ye jumped clothes and all into the Tay."
(There was evidently no extenuating feature, and
Peter's expression was hopeless.)

"Nor was that all. But the wicked speerit that's
in ye, Peter McGuffie, made ye swim out where the
river was running strongest and an able-bodied man
wouldna care to go. And what for did ye forget
yirsel and risk yir life?"   But for the first time
there was no bravery left in Peter to answer ; his
wickedness was beyond excuse, as he now felt.

"Just to save an orphan laddie frae a watery death.
And ye did it, Peter ; an' it . . . beats a'thing
ye've dune since ye came into Muirtown Academy .
As for you, Duncan Robertson, ye may say what ye

like, but it's my opinion that ye're no one grain better. Peter got in first, for he's a perfect genius for mischief—he's aye on the spot—but ye were after him as soon as ye could—you're art and part, baith o' ye, in the exploit." It was clear now that Dunc was in the same condemnation and would share the same reward ; whereat Peter's heart was lifted, for Robertson's treachery cried to Heaven for judgment.

"Boys of Muirtown, do you see those tablets ? " —and Bulldog pointed to the lists in gold of the former pupils who had distinguished themselves over the world—prizemen, soldiers, travellers, writers, preachers, lawyers, doctors. "It's a grand roll, and an honour to have a place in it, and there are two new names to be added.

"Laddies"—and Bulldog came down from his desk and stood opposite the culprits, whose one wish was that the floor might open beneath them and swallow them up—"you are the sons of men, and I knew you had the beginnings of men in you. I am proud . . . to shake hands with you, and to be . . . your master. Be off this instant, run like mad to yir homes and change yir clothes, and be back inside half an hour, or it will be the worse for ye! And, look ye here, I would like to know . . . how Nestie is."

His walk through the room was always full of majesty, but on that day it passed imagination, and from time to time he could be heard in a soliloquy. "A pair of young rascals ! Men of their hands, though, men of their hands! Their fathers' sons! Well done, Peter!" To which the benches listened with awe, for never had they known Bulldog after this fashion.

When the school assembled next Monday morning the boys read in fresh, shining letters—

"PETER MCGUFFIE and DUNCAN R. S. ROBERT-SON, who at the risk of their own lives saved a schoolfellow from drowning."

It stood before the school, so that all could see; but if any one dared to make a sign in that direction as he passed Speug's desk, his life was not worth living for seven days, and it was felt that Speug never completely recovered from the moral disgrace of that day.

III

NESTIE

IT was understood that Nestie's mother was dead and that his father was the Baptist minister of Muirtown—a denomination whose adherents were few and whose practices were vaguely associated with the mill lade—and for two years before he appeared at school Nestie and his father were quite familiar to the boys. Nestie began his education at a ladies' school, not far from the Seminary, where he was much petted by the big girls, and his father could be seen waiting for him every afternoon at dismissal time. A gentle timid little man, apt to blush on being spoken to, with a hesitating speech and a suggestion of lasting sorrow in his eyes, Mr. Molyneux would sooner have faced a cannon than Miss Letitia MacMuldrow's bevy of young women, and it was a simple fact that when, meditating his sermon one day in the North Meadow, he flopped into their midst, and his son insisted on introducing him to the boarders and to Miss Letitia, the poor man went home to bed and left the pulpit next Sunday to an amateur exhorter. His plan of campaign was to arrive on the opposite side of the terrace about a quarter to three, and, as the hour drew near, reconnoitre the door from behind a clump of bushes at the foot of the garden. Nestie usually made his appearance with a bodyguard of maidens, who kissed him shamelessly, and then, catching sight of the anxious face peeping through the laburnums, he would dash down the walk and, giving his slaves a last wave, disappear round the corner. The minister used to take a hasty survey lest they should become a sport to the barbarians in a land where for a father to kiss his boy was synonymous with mental incapacity, and then—it was a cat of a girl who oversaw the meeting —they hugged one another for the space of a whole minute, in which time it is wonderful what can be done if your heart is in it and your hat is allowed to go without care. Had a Seminary boy seen the sight—but the savages were caged at that hour—his feet would have been glued to the ground with amazement, and he had gone away full of silent gratitude that Providence had cast his lot north of the Tweed ; but of course he had not reckoned that the father and son had been separated for, say, six whole hours—or almost—and it was necessary to re-establish relations. When this had been done satisfactorily the two crossed a wooden bridge into the Meadow arm-in-arm—Mr. Molyneux unconsciously wearing his hat with a rakish air on the side of his

head. Between this hour and sunset was their pleasure in the summer time, and the things they did
were varied and remarkable. Sometimes they would
disappear into the woods above Muirtown, and return
home very dirty, very tired, very happy, laden with
wild flowers and dank, earthy roots, which they
planted in their tiny garden and watered together
with tender solicitude. Other times they played
what was supposed to be golf over a course of their
own selection and creation at the top of the Meadow,
and if by any chance the minister got a ball into a
hole, then Nestie danced for a space and the minister
apologised for his insolent success. Times there
were—warm, summer days—when the minister would
bring a book with him and read to Nestie as they lay
in a grassy hollow together. And on these days
they would fall a-talking, and it would end in a
photograph being taken from a case, and after they
had studied it together, both would kiss the face,
which was as if Nestie had kissed himself. Regular
frequenters of the North Meadow began to take an
interest in the pair, so that the golfers would cry
" Fore" in quite a kindly tone when they got in the
way of the balls, and one day old Peter Peebles, the
chief of the salmon fishers and a man of rosy countenance, rowed them up to Woody Island, and then
allowed the boat to drop down with the tide past
the North Meadow and beneath the two bridges,
and landed them at the South Meadow, refusing all

recompense with fierce words. Motherly old ladies
whose families were off their hands, and who took in
the situation at a glance, used to engage Mr. Molyneux in conversation in order to warn him about
Nestie's flannels and the necessity of avoiding damp
at nightfall. And many who never spoke to them,
and would have repudiated the idea of sentiment
with scorn, had a tender heart and a sense of the
tears of things as the pair, strange and lonely, yet
contented and happy, passed them in the evening.

When the time came that Nestie had to leave Miss
Letitia's, his father began to hang round the Seminary taking observations, and his heart was heavy
within him. After he had watched a scrimmage at
football—a dozen of the aboriginal savages fighting
together in a heap, a mass of legs, arms, heads—and
been hustled across the terrace in a rush of Russians
and English, from which he emerged without his hat,
umbrella, or book, and after he had been eye-witness
of an encounter between Jock Howieson and Bauldie
over a misunderstanding in marbles, he offered to
teach Nestie at home.

"Those Scotch boys are very . . . h-healthy,
Nestie, and I am not sure whether you are quite . . .
fit for their . . . habits. There is a master, too,
called . . . Bulldog, and I am afraid——" and Mr.
Molyneux looked wistfully at his boy.

"Why, pater, you are very n-naughty, and don't
d-deserve two lumps of sugar," for ever since they

were alone he had taken his mother's place and
poured out the tea. "Do you think I'm a coward?
A boy must learn to play games, you know, and they
won't be hard on a little chap at first. I'll soon learn
f-football and . . . the other things. I can play golf
a little now. Didn't you tell me, pater, that mother
was as bwave as . . . a s-soldier?"

"Of course she was, Nestie," and Mr. Molyneux
fell into the innocent little snare. "If you had only
seen the pony your mother used to ride on her
father's farm in Essex, where I saw her first! Do
you know, nobody could ride 'Gypsy' except its
mistress. It r-reared and . . . k-kicked, Nestie"—
the little man spoke with awe—"and once ran away;
but your mother could always manage it. She
looked so handsome on 'Gypsy'; and you have her
spirit. I'm very . . . t-timid."

"No, you aren't, not one little bit, pater, if there's
real d-danger." Nestie was now on his father's knee,
with a hand round his neck. "Who faced the cow
on the meadows when she was charging, and the nurse
had left the child, eh? Now, pater, tell the truth."

"That was because . . . the poor little man would
have been killed . . . any one would have d-done
that, and . . . I d-did not think what I was
d-doing . . ."

"Yes, I know," and Nestie mocked his father
shamefully, even unto his face; "and everybody read
in the paper how the child wasn't near the cow, and

the cow was quite nice and well-behaved, and you . . . ran away ; for shame, now !

"Did you go to the people that had the dip . . . dip . . . in the throat, or not ?—that's a word I can't manage yet, but I heard Miss Leti-titia and the girls say you were like the soldiers 'at got the Vic— Victoria Cwoss."

"That's d-different, Nestie ; that's my d-duty."

"Well, it's my d-duty to go to the S-Seminary, pater" ; and so he went.

"What's your name?" Nestie was standing in the centre of the large entrance hall where his father had left him, a neat, slim little figure in an Eton suit and straw hat, and the walls were lined by big lads in kilts, knickers, tweed suits, and tailless Highland bonnets in various stages of roughness and decay.

"Ernest Molyneux, and for short, Nestie," and he looked round with a bright little smile, although inwardly very nervous.

"Moly-havers," retorted Cosh, who had a vague sense that Nestie, with his finished little manner, his English accent, his unusual dress, and his high-sounding name, was an offence to the Seminary. "Get yir hat oot o' there," and Cosh sent Ernest's straw skimming into the forbidden "well."

Molyneux's face turned crimson, for he had inherited the temper which mistressed "Gypsy," and boys who remembered Speug's first exploit expected to see the newcomer spring at Cosh's face.

"You mean that for f-fun, I s'pose," he said an instant later, and he recovered his hat very neatly. "I can leap a little, you know, not m-much yet," and again he smiled round the ring.

Nothing quite like this had happened before in the Seminary, and there was a pause in the proceedings, which was the salvation of Nestie, and far more of Peter McGuffie. He had been arrested by the first sight of Nestie and had been considering the whole situation in silence. Peter had a sudden inspiration.

"Did ye say Nestie?" inquired Speug, with an almost kindly accent, moving a little forward as for purposes of identification.

"My pater calls me that, and . . . others did, but perhaps you would like to say Molyneux. What is your name?"

"We 'ill call ye 'Nestie'; it's no an ill word, an' it runs on the tongue. Ma name is Peter McGuffie, or Speug, an' gin onybody meddle wi' ye gie's a cry." And to show the celerity of his assistance Peter sent the remains of Cosh's bonnet into the "well" just as Bulldog came down to his room.

"Bulldog's in," as that estimable man identified the owner of the bonnet and passed on to his class-room. "In aifter him, an' gie yir name, afore the schule comes."

"Will you come with me, P-Peter?" and that worthy followed him mechanically, while the school held their breath; "it would be kind of you to intwodoosh—it's a little difficult, that word—me to the master."

" What's the meaning of this ? " demanded Bulldog at the sight of the two, for speech was paralysed in Speug and he was aghast at his own audacity.

" A new laddie . . . ca'ed Molly, Mol . . . a' canna mind it . . . Nestie . . . he didna know the way . . ." And Speug broke down and cast a despairing look at the cane.

" Peter pwotected me from the other boys, who were making fun of me, and I asked him to bwing me in to you, sir ; he was very p-polite."

" Was he ? " said Bulldog, regarding Speug's confusion with unconcealed delight; " that is quite his public character in this school, and there's nobody better known. My advice "—here Bulldog stopped, and looked from Speug to Nestie as one who was about to say something and had changed his mind— " is to . . . be friends with Peter."

So when the school took their places Nestie was seated next to Speug, and it was understood in a week that Nestie was ready to take his fair share in any honest fun that was going, but that if one of the baser sort tried to play the blackguard with Nestie, he had to balance accounts with Speug, and that the last farthing would be faithfully exacted.

As Nestie had at once settled in his mind that Speug was a young gentleman of high conduct and excellent manners—and Nestie, with all his sweet-

ness, was as obstinate as a mule—nothing remained
for Speug but to act as far as he could up to his new
character. With this example of diligence by his
side, he was roused to such exertion that he emerged
from long division and plunged into the rule of
three, while Nestie marvelled at his accomplishments—" for I'm not a clever chap like you, P-Peter."
Speug had also accumulated a considerable collection
of pencil sketches, mostly his own, in which life at
Muirtown Seminary was treated very broadly indeed,
and as he judged this portfolio unlikely to be appreciated by Nestie, and began himself to have some
scruple in having his own name connected with it, it
was consigned to the flames, and any offer of an addition, which boys made to Speug as a connoisseur in
Rabelaisean art, was taken as a ground of offence.
His personal habits had been negligent to a fault, and
Nestie was absurdly careful about his hands, so Peter
was reduced to many little observances he had overlooked, and would indeed have exposed himself to
scathing criticism had it not been that his sense of
humour was limited and, so far as it went, of a
markedly practical turn.

As Nestie never ceased to exalt this paladin of
chivalry and all the virtues which he had discovered
at school, Mr. Molyneux hungered to see him, and so
Speug was invited to tea on a Saturday evening—an
invitation he accepted with secret pride and outward
confusion of face. All the time which could be saved

that day from the sermons was devoted by Mr. Molyneux and his son to the commissariat, and it was pretty to see the Molyneuxs going from shop to shop collecting the feast. With much cunning Nestie had drawn from Speug that fried sausages (pork) with mashed potatoes, followed up by jam tarts and crowned with (raisin) cake, was a meal to live for, and all this they had, with shortbread and marmalade thrown in as relishes. When Nestie was not watching at the upper window for Peter's coming he was gloating over the table, and pater, putting last touches to his exposure of Infant Baptism, ran out and in to see that nothing had been forgotten, for they did not give many feasts, and this was one of gratitude. Peter was late, because he had gathered his whole establishment to dress him, including the old groom, who wished him to go in corduroy breeches and top boots, and Speug was polished to the extent of shining. He was also so modest that he would not speak, nor even look, and when Nestie began to discourse on his goodness he cast glances at the door and perspired visibly, on which occasions he wiped his forehead with a large red handkerchief. Amid all his experiences on land and water, on horseback and among boys—*i.e.*, savages—he had never yet been exalted as a hero and a philanthropist, and he felt uncomfortable in his clothes. He was induced, however, to trifle with the tea, and in the end did very fairly, regaining his native composure so far as to

describe a new horse his father had bought, and the
diabolical wickedness of the tame fox at the stables.
Afterwards Nestie took Speug to his room and
showed him his various treasures—a writing-desk
with a secret drawer; *The Sandalwood Traders*
by Ballantyne; a box of real tools, with nails and
tacks complete; and then he uncovered something
hidden in a case, whereat Speug was utterly astonished.

"Yes, it's a watch; my mother left it to me, and
some day I'll wear it, you know; your mother's
g-gone, too, Peter, isn't she?"

"Aye," replied Peter, "but a' dinna mind o' her."
And then, anxious to change the subject, he produced
a new knife with six blades. Before leaving he
promised to give Nestie a pair of rabbits, and to
guide him in their upbringing after a proper fashion.
Without having ventured into the field of sentiment,
there is no doubt Peter had carried himself in a way
to satisfy Mr. Molyneux, and he himself gave such an
account of the tea to Mr. McGuffie senior, that night,
that the horsedealer, although not given to Pharisaical
observance of the Sabbath, attended the little Baptist
chapel next day in state, sleeping through the sermon,
but putting five shillings in the plate, while Peter,
sitting most demurely at his father's side, identified
two of his enemies of McIntyre's Academy and
turned various things over in his mind.

If any one, however, supposed that the spirit had

gone out of Peter through his friendship with Nestie, he erred greatly, and this Robert Cosh learned to his cost. What possessed him no one could guess, and very likely he did not know himself, but he must needs waylay Nestie in Breadalbane Street one day after schooltime and speak opprobriously to him, finishing up—

"Awa' wi' ye; yir father's a meeserable yammering (stammering) dookie (Baptist) minister."

"My father's one of the best men living"—Nestie was in an honourable temper—"and you are an ill-bred c-cad."

Poor Nestie would have been half killed before Cosh had done with him had not Speug arrived on the scene, having been in the gundy (candy) shop not far off, and then there were circumstances. Cosh had a poor chance at any time with Peter, but now that worthy's arm was nerved with fierce indignation, and Nestie had to beg for mercy for Cosh, whose appearance on arriving home was remarkable. His story was even more so, and was indeed so affecting, not to say picturesque, that Bailie Cosh came into Bulldog's room with his son two days afterwards to settle matters.

"A' called, Maister MacKinnon," he said, in tones charged with dignity, "to explain the cause of my son Robert's absence; he was in bed with a poultice on his face twenty-four hours, an' he'll no be himself for days."

"He is no in a condeetion to lose time wi' his lessons, a' can tell ye, Bailie ; ye're richt to bring him back as sune as ye could ;. was't toothache ? "

"No, it wasna toothache, but the ill-usage o' one of your scholars, the maist impudent, ill-doing, aggravating little scoondrel in Muirtown."

"Peter McGuffie, come out here," which showed Bulldog's practical acquaintance with affairs. "Did ye give Robert Cosh a licking ? " ·

No answer from Speug, but a look of satisfaction that was beyond all evidence.

"Was that just yir natural iniquity, Peter, or had ye a justification ? "

Dogged silence of Speug, whose code of honour had one article at least—never to tell on a fellow.

"Please, sir, may I speak ? " cried Nestie, as he saw the preparations for Peter's punishment and could not contain himself.

"Were you in this job, too, Nestie ? You didn't tell me that there were two at puir Robert, Bailie ; if Nestie got his hand on your son, he's sic a veeciously inclined character that it's a wonder Robert's leevin'.

"Now, Bailie, we'll conduct a judeecial investigation. Robert Cosh, what have ye to say ? Speak up like a man, and I'll see justice done ye, be sure o' that ; but mind ye, the truth, the whole truth, and nothing but the truth."

Robert Cosh declined to contribute even the smallest morsel of truth in any shape or form, and in spite of strong encouragement from the magistrate, preserved an impenetrable silence.

"This," said Bulldog, with a shrewd glance, "is mair than ordinary modesty; we 'ill take another witness. Ernest Molyneux, what have ye got to say?"

"Cosh called my father names, and . . . I lost my t-temper, and . . . and . . . I said things . . . the pater's ill, sir, so I . . . and Cosh stwuck me once or twice—but I don't mind that; only Peter, you see, sir, wanted to help me. I'm afraid he h-hurtit Cosh, but that was how it happened."

"Stand beside Nestie, Cosh . . . so; half a head taller and much broader and four years older. Ye called his father names, and then cut his lip when he answered. Just so. There are some pretty little scratches on yir own face. That would be Peter. Well, Bailie, the case is pretty plain, and we 'ill go to judgment.

"Ernest Molyneux, yir father's a good man, and it does not matter two brass peens what Robert Cosh says about him, and ye're no an ill-disposed laddie yersel'. Ye may go to your seat.

"Peter McGuffie, ye're aye meddlin' wi' what doesna concern ye, and ye seem to think that Providence gave Nestie into yir chairge. One day ye pull him oot o' the river, and anither ye take him oot o' the hands o' Robert Cosh. But ye've done your wark sae neatly this time that I havena the heart to thrash

ye. Ye may go to yir seat, too; and, Peter, ma
man, just one word of advice. Yir head is thick,
but yir heart is richt; see that ye always use yir
fists as well as ye did that day.

"Robert Cosh, ye've had a fair trial, and ye have
been convicted of three heinous sins. First, ye
miscalled a good man—for that three strokes with
the cane; next, ye ill-used the quietest laddie in
the whole school—for that three strokes; and, lastly,
being moved of the devil, ye went home and told
lies to a magistrate—for that six strokes. Three on
each hand to-day and to-morrow will just settle the
count. Right hand first."

"Mr. MacKinnon, I protest. . . ."

"What?" and Bulldog turned on the magistrate;
"would ye interfere with the course o' justice in
another man's jureesdiction, and you a magistrate?"
And Bulldog's eyes began to rotate in a fearsome
manner.

The Bailie allowed it to be understood that he had
changed his mind, and Robert, who had expected
great things from the magistrate's protection, abandoned himself to despair and walked humbly for
many days to come.

Next day Nestie was not in his place, and Bulldog,
growing uneasy, called on his way home.

"Aye, aye," and the landlady's voice sank into the
minor key of Scots sympathy, "Maister Mollynoox
(for such an outlandish name was ever a trial) is far

through wi't ; the doctor says he never 'had much to
come an' go on, and noo this whup o' inflammation is
the feenish.

"The doctor doesna expect him to see mornin', an'
he's verra sober (weak) ; but his head's clear, an' the
laddie's wi' him. Ma hert is wae (sorry) for him, for
the twa hev been that bund up thegither that a'm
dootin' Nestie 'ill never get ower the pairtin'."

The gentle little minister was not far from his end,
and Nestie was nursing him as best he could. He
sponged his father's face—threatening to let the soap
get into his eyes if he were not obedient—and dried
it with a soft towel ; then he brushed the soft, thin
brown hair slowly and caressingly, as he had often
done on Sundays when his father was weary.
Turning round, he saw Bulldog, and instead of
being afraid, Nestie smiled a pathetic welcome, which
showed either what a poor actor the master was, with
all his canings, or that his English scholar was a very
shrewd little man.

"Th-thank you f-for coming to see father, sir ; he
was n-naughty and got cold, and he has been so ill ;
but he must get better, for you know there are . .
just the two of us, and . . . I would be . . . lonely
without the pater."

"Nestie does not wish to part with me, Mr.
MacKinnon, for we h-have been . . . dear friends,
that's how it was, and we loved . . . mother ; but he
is a . . . brave little man, as you know, and mother

and I will not forget him . . . you came to ask for Nestie, and it was God's will, for I h-have a f-favour to ask of you."

Bulldog went over and sat down by the bed, but said nothing. Only he took the minister's hand in his and waited. He also put his other arm round Nestie, and never did he look fiercer.

" I have no relatives, and his m-mother's family are all dead; there is nobody to be g-guardian to Nestie, and he cannot live alone. C-could you get some family who would be . . . where he might be at . . . h-home ?

" You know we are not rich, but we've s-saved a little, for Nestie is a famous little house-k-keeper; and maybe there's enough to keep him . . . till he grows big ; and I'll give you the receipt at the bank, and you'll . . . manage for him, won't you ? "

Bulldog cleared his throat to speak, but could not find his voice—for a wonder, but his hand tightened on the minister's, and he drew Nestie nearer to him.

" Of course, Mr. MacKinnon, I know that we have no c-claim on you, for we are strangers in Muirtown, and you . . . have many boys. But you've been kind to Nestie, and he . . . loves you."

The minister stopped, breathless, and closed his eyes.

" Mr. Molyneux," began Bulldog in a stern voice, " I'm willing to manage Nestie's estate, big or small, and I'll give an account of all intromissions to the

Court, but I must decline to look out a home for Nestie.

"Nestie and me" (bad grammar has its uses, and some of them are very comforting) "are good freends. My house has just an auld schoolmaster and an housekeeper in it, and whiles we would like to hear a young voice."

Bulldog paused and then went on, his voice sterner than ever—in sound.

"Now Bell's bark is worse than her bite, and maybe so is mine (Nestie nodded), so if the wee man wouldna be feared to live wi' . . . Bulldog—oh, I know fine what the rascals call me—he 'ill have a heart welcome, and . . . I'll answer to ye baith, father and mother, for yir laddie at the Day o' Judgment."

"'What shall I render . . . unto the Lord . . . for all His benefits?' I cannot thank you . . . (the minister was now very weak); but you will not . . . miss your reward. May the God of the orphan . . . Kiss me, Nestie."

For a short while he slept, and they watched for any sign of consciousness.

"It was too soon"—he was speaking, but not to them—"for Nestie . . . to come, Maud; he must stay . . . at school. He is a good boy, and . . . his master will . . . take care of him. . . . Nestie will grow to be a man, dear."

The minister was nearing the other side, and seeing the face he loved and had lost awhile.

"It's mother," whispered Nestie, and a minute later he was weeping bitterly and clinging with all his might to the schoolmaster, who came perilously near to tears himself.

"They're together now, and . . . I'll be father and mother to ye, Nestie," said Mr. Dugald MacKinnon, master of mathematics in Muirtown Seminary, and known as Bulldog to three generations of Muirtown lads.

IV

A FAMOUS VICTORY

THE Seminary perfectly understood that, besides
our two chief enemies, the " Pennies " and
McIntyres, there were, in the holes and corners of
the town, obscure schools where little companies of
boys got some kind of education and were not quite
devoid of proper spirit. During a really respectable
snowstorm—which lasted for a month and gave us
an opportunity of bringing affairs to a temporary
settlement with our rivals, so that the town of
Muirtown was our own for the next seven days—a
scouting party from the Seminary in search of adventures had an encounter with a Free Kirk school,
which was much enjoyed and spoken about for weeks
beside the big fire. Speug began, indeed, to lay out
a permanent campaign by which the boys going
home southwards could look in from time to time on
the Free Kirkers, and he indicated his willingness to
take charge of the operation. It was also said that
an Episcopal or Papist school—we made no subtile
distinctions at the Seminary—in the northern district

might afford some sport, and the leadership in this case was to be left to Duncan Robertson, the other captain of the commonwealth. Snow did not last the whole year round even in a Scots town ; but it was wonderful what could be done in summer by the use of book-bags, well stuffed out with Cæsar and Lennie's English Grammar, and at the worst there always remained our fists. The pleasure of planning these forays is still a grateful recollection, for it seemed to us that by spreading our forces we might have perpetual warfare from January to December and over the length and breadth of the town, so that no one would be compelled to return to his home of an evening without the hope of a battle, and every street of the town would be distinguished by conflict. Nothing came, however, of those spirited enterprises that year, because our two rivals, laying aside their mutual quarrels, which, we understood, were very bitter, and entering into a covenant of falsehood— their lying filled us with holy indignation—attacked us front and rear while we were having an innocent game of Russians and English on the north meadow. Although taken unawares and poorly provided with weapons we made a good fight ; but in the end we were scattered so completely that Speug never reached the school again that day, for which he was thrashed by Bulldog next morning, and Dunc came in with a front tooth gone and one black eye, for which he was soundly thrashed at once.

During all that summer we denounced the amazing meanness of the other side, and turned over plans for splitting the alliance, so that we might deal with each power separately and finally. Speug even conducted a negotiation—watchfully and across the street, for the treachery of the other side was beyond description—and tried to come to terms with the representative of our least hated opponent. He even thought, and Peter was not guileless, that he had secured their neutrality, when they suddenly burst forth into opprobrious language, being a very vulgar school indeed, and exposed Peter's designs openly. His feelings were not much hurt by the talk, in which, indeed, he scored an easy victory after he had abandoned negotiation and had settled down to vituperation, but Seminary boys whose homeward route took them past the hostile territories had to be careful all that summer. It was, indeed, a time of bitter humiliation to the premier school of Muirtown, and might have finally broken its spirit had it not have been for the historical battle in the beginning of November, when McGuffie and Robertson led us to victory, and the power of the allies was smashed for years. So great, indeed, was their defeat that in early spring Peter has been known to withdraw himself from marbles in the height of the season and of his own personal profit, for the simple purpose of promenading through the enemies' sphere of influence alone and flinging words of gross insult in at their gates.

One of the schools must have been a charity for the education of poor lads, since it was known to us as the " Penny School," and it was a familiar cry ringing through the yard of the Seminary, " The Pennies are coming !" when we promptly turned out to give them the welcome which, to do them justice, they ardently desired. Whether this was a penny a week or a penny a month we did not know, or whether, indeed, they paid a penny at all, but it pleased us to give this name, and it soon passed beyond the stage of correction. Our enemies came at last to wear it proudly, like many other people who have been called by nicknames and turned the nickname into an honour, for they would follow up a particularly telling snowball with the cry, " There's a penny for ye!" They were sturdy varlets, quite indifferent as to boots and stockings, and equally so as to blows. Through their very regardlessness the Pennies would have been apt to rout the Seminary— whose boys had given pledges to respectability, and who had to answer searching questions as to their personal appearance every evening—had it not been for stalwarts like McGuffie, whose father, being a horsedealer, did not apply an over strict standard of judgment to his son's manners or exploits, and Robertson, who lived in lodgings and, being a soldier's son, was supposed to be in a state of discipline for the Army.

Our feeling towards the Pennies was hardly cordial,

but it was as nothing to our hatred of McIntyre's school, which called itself an academy, and had a Latin master and held examinations and affected social equality with the Seminary. Every one knew that the Seminary had existed in the time of Queen Mary, and some said went back to the days of William Wallace, although we had some doubts as to whether the present building was then in existence. Every one also knew that McIntyre's whole concern belonged to himself, and that he collected the fees in every class on Friday morning, that he took home what was over after paying his assistants, and that butcher meat for the McIntyre family next week depended on the result. McIntyre drew his supplies from the small tradesmen, and a Seminary lad going in to get a new pair of boots at Meiklewham's would have a fine sense of pride in being measured by an old opponent whose face had often looked out on him from the mist of battle. This pretentious and windy institution even attempted the absurdity of a yearly prizegiving, when, instead of the Provost sitting in state and glaring before him with a Horace in his hands upside down, McIntyre's minister would hold forth on diligence and tidiness and courtesy and suchlike contemptible virtues. Had a Seminary boy been offered the painful choice, he would almost as soon have gone to the Pennies as to McIntyre, for in that case he had not been an impostor and a fraud

For a week the weather had been hovering on frost,

and on Wednesday afternoon the snow began to fall
with that quiet and steady downpour which means a
lasting storm.   Speug went home in great spirits,
declaring to an admiring circle of junior boys that if
Providence were kind and the snow continued there
would be something worth living for at the dinner
hour on Friday.   As the snowball war was a serious
affair, and was conducted after a scientific fashion,
it never commenced until there was a good body
of snow upon the ground and pure snow could be
gathered up without earth and stones.   The unpar-
donable sin of our warfare was slipping a stone into
a snowball : this was the same as poisoning the
wells, and the miscreant who perpetrated this crime
was cast out from every school.   There was a general
understanding between parties that the mercies were
not to be wasted, and that the schools were to refrain
themselves until there was a fair and lasting supply
of ammunition.   It was still snowing on Thursday
morning, and there were some who said that war
might now be declared ; and Jock Howieson, ever a
daring and rash spirit, declared we should repent it if
we were not ready against one o'clock.   Speug and
Dunc were however of opinion that nothing was
likely to take place that day except desultory skirmishes, and that the whole day ought to be spent in
accumulating a store of snowballs against Friday,
when there was no question that we should have to
face the united schools in a decisive battle.   This

was the only instance where our captains ever made a mistake, and they atoned for their error of judgement by the valour and skill with which they retrieved what seemed a hopeless defeat.

As the hours wore on to one o'clock Speug could be seen glancing anxiously out at the window, and he secured an opportunity with Dunc for a hasty conference during the geometry lesson. About a quarter to one he turned from his slate and cocked his ear, and in two minutes afterwards every boy in Bulldog's classroom understood that the war had begun and that we had been taken by surprise. Scouts from McIntyre's, as we afterwards learned, had risked the danger of playing truant, which in a school like theirs cost nothing, and had visited our playground. They had carried back news that we were not yet prepared for battle, and our firm opinion was that the authorities of Penny's and McIntyre's had allowed their schools out at half-past twelve, in order to take us at a disadvantage. Before the bell rang, and the senior classes were dismissed the Seminary knew that our enemies had seized the field of battle, but we did not know until we came out the extent of the disaster.

The Pennies had come down the back street and had established themselves opposite the narrow entrance between two sheds through which three only could walk abreast from our playground to the street. They had also sent a daring body of their lighter and more agile lads to the top of the sheds which separated our playground from the street, and they had conveyed down an enormous store of ammunition, so that the courtyard was absolutely at their mercy, and any one emerging from the corridor was received with a shower of well made and hard snowballs against which there was no standing. Even if we ran this risk and crossed the open space we could then be raked by the fire from the shed, and a charge through the narrow passage to the street would be in the last degree hazardous. There were twelve feet of passage, and there were not many who would care to face a stream of snowballs driven by the vigorous hands of the Pennies down this passage as through a pipe. Instead of meeting our enemies on the street, we had been penned up within our own school. McIntyre's had come down the terrace and seized an excellent position behind two Russian guns which stood opposite our school and about twenty feet from our front entrance. They had made these guns into a kind of fort, from behind whose shelter, reinforced by a slight barricade of jackets, they commanded our entrance, and had driven in the first boys who emerged, in hopeless discomfiture. It came upon us that we had been shut up back and front, and shut up with the poorest supply of snowballs and very little snow with which to repair our resources.

While the younger boys raged and stormed in the

safety of the corridors, Dunc and Speug retired for
consultation. In two minutes they came out and
gave their orders to the mass of boys gathered
together round the "well" and in the "well," and
on the stairs and along the corridors. It was at this
moment that Nestie Molyneux obtained a name
which he covered with glory before the close of the
day. As he had no class between twelve and one,
he had been observing events, and with the aid of two
or three other little boys had done what he could to
repair the neglect of yesterday. In spite of a rain of
snowballs he had availed himself of a sheltered
corner in the playground and had worked without
ceasing at the preparation of the balls. Every ball
as it was made was dipped into a pail of water and
then, half frozen, was laid in a corner where it was
soon frozen altogether. "There'll be the feck o' twa
hundred balls ready. Ma certes! Nestie has a head
on his shoulders. Now," said Speug, speaking from
halfway up the stair, "we'll start with thae balls for
a beginnin', and wi' them we'll fecht our way out to
the open. As soon as we've cleared the background
every ane o' the two junior classes is to mak' balls as
hard as he can lick and bring them forward to the
fighting line.

"We'll divide the senior school into three divisions;
Dunc will take thirty of ye and drive McIntyre frae
the guns and along the terrace till ye turn them
into Breadalbane Street. Thirty o' ye—and I want

nae Dowbiggins—'ill come with me, and we'll bring
the Pennies aff the shed quicker than they got up,
and drive them up the back streets till we land them
wi' the rest in Breadalbane Street; and the juniors
ill keep us well supplied with balls, else Dunc and
me will ken the reason at two o'clock.

"Jock Howieson, ye're to tak' thirty swank fellows
that can run and are no 'feart to be left alane. Ye'll
rin round by the North Street and the Cathedral and
come down the top of Breadalbane Street till ye cut
off McIntyre's and the Pennies frae their schools.
Dae nothin' till ye see Dunc and me drivin' the lot
up Breadalbane Street, then come down from the
back end of them wi' all your might, and I'm thinkin'
they'll be wanting to be inside their ain yard afore a'
be done."

Dunc assembled his corps inside the front porch,
each boy supplied with two balls and with twenty
youngsters behind bringing up more. McIntyre's
balls were falling on the front wall and coming in
through the porch. One of them struck Dunc on the
side of the head, but he forbade any return fire.
"They're wastin' their balls," he said; "it'll be the
better for us"; and then, looking round, "Are ye
ready? Charge!" and shouting "Seminary! Seminary!" he led his division across the terrace and fell
upon McIntyre's behind the guns. It was a short
sharp scrimmage, during which Dunc levelled the
leader of McIntyre's, and then the enemy began to

retreat slowly down the terrace, with many a hand-to-hand encounter and scuffle on the snow. As soon as Dunc's division had cleared the front, Jock Howieson collected his lads and started along the terrace in the opposite direction at a sharp run, carrying no balls, for they intended to make them on the scene of operation. When the other two divisions were off, Speug addressed his faithful band. "MacFarlane, take six birkies, climb up the water-spout, and clean the richt-hand shed, couping the Pennies into the street. Mackenzie, ye're no bad at the fightin'; tak anither sax and empty the roof o' the left-hand shed, and 'gin ye can clout that Penny that's sittin' on the riggin' it'll teach him to keep in the street next day.

"Noo, that leaves eighteen, and me and Bauldie and Jamie Johnston 'ill lead ye down the passage. We'll need six balls each, as hard as ye mak 'em, and the rest o' ye tak two in yer arms and one in yer hand. Pit yer bonnits in yer pocket—they'll no be muckle use—button yer jackets, and when the three o' us gae down the passage for ony sake follow close in behind. Just ae thing more," said Speug, who was in his glory that day. "I'll need a laddie to keep me gaein' with balls, and I want a laddie that has some spunk, for he'll hae a rough time." Below thirty of the junior school were waiting and looking at Speug like dogs for a biscuit. He threw his eye over the group, any one of which would have

given his best knife and all his marbles, and thrown
in a cricket bat and his last kite, to have been chosen.

"Nestie," said Speug, "ye're little and ye're white
and ye're terrible polite, but there's a sperit in ye.
Ye'll carry ma balls this day, and noo, you juniors,
aff to the ball-making, and see that Nestie's bonnet's
well filled, and there's no any of us wanting for a
ball when we drive the Pennies down the back road."
Then Speug moved to the back corridor and arranged
his division, with Nestie behind him, and Bauldie and
Jamie Johnston on the right hand and on the left,
Mackenzie's and MacFarlane's detachments close
behind, who were to turn off to the right hand and
the left as they emerged from the corridor ; the rest
were to follow Speug through the passage of danger.
Speug took two balls and placed them in the hollow
of his left arm, feeling them carefully to see that they
would leave a mark when they struck a Penny. The
third he took in his right hand, and Nestie had the
reserve.

"Noo," he said, "gin anybody be feared he'd better
gae in and sit doun beside the fire with the Dowbiggins," and since nobody responded to this genial
invitation Speug gave one shout of "Seminary!"
and in a minute was across the playground and at
the mouth of the passage, while Mackenzie and
MacFarlane were already scrambling up the walls of
the sheds. Covering his face with his left arm and
sending his first ball direct into the face of the fore-.

most Penny, and following it up with a second and
a third driven with unerring aim and the force of a
catapult, and receiving anything from twelve to
twenty balls between him and Bauldie and Johnston,
the three led the way down the passage, Nestie close
behind Speug and handing him a new supply of
balls. They met at the outer end of the passage—
the Pennies and Speug's lot—and for about thirty
seconds they swayed in one mass of struggling, fighting, shouting boy life, and then, so steady was the
play of Speug's fists, so able the assistance of the
other two, so strong the pressure from behind, and so
rapid the shower of balls sent over Speug's head
among the Pennies, the Pennies gave way and Speug
and his band burst into the back street, the leader
with his jacket torn off his back, and his face bearing
the scars of conflict, but full of might, and Nestie
with the balls behind him.

The Seminary lads and the Pennies were now face
to face in the back street, with a space of about ten
yards between, and both parties made arrangements
for the final conflict. The scouts of the Pennies
could be seen bringing balls from Breadalbane Street,
and the Pennies themselves made such hasty readjust-
ments of their negligent attire as were rendered
necessary by the vigour of the last fighting. Their
commander was a sturdy lad about fifteen years of
age, with a great shock of red hair and fists like iron.
His favourite method of charge was to lead his army

in the form of an inverted V, he being himself at the apex, and to force his way through the other side on the principle of a wedge. Speug did not believe in this arrangement. He led himself in the centre and threw out his two lieutenants far out on the right hand and on the left, so that when the Pennies forced their way into the middle of his division, Bauldie and Johnson were on their right and left flanks—tactics which in Speug's experience always caused dismay in the attacking force. The younger boys of the Seminary had by this time ample resources of ammunition ready, working like tigers without jackets now or bonnets, and as they brought out the supplies of balls through the passage of victory they received nods of approval from Speug, each nod being something like a decoration. It was fine to see Speug examining the balls to see that they were properly made and of a hardness which would give satisfaction to the expectant Pennies.

Some pleasant incidents occurred during this interlude. When the Seminary lads fought their way through the passage they cut off the retreat of three Pennies who were still fighting with MacFarlane on the top of the right-hand shed.

"What are ye daein' up there?" said Speug, with ironic politeness; "that's no' the ordinar' road into the Seminary"; and then, as they hesitated on the edge of the water pipe, Speug conceived what was in these days a fine form of humour. "Come down," he said, " naebody 'ill touch ye " ; and then he ordered an open passage to be made through the ranks of the Seminaries. Down between two lines the unfortunate Pennies walked, no one laying a hand upon them, but various humorists expressing their hopes that they had enjoyed the top of the shed, that it wasn't MacFarlane that had given one of them a black eye, that they hoped one of them hadn't lost his jacket on the roof of the shed, and that they were none the worse of their exertion, and that they expected to meet them later on—which gracious salutations the Pennies received in bitter silence as they ran the gauntlet; and when they had escaped clear of the Seminaries and stood half way between the two armies they turned round with insulting gestures, and one of them cried, "Ye'll get yer paiks (thrashing) for this or the day be done ! "

Their arrival among their friends and the slight commotion which it caused in the front ranks of the Pennies was a chance for Speug, who gave the signal for the charge and made himself directly for the leader of the Pennies. No pen at this distance of time can describe the conflict between the two leaders, who fired forth balls at each other at close distance, every one going to its mark, and one leaving an indelible impress upon Speug's ingenuous forehead. They then came to close grip, and there was a tussle, for which both had been waiting for many a day. From fists, which were not quite ineffectual, they fell upon wrestling, and here it seemed that Redhead must have the advantage, for he was taller in stature and more sinuous in body. During the wrestle there was something like a lull in the fighting, and both Pennies and Seminaries, now close together, held their hands till Speug, with a cunning turn of the leg that he had been taught by an English groom in his father's stable, got the advantage, and the two champions came down in the snow, Redhead below. The Seminaries set up a shout of triumph, and the scouts running to and fro with the balls behind joined in with, " Well done, Speug ! "

Speug had all the instincts of a true general and was not the man to spend his time in unprofitable exultation. It was a great chance to take the Pennies when they were without their leader and discomfited by his fall, and in an instant Speug was up, driving his way through the midst of the enemy, who were now divided in the centre, whilst Johnston and Bauldie had crept up by the side of the houses on either side and were attacking them in parallel lines. MacFarlane and Mackenzie had come down from the shed with their detachment and were busy in the rear of the Seminaries. Redhead fought like a hero, but was almost helpless in the confusion, and thought it the best strategy to make a rush to the clear ground in the rear of his position, calling his followers after him ; and now the Pennies gathered at the far end of the street, beaten in tactics and in fighting, but ever

strong in heart, and full of insolence. " That," said
Speug, wiping his face with his famous red handkerchief which he carried in his trousers pocket, and
hastily attending to some of his wounds, " that wesna'
bad " ; and then turning to Nestie, " Ye keepit close,
my mannie." Speug's officers, such mighties as
Bauldie and Johnston, MacFarlane and Mackenzie,
all bearing scars, clustered round their commander
with expressions of admiration. " Yon was a bonny
twirl, and you coupit him weel." " Sall, they've gotten
their licks," while Speug modestly disclaimed all
credit, and spoke generously of the Pennies, declaring
that they had fought well, and that Redhead nearly
got the mastery.

At that moment a shout of " Seminary!" was
heard in the rear of the Pennies, and Speug knew
that Duncan Robertson had driven McIntyre's the
full length of the terrace and was now fighting them
in Breadalbane Street. " Forward!" cried Speug.
" Dunc's on the back of them," and Redhead at the
same moment hurriedly withdrew his forces, covering
his retreat with a shower of balls, and united with
McIntyre's, who were retiring before Robertson and
the second division of the Seminaries. Amid cries of
" Seminary! Seminary!" Speug and Duncan met
where the back street opens into Breadalbane Street,
and their divisions amalgamated, exchanging notes
on the battle and examining one another's personal
appearance. There was not a bonnet to be seen, and

not many jackets, which had either been left behind
or thrown off or torn off in personal conflict with the
Pennies; collars may have remained, but that no one
could tell, and there were some whose waistcoats
were now held by one button. Two or three also
had been compelled to drop out of active battle and
were hanging in the rear, rubbing their faces with
snow and trusting to be able to see clear enough for
the final charge; and still the juniors were making
their balls and had established a new magazine at the
end of the terrace. Several of these impenitent
little wretches had themselves been in the thick of
the fight, and could be seen pointing proudly to a
clout on the forehead and a cut on the lip. What a
time certain mothers would have that evening when
their warriors came home, some of them without caps,
which would never be recovered, most of them with
buttonless waistcoats and torn jackets, half of them
with disfigured faces, all of them drenched to the skin,
and every one of them full of infinite satisfaction and
gladness of heart! Their fathers, who had heard
about the battle before they came home and had not
failed to discover who had won, being all Seminary
lads themselves, would also be much lifted, but would
feign to be extremely angry at the savagery of their
boys, would wonder where the police were, would
threaten their sons with all manner of punishments if
this ever happened again, and would declare their
intention of laying a complaint before the chief

constable. As, however, it was absolutely necessary in the interests of justice that the whole facts should be known before they took action, they would skilfully extract the whole Homeric narrative, with every personal conflict and ruse of war, from their sons, and only when the last incident had been related would announce their grave and final displeasure.

As for the police, who were not numerous in Muirtown, and who lived on excellent good terms with everybody, except tramps, they seemed to have a prophetic knowledge when a snow-fight was coming on, and were detained by important duty in distant streets. It was always, however, believed by the Seminary that two of the police could be seen, one at the distance of the bridge over the Tay, the other at the far extremity of Breadalbane Street, following the fight with rapt attention, and in the case of the Pennies winning, which had been their own school smacking their lips and slapping their hands under pretence of warming themselves in the cold weather, and in the event of the Seminaries winning marching off in opposite directions, lest they should be tempted to interfere, which they would have considered contrary to the rules of fair play, and giving their own school a mean advantage. Perhaps some ingenuous modern person will ask, "What were the masters of the Seminary about during this hour?" The Rector was sitting by the fire in his retiring-room, reading a winter ode of Horace, and as faint

sounds of war reached his ears he would stir the fire
and lament, like the quiet old scholar that he was,
that Providence had made him ruler of such a band
of barbarians ; but he would also cherish the hope
that his barbarians would not come off second.   As
for Bulldog, his mind was torn between two delights
—the anticipation of the exercise which he would
have next day, and the pleasure which his lads were
having to-day—and nothing more entirely endeared
Bulldog to his savages than the fact that, instead of
going home to dinner during this hour, which was
his usual custom, he contented himself with a biscuit.
He was obliged to buy it in a baker's shop in Breadalbane Street, from which he could command a perfect
view of the whole battle, especially as he happened to
stand in the doorway of the shop, and never returned
to school till the crisis of war was over.   He was
careful to explain to the school that he had himself
gone for the purpose of identifying the ringleaders in
mischief, and it was on such an occasion that Speug,
keeping his right cheek immovable towards Bulldog,
would wink to the assembled school with irresistible
effect.

Nor ought one to forget the janitor of Muirtown
Seminary, who had been a sergeant in the Black
Watch and had been wounded three times in the
Crimean War.   His orders, as given him by the
Rector and reinforced by all law-abiding parents,
were to prevent any boy of the Seminary leaving the

school for the purpose of a snowball fight, and should
such an unfortunate affair take place he was directed
to plunge into the midst and by force of arm to bring
the Seminaries home to their own fireside, leaving
rough and rude schools like the Pennies and
McIntyre's to fight at their wicked will. For did
not the Seminary lads move in polite society, except
Speug, and were they not going to be, as they have
become, clergymen and lawyers, and physicians, to
say nothing of bailies on the bench and elders of the
Kirk? These orders Sergeant Dougal McGlashan
carried out, not so much in the bondage of the letter
as in the fulness of the spirit. Many were the con-
versations which Speug and he had together in
anticipation of the snow time, when you may believe
if you please that that peaceable man was exhorting
Speug to obedience and gentleness, or if you please
that he was giving the commander of the Seminary
certain useful hints which he himself had picked up
from the "red line" at Balaclava. Certain it is that
when the Seminaries went out that day in battle
array the sergeant was engaged mending the fires
with great diligence, so that he was not able to see
them depart. Afterwards it was the merest duty for
him to stand at the end of the passage of victory, lest
the Pennies or any other person should venture on
another outrage; and if he was late in calling his
boys back from Breadalbane Street, that was only
because the cold had made his wounds to smart again,

and he could only follow them in the rear till the battle was over. When the evil was done there was no use of vain regret, and in the afternoon the sergeant stood beside the big fire and heard accounts of the battle from one and another, and then he would declare that there were lads in Muirtown Seminary who would have done well at Inkermann and the storming of the Redan.

Breadalbane Street, which was broad and straight, with the back road to the Seminary on the right hand, and the street to McIntyre's and the Pennies on the left, had been the battle-ground of generations, for it gave opportunity for deploying in divisions, for front attack and for flank, as well as for royal charges which extended across the street. McIntyres and Pennies had been recruited from their several schools and supplied afresh with ammunition. Redhead took command of the united force and arranged them across the street in his favourite wedge, with the base resting on the home street, and this time he gave the signal, and so impetuous was their charge that they drove their way almost through the ranks of the Seminaries, and Speug himself, through sheer weight of attack, was laid flat in the middle of the street. Robertson and his officers rallied their forces, but it was possible that the Seminaries might have lost the day had it not been for the masterly foresight of Speug and the opportune arrival of Jock Howieson. That worthy

had taken his division by a circuitous route, in which
they had been obstructed by a miserable Episcopal school which wanted a fight on its own account
and had to receive some passing attention. A little
late, Howieson reached the Cathedral, and then,
judging it better not to come down Breadalbane
Street, where his attack would have been exposed,
he made his way on the right of the street by
passages known only to himself, and having supplied
his division with ammunition from a snow-drift in a
back entry, he came into the home street, which was
the only line of retreat for the enemy, and cut them
off from their base. Leaving a handful of lads to
prevent the scouts coming out from the Pennies or
the McIntyres with information, and driving before
him the ammunition train of the enemy, he came
round into Breadalbane Street with twenty-five tough
fighters raging and fuming for the battle and just in
the nick of time. It was hard for any fighting man
to have spent something like half an hour wandering
round circuitous streets and holding ridiculous
conflicts with unknown schools when the battle of
Waterloo, with the fate of the Empire of Muirtown,
was hanging in the balance.

Before Redhead had notice of the arrival of the
new division they were upon his rear, and a play of
snowballs fell upon the back of the Pennies. This
was more than even veteran forces could endure, and
in spite of the heroic efforts of Redhead, who fired

his balls alternately back and forward, his forces fell
into a panic. They broke and drove their way
through Howieson's division, receiving severe punishment from balls fired at a distance of a few feet, and
then, in spite of the efforts of their officers, who fought
till they were black and blue, but chiefly red, the
enemy rushed down the home street and, sweeping
the rearguard of Howieson's before them like straws
in a stream, made for their respective schools. The
Seminaries in one united body, headed by the three
commanders and attended by the whole junior school,
visited the Pennies' school first, whose gates were
promptly closed, and having challenged the Pennies
with opprobrious words to come out and fight like
men—Redhead being offered the chance of single
combat with Dunc or Speug or Jock Howieson—the
Seminaries then made their way to McIntyre's
Academy. As this unfortunate place of learning had
no gate, Speug led the Seminaries into the centre of
their courtyard, McIntyre's boys having no spirit left
in them and being now hidden in the class-rooms.
As they would not come out, in spite of a shower of
courteous invitations, Speug stood in the centre of
their courtyard and called the gods to witness that it
had been a fair fight and that the Seminaries had
won. A marvellous figure was he, without bonnet,
without collar, without tie, without jacket, without
waistcoat, with nothing on him but a flannel shirt
and those marvellous horsey trousers, but glorious in

victory. Taking a snowball from Nestie, who was standing by his side, openly and in face of McIntyre's masters, gathered at a window, he sent it with unerring aim through the largest pane of glass in McIntyre's own room. " That," said Speug, " 'ill tell ye the Seminaries have been here." Then he collected his forces and led them home down the cross street and into Breadalbane Street, down the middle of Breadalbane Street, and round the terrace, and in by the front door into the Seminary. As they came down they sang, " Scots wha hae," and the juniors, who had rushed on before, met them at the door and gave three cheers, first for Speug, then for Dunc, and then for Jock Howieson, which homage and tribute of victory Speug received with affected contempt but great pride of heart. In order to conceal his feelings he turned to his faithful henchman, little Nestie Molyneux, who, always a delicate-looking little laddie, was now an altogether abject spectacle, with torn clothes, dripping hair, and battered face. " Nestie," said Speug, in hearing of the whole school, " ye're a plucky little deevil," and although since then he has been in many places and has had various modest triumphs, that still remains the proudest moment in Nestie Molyneux's life.

V

HIS PRIVATE CAPACITY

IT is well enough for popular rulers like presidents
to live in public and shake hands with every
person ; but absolute monarchs, who govern with an
iron hand and pay not the slightest attention to the
public mind, ought to be veiled in mystery. If Bulldog had walked homeward with his boys in an affectionate manner, and inquired after their sisters, like
his temporary assistant, Mr. Byles, or had played with
interesting babies on the North Meadow, as did Topp,
the drawing-master—Augustus de Lacy Topp—who
wore a brown velvet jacket and represented sentiment
in a form verging on lunacy ; or if he had invited his
classes to drink coffee in a very shabby little home,
as poor Moossy did, and treated them to Beethoven's
Symphonies, then even Jock Howieson, the stupidest
lad in the Seminary, would have been shocked, and
would have felt that the Creation was out of gear.
The last thing we had expected of Bulldog was
polite conversation, or private hospitality. His speech
was confined to the class-room, and there was most

practical ; and his hospitality, which was generous and widespread, was invariably public. His *rôle* was to be austere, unapproachable, and lifted above feeling, and had it not been for Nestie he had sustained it to the day of his death.

Opinion varied about Bulldog's age, some insisting that he had approached his century, others being content with " Weel on to eighty." None hinted at less than seventy, No one could remember his coming to Muirtown, and none knew whence he came. His birthplace was commonly believed to be the West Highlands, and it was certain that in dealing with a case of aggravated truancy he dropped into Gaelic. Bailie McCallum used to refer in convivial moments to his schooldays under Bulldog, and always left it to be inferred that had it not been for that tender, fostering care, he had not risen to his high estate in Muirtown. Fathers of families who were elders in the kirk, and verging on grey hair, would hear no complaints of Bulldog, for they had passed under the yoke in their youth, and what they had endured with profit—they now said—was good enough for their children. He seemed to us in those days like Melchizedek, without father or mother, beginning or end of days ; and now that Bulldog has lain for many a year in a quiet Perthshire kirkyard, it is hardly worth while visiting Muirtown Seminary.

Every morning, except in vacation, he crossed the bridge at 8.45, with such rigid punctuality that the clerks in the Post Office checked the clock by him, and he returned by the way he had gone, over the North Meadow, at 4.15, for it was his grateful custom to close the administration of discipline at the same hour as the teaching, considering with justice that any of the Muirtown varlets would rather take the cane than be kept in, where from the windows he could see the North Meadow in its greenness, and the river running rapidly on an afternoon. It would have been out of place for Bulldog to live in a Muirtown street, where he must have been overlooked and could not have maintained his necessary reserve. Years ago he had built himself a house upon the slope of the hill which commanded Muirtown from the other side of the river. It was a hill which began with wood and ended in a lofty crag ; and even from his house, half way up and among the trees, Bulldog could look down upon Muirtown, compactly built together on the plain beneath, and thinly veiled in the grey smoke which rose up lazily from its homes. It cannot be truthfully said that Bulldog gave himself to poetry, but having once varied his usual country holiday by a visit to Italy, he ever afterwards declared at dinner-table that Muirtown reminded him of Florence as you saw that city from Fiesole, with the ancient kirk of St. John rising instead of the Duomo, and the Tay instead of the Arno. He admitted that Florence had the advantage in her cathedral, but he stoutly insisted that the Arno was but a poor, shrunken river com-

pared with his own; for wherever Bulldog may have
been born, he boasted himself to be a citizen of Muirtown, and always believed that there was no river to
be found anywhere like unto the Tay. His garden
was surrounded with a high wall, and the entrance
was by a wooden door, and how Bulldog lived within
these walls no one knew, but many had imagined.
Speug, with two daring companions, had once traced
Bulldog home and seen him disappear through the
archway, and then it was in their plan to form a
ladder one above the other, and that Peter, from the
top thereof, should behold the mysterious interior and
observe Bulldog in private life; but even Speug's
courage failed at the critical moment, and they returned without news to the disappointed school.

Pity was not the characteristic of Seminary life in
those days, but the hardest heart was touched with
compassion when Nestie Molyneux lost his father
and went to stay with Bulldog. The Seminary rejoiced in their master ; but it was with trembling,
and the thought of spending the evening hours and
all one's spare time in his genial company excited
our darkest imagination. To write our copybooks
and do our problems under Bulldog's eye was a
bracing discipline which lent a kind of zest to life,
but to eat and drink with Bulldog was a fate beyond
words.

As it was an article of faith with us that Bulldog
was never perfectly happy except when he was plying

the cane, it was taken for granted that Nestie would be his solitary means of relaxation, from the afternoon of one day to the morning of the next, and when Nestie appeared, on the third morning after his change of residence, the school was waiting to receive him.

His walking across the meadow by Bulldog's side, with his hands in his pockets, talking at his ease and laughing lightly, amazed us on first sight, but did not count for much, because we considered this manner a policy of expediency and an act of hypocrisy. After all, he was only doing what every one of us would have done in the same circumstances—conciliating the tyrant and covering his own sufferings. We kept a respectful distance till Nestie parted with his guardian, and then we closed in round him and licked our lips, for the story that Nestie could tell would make any Indian tale hardly worth the reading.

Babel was let loose, and Nestie was pelted with questions which came in a fine confusion from many voices, and to which he was hardly expected to give an immediate answer.

"What like is the cane he keeps at home?" "Has Bulldog tawse in the house?" "Div ye catch it regular?" "Does he come after you to your bedroom?" "Have ye onything to eat?" "Is the garden door locked?" "Could ye climb over the wall if he was thrashing you too sore?" "Did he let ye bring yir rabbits?" "Have ye to work at yir lessons a' night?" "What does Bulldog eat for his dinner?" "Does he ever speak to you?" "Does he ever say onything about the school?" "Did ye ever see Bulldog sleeping?" "Are ye feared to be with him?" "Would the police take ye away if he was hurting ye?" "Is there ony other body in the house?" "Would he let ye make gundy (candy) by the kitchen fire?" "Have ye to work all night at yir books?" "Does he make ye brush his boots?" "What do ye call him in the house?" "Would ye call him Bulldog for a shilling's-worth of gundy if the garden gate was open?" "Has he ony apples in the garden?" "Would ye daur to lay a finger on them?" "How often have ye to wash yir hands?" "Would ye get yir licks if yir hair wasna brushed?" And then Speug interfered, and commanded silence that Nestie might satisfy the curiosity of the school.

"Haud yir blethering tongues!" was his polite form of address. "Noo, Nestie, come awa' wi' yir evidence. What like is't to live wi' Bulldog?"

"It's awfully g-good of you fellows to ask how I'm getting on with Bully," and Nestie's eyes lit up with fun, for he'd a nice little sense of humour, and never could resist the temptation of letting it play upon our slow-witted, matter-of-fact intellects. "And I declare you seem to know all about what h-happens. I'll j-just tell you something about it, but it'll make you creepy," and then all the circle gathered in round Nestie. "I have to rise at five in the morning, and

if I'm not down at half-past, Bulldog comes for me
with a c-cane " (Howieson at this point rubbed himself behind gently). " Before breakfast we have six
' p-props ' from Euclid and two vulgar f-fractions "
(a groan from the school): " for breakfast we've
porridge and milk, and I have to keep time with
Bulldog—one, two, three, four—with the spoonfuls.
He's got the c-cane on the table." (" Gosh " from a
boy at the back, and general sympathy.) " He has
the t-tawse hung in the lobby so as to be handy."
(" It cowes all.") " There are three regular c-canings
every day, one in the morning, and one in the afternoon, and one before you go to bed." At this point
Speug, who had been listening with much doubt to
Nestie's account, and knew that he had a luxuriant
imagination, interfered.

" Nestie," he said, " ye're an abandoned little
scoundrel, and ye're telling lees straicht forward,"
and the school went into the classroom divided in
opinion. Some were suspicious that Nestie had been
feeding their curiosity with highly spiced meat, but
others were inclined to believe anything of Bulldog's
household arrangements. During the hour Speug
studied Nestie's countenance with interest, and in
the break he laid hold of that ingenious young
gentleman by the ear and led him apart into a quiet
corner, where he exhorted him to unbosom the truth.
Nestie whispered something in Speug's ear which
shook even that worthy's composure.

"Did ye say rabbits?"

"Lop-ears," said Nestie after a moment's silence, and Speug was more confounded than he had ever been in all his blameless life.

"Ernest Molyneux, div ye kin whar ye 'ill go to if ye tell lees."

"I'm telling the t—truth, Speug, and I never tell lies, but sometimes I compose t—tales. Lop-ear rabbits, and he feeds them himself."

"Will ye say 'as sure as death'?"—for this was with us the final and awful test of truth.

"As sure as death," said Nestie, and that afternoon Speug had so much to think about that he gave almost no heed when Bulldog discovered him with nothing on the sheet before him except a remarkably correct drawing of two lop-eared rabbits.

Speug and Nestie crossed the North Meadow together after school, and before they parted at the bridge Nestie entreated the favour of a visit in his new home that evening from Speug; but, although modesty was not Speug's prevailing characteristic, he would on no account accept the flattering invitation. Maybe he was going to drive with his father, who was breaking-in a new horse, or maybe he was going out on the river in a boat, or maybe the stable gates were to be shut and the fox turned loose for a run, or maybe——

"Maybe you are going to learn your l—lessons, Speug, for once in your life," said Nestie, who, his head on one side, was studying Speug's embarrassment.

"A'm to do naething o' the kind," retorted Speug, turning a dark red at this insult.   "Nane o' yir impidence."

"Maybe you're f-frightened to come," said Nestie, and dodged at the same time behind a lamp-post. "Why, Speug, I didn't know you were f-frightened of anything."

"Naither I am," said Speug stoutly; "an' if it had been Jock Howieson said that, I'd black his eyes. What sud I be frightened of, ye miserable little shrimp?"

"Really, I don't know, Speug," said Nestie; "but just let me g-guess. It might be climbing the hill; or did you think you might meet one of the Pennies, and he would fight you; or, Speug—an idea occurs to me—do you feel as if you did not want to spend an hour—just a nice, quiet hour—all alone with Bulldog? You and he are such f-friends, Speug, in the Seminary. Afraid of Bulldog? Speug, I'm ashamed of you, when poor little me has to live with him now every day."

"When I get a grip o' you, Nestie Molyneux, I'll learn ye to give me chat. I never was afraid of Bulldog, and I dinna care if he chases me round the garden wi' a stick, but I'm no coming."

"You *are* afraid, Speug; you *dare* not come." And Nestie kept carefully out of Speug's reach.

"You are a liar," cried Speug. "I'll come up this very night at seven o'clock, but I'll no come in unless ye're at the garden door."

Speug had fought many pitched battles in his day, and was afraid neither of man nor beast, but his heart sank within him for the first time in his life when he crossed the bridge and climbed the hill to the residence of Mr. Dugald MacKinnon. Nothing but his pledged word, and a reputation for courage which must not be tarnished, since it rested on nothing else, brought him up the lane to Bulldog's door. He was before his time, and Nestie had not yet come to meet him, and he could allow his imagination to picture what was within the walls, and what might befall his unfortunate self before he went down that lane again. His one consolation and support was in the lop-eared rabbits; and if it were the case, as Nestie had sworn with an oath which never had been broken at the Seminary, that there were rabbits within that dreadful enclosure, there was hope for him; for if he knew about anything, he knew about rabbits, and if any one had to do with rabbits—and although it was incredible, yet had not Nestie sworn it with an oath? —there must be some bowels of mercy even in Bulldog. Speug began to speculate whether he might not be able, with Nestie's loyal help, to reach the rabbits and examine thoroughly into their condition, and escape from the garden without a personal interview with its owner; and at the thought thereof Speug's heart was lifted. For of all his exploits which had delighted the Seminary, none, for its wonder and daring, its sheer amazingness, could be compared with a stolen visit to Bulldog's rabbits. "Nestie," he murmured to himself, as he remembered that little Englishman's prodigal imagination, "is a maist extraordinary leear, but he said 'as sure as death.'"

"Why, Speug, is that you? You ought to have opened the door. Come along and shake hands with the master; he's just l-longing to see you." And Speug was dragged along the walk between the gooseberry bushes, which in no other circumstances would he have passed unnoticed, and was taken up to be introduced with the air of a dog going to execution. He heard some one coming down the walk, and he lifted up his eyes to know the worst, and in that moment it appeared as if reason had deserted the unhappy Speug. It was the face of Bulldog, for the like of that countenance could not be found on any other man within the United Kingdom of Great Britain and Ireland. Yes, it was Bulldog, and that Speug would be prepared to swear in any court of justice. The nose and the chin, and the iron-grey whiskers and hair, and above all those revolving eyes. There could not be any mistake. But what had happened to Bulldog's face, for it was like unto that of another man? The sternness had gone out of it, and—there was no doubt about it—Bulldog was smiling, and it was an altogether comprehensive and irresistible smile. It had taken the iron lines out of his face and shaped his lips to the kindliest curve, and deprived his nose of its aggressive air, and robbed the judicial appearance of his whiskers, and it had given him—it was a positive fact—another pair of eyes. They still revolved, but not now like the guns in the turret of a monitor dealing destruction right and left. They were shining and twinkling like the kindly light from a harbour tower. There never was such a genial and humoursome face, so full of fun and humanity, as that which looked down on the speechless Speug. Nor was that all ; it was a complete transformation. Where were the pepper-and-salt trousers and the formal black coat and vest, which seemed somehow to symbolise the inflexible severity of Bulldog's reign ? and the hat, and the gloves, and the stick— what had become of his trappings ? Was there ever such a pair of disreputable old slippers, down at the heel, out at the sides, broken at the seams, as those that covered the feet of Bulldog in that garden. The very sight of those slippers, with their suggestion of slackness and unpunctuality and ignorance of all useful knowledge and general Bohemianism, was the first thing which cheered the heart of Speug. Those slippers would tolerate no problems from Euclid and would laugh a cane to scorn. Where did he ever get those trousers, and from whose hands did they origin- ally come, baggy at the knee and loose everywhere

stained with garden mould and torn with garden
bushes ?

Without question it was a warm night in that
sheltered place on the side of the hill ; but would
any person believe that the master of mathematics,
besides writing and arithmetic, in Muirtown Seminary,
was going about in his garden, and before the eyes of
two of his pupils, without the vestige of a waistcoat ?
Speug now was braced for wonders, but even he was
startled with Bulldog's jacket, which seemed of earlier
age than the trousers, with which it had no connexion
in colour. It may once have had four buttons, but
only two were left now ; there was a tear in its side
that must have been made by a nail in the garden
wall, the handle of a hammer projected from one
pocket, and a pruning-knife from the other. And if
there was not a pipe in Bulldog's mouth, stuck in the
side of his cheek, "as sure as death ! " There was a
knife in his hand, with six blades and a corkscrew
and a gimlet and the thing for taking the stones out
of a horse's hoof—oath again repeated—and Bulldog
was trying the edge of the biggest blade upon his
finger. Speug, now ascending from height to height,
was not surprised to see no necktie, and would have
been prepared to see no collar. He had now even a
wild hope that when he reached Bulldog's head it
might be crowned with a Highland bonnet, minus the
tails ; but instead thereof there was a hat, possibly
once a wide-awake, so bashed, and shapeless, and

discoloured, and worn so rakishly, partly on the back and partly on the side of his head, that Speug was inwardly satisfied, and knew that no evil could befall him in that garden.

"Speug, my mannie, how are ye?" said this amazing figure. "Ye've been long of coming. There's something like a knife, eh!" and Bulldog opened up the whole concern and challenged Speug to produce his knife, which was not so bad after all, for it had six departments, and one of them was a file, which was wanting in Bulldog's.

"Show the master your peerie, Speug," said Nestie. "It's split more tops than any one in the school; it's a r-ripper," and Nestie exhibited its deadly steel point with much pride, while Speug endeavoured to look unconscious as the owner of this instrument of war.

"Dod, I'll have a try myself," said Bulldog. "It's many a year since I've spun a top. Where's yir string?" and he strode up the walk winding the top, and the boys behind looked at one another, while Nestie triumphed openly.

"Are you frightened, Speug?" he whispered. "Ain't he great? And just you wait; you haven't begun to see things yet, not h-half."

Upon the doorstep Bulldog spun the top with a right hand that had not lost its cunning, but rather had been strengthened by much cane exercise. "It's sleeping," he cried in huge delight. "If you dare to touch it, pity you!" but no one wished to shorten its time, and the three hung over that top with fond interest, as Bulldog timed the performance with his watch, which he extricated from his trouser pocket.

" Ye're a judge of rabbits, Speug," said the master. " I would like to have yir advice," and as they went down through the garden they halted at a place, and the robins came and sat on Bulldog's shoulder and took crumbs out of his hand, and a little further on the thrushes bade him welcome, and he showed the boys where the swallows had built every year, and they also flew round his head.

" If ye dinna meddle with them, the birds 'ill no be afraid o' you, will they, Dandie ? " and the old terrier which followed at his heels wagged his tail and indicated that he also was on good terms with every living thing in the garden.

No one in the Seminary ever could be brought to believe it, even although Speug tried to inculcate faith with his fists, that Bulldog had carried out a litter of young rabbits in his hat for inspection, and that, before the three of them laid themselves out for a supper of strawberries, Speug had given to his master the best knowledge at his command on the amount of green food which might be given with safety to a rabbit of adult years, and had laid it down with authority that a moderate amount of tea-leaves and oatmeal might be allowed as an occasional dainty.

After the attack on the strawberries, in which

Speug greatly distinguished himself, and Bulldog
urged him on with encouraging words, they had
tarts and lemonade in the house, where not a sign
of cane or tawse could be found. Bulldog drew the
corks himself, and managed once to drench Speug
gloriously, whereat that worthy wiped his face with
his famous red handkerchief and was inordinately
proud, while Nestie declared that the thing had been
done on purpose, and Bulldog threatened him with
the tawse for insulting his master.

"Div ye think, Speug, ye could manage a piece of
rock before ye go," and Bulldog produced the only
rock that a Muirtown man will ever think worth
eating—Fenwick's own very best, thick, and pure,
and rich, and well-flavoured ; and when Speug knew
not whether to choose the peppermint, that is black
and white, or the honey rock, which is brown and
creamy, or the cinnamon, which in those days was
red outside and white within, his host insisted that
he should take a piece of each, and they would last
him till he reached his home.

"Speug," and Bulldog bade farewell to his pupil at
the garden gate, "ye're the most aggravating little
scoundrel in Muirtown Seminary, and the devilry
that's in ye I bear witness is bottomless ; but ye're
fine company, and ye 'ill, maybe, be a man yet, and
Nestie and me will be glad to see ye when ye're no
engaged with yir study. Ye 'ill no forget to come,
Peter."

Peter's tongue, which had been wagging freely among the rabbits, again forsook him, but he was able to indicate that he would seize an early opportunity of again paying his respects to Mr. Dugald MacKinnon in his own home ; and when Bulldog thrashed him next day for not having prepared an exercise the night before, the incident only seemed to complete Speug's pride and satisfaction.

VI

THE DISGRACE OF MR. BYLES

BULLDOG'S southern assistant had tried the patience of the Seminary by various efforts to improve its mind and manners, but when he proposed at the beginning of the autumn term to occupy Saturdays with botanical excursions to Kilspindie Woods, which, as everybody knows, are three miles from Muirtown, and a paradise of pheasants, it was felt that if there was any moral order in the universe something must happen. From the middle of September, when the school opened, on to the beginning of October, when football started, our spare time was given to kites, which we flew from the North Meadow in the equinoctial gales gloriously. Speug had one of heroic size, with a figure of a dragon upon it painted in blue and yellow and red—the red for the fire coming out of his mouth—and a tail of eight joints, ending in a bunch of hay fastened with a ribbon. None but a sportsman like Speug could have launched the monster from the ground—bigger than Peter by a foot—and nursed it through the lower spaces till it caught the wind, and held it in the higher as it tore upwards and forwards till the dragon was but the size of a man's hand in the clear autumn sky. Then Peter would lie down upon his back, with his hands below his head, and the stick with the kite string beneath his feet, and gaze up at the speck above, with an expression so lifted above this present world that a circle of juniors could only look at him with silent admiration and speculate whether they would ever become so good and great.

It must not be thought, however, that kite-flying was chiefly done upon your back, for it gave endless opportunities for intricate manœuvres and spectacular display. When Peter was in the vein he would collect twelve mighties—each with a kite worth seeing—and bringing the kites low enough for the glory of their size and tails to be visible they would turn and wheel and advance and retire, keeping line and distance with such accuracy that Sergeant McGlashan would watch the review with keen interest and afterwards give his weighty approval. Then the band would work their way up to the head of the Meadow in the teeth of a north-wester, and forming in line, with half a dozen yards between each boy, would let the kites go and follow them at the run as the kites tore through the air and almost pulled their owners' arms out of the sockets. It was so fine a demonstration that the women bleaching their clothes

would pick up half a dozen of the goodman's shirts
to let Speug keep his course—knowing very well
that he would have kept it otherwise over the shirts
—and golfers, who expect every one to get out of
their way on pain of sudden death, would stop upon
the putting green to see the kites go down in the
wind with the laddies red-faced and bare-headed at
their heels. If the housewives shook their heads as
they spread out the shirts on the grass again—weigh-
ing them down with clean stones that they might not
follow the kites—it was with secret delight, for there
is no wholesome woman who does not rejoice in a
boy and regard his most vexatious mischief with
charity. And old Major MacLeod, the keenest of
golfers and the most touchy of Celts, declared that
this condemned old Island was not dead yet when it
could turn out such a gang of sturdy young ruffians.
And it was instead of such a mighty ploy that
Mr. Byles proposed to take the Seminary for a
botanical excursion.

It was in the mathematical class-room that Mr.
Byles announced the new departure, and, even if
Bulldog had not been keeping watch with an inscrutable countenance, the school was too much amazed
to interrupt. Having touched on the glories of the
creation amid which we lived, Mr. Byles pointed out
in what the newspapers call "neat and well chosen
terms," that it was not enough to learn mathematics
as they all did so diligently—Jock Howieson's eye

turned instinctively to Bulldog's cane—but they must also know some natural science in order to become, as he hoped they would, cultured men—Speug was just able to cast a longing glance at Thomas John. That no pursuit was easier and more delightful than botany, especially among wild flowers. That on Saturday he proposed to go with as many as would join him to ransack the treasures of Kilspindie Woods. That these woods were very rich, he believed, in flowers, among which he mentioned wild geraniums —at which the school began to recover and rustle. That the boys might dry the geraniums and make books for Christmas presents with them, and that he hoped to see a herbarium in the Seminary containing all the wild flowers of the district. The school was now getting into good spirits, and Bulldog allowed his eye to fall on Speug. That any boy who desired to improve his mind was to put on his oldest suit and bring a bag to carry the plants in and be in front of the Seminary at nine to-morrow. Then Bulldog brought his cane down on the desk with energy and dismissed the school, and Nestie told Peter that his mouth had begun to twitch.

Outside the school gathered together on the terrace around the Russian guns, which was our Forum, and after five seconds' pause, during which we gathered inspiration from each other's faces, a great shout of laughter went up to the sky, full-toned, unanimous, prolonged. Any sense of humour in the Seminary was practical, and Mr. Byles's botany class, with expeditions, was irresistible.

"Geranniums!" cried Howieson, who was immensely tickled; "it cowes a'. An' what was the ither flooer—'herbarries'? It's michty; it'ill be poppies an' mustard seed next. Speug, ye'ill be making a book for a present to Bulldog."

"Tak care o' yirsel," Bauldie shouted to the Dowbiggins, who were making off, as mass meetings did not agree with them, "an' see ye dinna wet yir feet or dirty yir hands. Ye'ill get yir wheeps at home if ye do. Give us a bit o' Byles, Nestie," and then there was instant silence, for Nestie had a nice little trick of mimicry which greatly endeared him to a school where delicate gifts were rare.

"S-silence, if you please," and Nestie held up his hand with Mr. Byles's favourite polite deprecating gesture. "I hear a smile. Remember, d-dear boys, that this is a serious s-subject. Do p-please sit quiet, Peter McGuffie; your fidgetin' is very t-tryin' indeed and I 'ope, I mean h-hope, you will make an effort to l-learn. This, my l-lads, is a common object of Nature which I 'old, that is hold, in my h-hands—Howieson, I must ask you not to annoy Thomas John Dowbiggin —the c-colour is a lovely gold, and yet—no talking, if you please, it is r-rude—we pass it every day without n-notice. Each boy may take a dandelion h-home to his sister. Now go hout . . . or rather out, quietly."

"Gosh, it's just Byles to the ground!" cried Bauldie; and Johnston passed a half stick of gundy to Nestie to refresh him after his labours. "Are ony o' you chaps goin'? It wud be worth seein' Byles traking thro' the Kilspindie woods, with thae bleatin' sheep o' Dowbiggins at his heels, carryin' an airmful o' roots and sic like."

"You'ill no catch me tramping oot at the tail o' Byles and a litter o' Dowbiggins!"—and Jock was very emphatic. "Dod, it'ill just be like a procession o' MacMuldrow's lassies, two and two, and maybe airm in airm!"

This fearful and malignant suggestion settled the matter for the Seminary, as a score of its worthies marching across the bridge in the interests of science, like a boarding-school, would be a scandal for ever. So it was agreed that a body of sympathisers should see the Byles expedition off next morning, and then hold a field day of kites in the meadow.

The deterioration of the best is the worst, and that means that when a prim, conventional, respectable man takes in his head to dress as a Bohemian, the effect will be remarkable. Byles had been anxious to show that he could be quite the gay rustic when he pleased, and he was got up in a cap, much crushed, and a grey flannel shirt, with a collar corresponding, and no tie, and a suit of brown tweeds, much stained with futile chemical experiments. He was also equipped with a large canvas bag, slung over his shoulder, and a hammock net, which he explained could be slung from a tree and serve as a resting-place if it were damp beneath. The Dowbiggins had entered into the spirit of the thing, and were in clothes reserved for their country holidays. They had each an umbrella, large and bulgy, and altogether were a pair of objects to whom no one would have lent a shilling. Cosh, whose attack on Nestie made him a social outcast, had declared himself a convert to natural science, and was sucking up to Byles, and two harmless little chaps, who thought that they would like to know something about flowers, made up the Botanical Society.

They were a lonely little group standing on the terrace, while Mr. Byles was securing a trowel and other instruments of war from his room, but a large and representative gathering of the Seminary did their best to cheer and instruct them.

Howieson insisted that the bottle of milk which bulged from the bag of the younger Dowbiggin contained spirituous liquors, and warned the two juniors to keep clear of him and to resist every temptation to drinking. He also expressed an earnest hope that a rumour flying round the school about tobacco was not true. But the smell on Dowbiggin's clothes was horrid. Cosh was affectionately exhorted to have a tender care of his health and personal appearance, not to bully Lord Kilspindie's gamekeepers, nor to put his foot into a steel trap, nor to meddle with the rabbits, nor to fall into the Tay, but above all things not to tell lies.

Thomas John was beset with requests—that he would leave a lock of his hair in case he should not return, that he would mention the name of the pawn-broker from whom he got his clothes, that he would bring home a bouquet of wild flowers for Bulldog, that he would secure a supply of turnips to make lanterns for Halloween, that he would be kind to Mr. Byles and see that he took a rest in his net, that he would be careful to gather up any "h's" Mr. Byles might drop on the road, and that he should not use bad language under any circumstances.

"Never mind what those boys say, Thomas," said Mr. Byles, who had come out in time to catch the last exhortation : "it is far better to himprove, I mean cultivate, the mind than to fly kites like a set of children ; but we all hope that you will have a nice fly, don't we, boys?" And sarcasm from so feeble a quarter might have provoked a demonstration had not Byles and his flock been blotted out by an amazing circumstance. As the botanists started, Speug, who had maintained an unusual silence all the morning, joined the body along with Nestie, and gave Mr. Byles to understand that he also was hungering for scientific research. After their friends had recovered themselves they buzzed round the two, who were following the Dowbiggins with an admirable affectation of sedateness, but received no satisfaction.

Speug contented himself with warning off a dozen henchmen who had fallen in by him with the idea of forming a mock procession, and then giving them a wink of extraordinary suggestiveness. But Nestie was more communicative, and explained the situation at length—

"Peter was a b-botanist all the time, but he did not know it ; he fairly loves g-geraniums, and is sorry that he wasted his time on k-kites and snowballs. We are going to himpwove our m-minds, and we don't want you to trouble us." But this was not knowledge.

It remained a mystery, and when Jock and Bauldie tailed off at the bridge, and Speug, half way across, turned round and winked again, it was with regret that they betook themselves to their kites, and more than once they found themselves casting longing glances to the distant woods, where Speug was now pursuing the study of botany.

"Bauldie," said Jock suddenly, as the kites hung motionless in the sky, "this is weel enough, but tak' my word for't it's nothing to the game they're playin' in yon woods."

"Div ye mean howkin' geranniums ? for I canna see muckle game in that : I would as soon dig potatoes." Bauldie, though a man of his hands, had a prosaic mind and had little imagination.

"Geranniums ! ger—— havers, that's no' what Speug is after, you bet. He's got a big splore (exploit) on hand or he never crossed Muirtown Brig in such company. Man, Bauldie, I peety Byles, I do. Peter'ill lose the lot o' them in the woods or he'ill stick them in a bog, or "—and Jock could hardly hold his kite—" what div ye say to this, man ? he'ill row them over to Woody Island and leave them there till Monday, with naething but bread and milk and the net to sleep in." And the joy of Jock and Bauldie at this cheerful prospect was rather a testimony to their faith in Peter's varied ability than a proof of sympathy with their fellow-creatures.

If Speug was playing the fox he gave no sign on the way to the woods, for he was a model of propriety and laid himself out to be agreeable. He showed an unwonted respect for the feelings of the Dowbiggins, so that these two young gentlemen relaxed the vigilant attention with which they usually regarded Speug, and he was quite affable with Cosh. As for the master, Peter simply placed himself at Mr. Byles's service, expatiating on the extent of the woods and their richness in flowers— "just fair scatted up wi' geranniums and the rest o' them" : offering to take the expedition by the nearest way to the treasures, and especially insisting on the number and beauty and tameness of the pheasants, till Mr. Byles was charmed and was himself surprised at the humanising influence of scientific pursuits.

Nor had Peter boasted vainly of his wood lore,

for he led them by so direct a way that, before
they came to the place of flowers, the expedition
—except the two little chaps, whom Speug sent
round in Nestie's charge, to a selected rendezvous
as being next door to babies—had climbed five
dykes, all with loose stones, fought through three
thickets very prickly indeed, crawled underneath
two hedges, crossed three burns, one coming up to
the knees, and mired themselves times without
number. Cosh had jostled against Speug in leaping
from one dry spot to another and come down
rolling in the mud, which made his appearance from
behind wonderful; Speug, in helping Thomas John
out of a very entangling place, had been so zealous
that the seat had been almost entirely detached
from Thomas John's trousers, and although Mr.
Byles had done his best with pins, the result was
not edifying; his brother's straw hat had fallen in
the exact spot where Speug landed as he jumped
from a wall, and was of no further service, and so
the younger Dowbiggin—"who is so refined in his
ways," as his mother used to say—wore as his head-
gear a handkerchief which had been used for cleaning the mud from his clothes. Upon Mr. Byles,
whom fate might have spared, misfortunes had
accumulated. His trousers had been sadly mangled
from the knee downwards as he crawled through
a hole, and had to be wound round his legs with
string, and although Speug had pulled his cap out

of a branch, he had done his work so hastily as to leave the peak behind, and he was so clumsy, with the best intentions, that he allowed another branch to slip, which caught Mr. Byles on the side of the head and left a mark above his eye, which distinctly suggested a prizefight to any one not acquainted with that gentleman's blameless character. Peter himself had come unscathed from the perils of land and water, save a dash of mud here and there and a suspicion of wet about his feet, which shows how bad people fare better than good. The company was so bedraggled and discouraged that their minds did not seem set on wild flowers, and in these circumstances Peter, ever obliging and thoughtful, led the botanists to a pleasant glade, away from thickets and bogs, where the pheasants made their home and swarmed by hundreds. Mr. Byles was much cheered by this change of environment, and grew eloquent on the graceful shape and varied plumage of the birds. They were so friendly that they gathered round the party, which was not wonderful, as a keeper fed them every day, but which Mr. Byles explained was due to the instinct of the beautiful creatures, " who know, my dear boys, that we love them." He enlarged on the cruelty of sport, and made the Dowbiggins promise that they would never shoot pheasants or any other game, and there is no reason to doubt that they kept their word, as they did not know one end of a gun from another, and would no sooner have dared to fire one than they would have whistled on Sunday. A happy thought occurred to Mr. Byles, and he suggested that they should now have their lunch and feed the birds with the fragments. He was wondering also whether it would be wrong to snare one of the birds in the net, just to hold it in the hand and let it go again.

When things had come to this pass—and he never had expected anything so good—Speug withdrew unobtrusively behind a clump of trees, and then ran swiftly to a hollow where Nestie was waiting with the juniors.

"Noo, my wee men," said Peter to the innocents, "div ye see that path? Cut along it as hard as ye can leg, and it 'ill bring you to the Muirtown Road, and never rest till ye be in your own houses. For Byles and these Dowbiggins are carryin' on sic a game wi' Lord Kilspindie's pheasants that I'm expectin' to see them in Muirtown jail before nicht. Ye may be thankful," concluded Peter piously, "that I savit ye from sic company."

"Nestie," Peter continued, when the boys had disappeared, " I've never clypit (told tales) once since I cam to the Seminary, and it's no' a nice job, but div ye no think that the head keeper should know that poachers are in the preserves ? "

"It's a d-duty, Peter," as they ran to the keeper's house, "especially when there's a g-gang of them

and such b-bad-looking fellows—v-vice just written
on their faces. It's horrid to see boys so young
and so w-wicked."

"What young prodigals are yon comin' skelpin'
along, as if the dogs were aifter them?" and the
head keeper came out from the kennels. "Oh, it's
you, Speug—and what are you doin' in the woods
the day? there's no eggs now." For sporting people
are a confederacy, and there was not a coachman
or groom, or keeper or ratcatcher, within twelve
miles of Muirtown, who did not know Mr. McGuffie
senior, and not many who did not also have the
acquaintance of his hopeful son.

"Nestie and me were just out for a run to keep
our wind richt, an' we cam on a man and three
boys among the pheasants in the low park."

"Among the what? Meddlin with Lord Kilspindie's birds?"

"Well, I dinna ken if they were juist poachin',
but they were feedin' them, and we saw a net."

"Sandie," shouted the head keeper, "and you,
Tom, get up out of yir beds this meenut; the
poachers are after the pheasants. My word, takin'
them alive, as I'm a livin' man, to sell them for
stock: and broad daylight; it beats everything. He
'ill be an old hand, frae Dundee maist likely. And
the impidence o't, eleven o'clock in the forenoon
an' the end o' September. Dod: it's a depairture
in poachin'." And as the sight of Mr. Byles burst

on his view, surrounded by trustful birds, and the two Dowbiggins trying very feebly to drop the net on a specially venturesome one, the head keeper almost lost the power of speech.

"Dinna let us interrupt you," and Mr. Byles looked up to see three armed keepers commanding their helpless party, and one of them purple with rage. "I hope we don't intrude; maybe we could give you a hand in catchin' the birds, and if a spring-cart would be of ony use . . . confound your cheek!

"Gathering flowers, are ye, and gave the pheasants a biscuit, did ye, and the boys thought they would like to stroke one, would they? How is that, lads? I've seen two or three poachers in my time, but for brazen-faced lyin' I've never seen your match. Maybe you're a Sabbath-school out for a trip, or an orphan asylum?

"Assistant mathematical master at the Seminary, that's what you are, is it, ye awfu' like blackguard, an' the laddies are the sons o' a respectable Free Kirk minister, the dirty dogs? Are ye sure ye're no' the principal o' Edinburgh University? Tak yir time and try again. I'm enjoying it. Is't by the hundred ye sell them, and wud it be a leeberty to ask for whose preserves? Dash the soople tongue o' ye.

"If ye dare to put yir hand in a pocket, I'll lodge a charge o' shot in ye: we'ill hae nae pistol-work in

Kilspindie Woods.   Come along wi' ye, professor an'
students, an' I'll give ye a ride into Muirtown, an'
we 'ill just be in time to catch the magistrate.   He
hasna tried a learned institution like this since he
mounted the bench.   March in front, but dinna try
to run, or it will be the waur for ye.   Ma certes, sic
a band o' waufies ! "

Then those two officers of justice, Peter and Nestie,
having seen all without being seen, now started for
Muirtown to gather the kite-players and as many of
the Seminary as could be found to see the arrival of
the botanists.   They were brought in a large spring-
cart—Mr. Byles seated between the head keeper and
the driver, in front, and the other three huddled like
calves in the space behind—a mass of mud, tatters,
and misery, from which the solemn, owl-like face of
Thomas John, whose cap was now gone also, looked
out in hopeless amazement.   As they were handed
over to the police the Seminary, which had been at
first struck dumb, recovered speech and expressed
itself with much vivacity.

" Who would have thought Byles had as much
spirit ?   Sall, he 'ill be rinnin' horses at Muirtown
Races yet " ;   " For ony sake walk backwards,
Thomas — yir breeks are barely decent " ;   " The
pheasants have been hard on yir legs, Cosh " ;
"Where's the geranniums ? "   " Has his Lordship kept
yir bonnet, Dowbiggin ? "   " It 'ill be a year's hard
labour."   For boys are only in the savage state, and

the discomfiture of such immaculate propriety was very sweet to the Seminary.

So powerful was the evidence of the head keeper, who saw in Mr. Byles's effort a new and cunning form of poaching he was not prepared for, and so weird was the appearance of the prisoners, that the Bailie on duty was for sentencing them at once, and would hardly wait for the testimony of friends. It took the sworn testimony of the Rector of the Seminary and poor Dr. Dowbiggin, summoned from their studies in hot haste and confusion of face, to clear the accused, and even then the worthy magistrate thought it proper, as Scots magistrates do, to administer a rebuke and warning so solemn that it became one of the treasures of memory for all Seminary lads.

" After what I have heard I cannot convict you, and you may go this time ; but let me never see you here again in such circumstances. It's fearsome to think that an educated man "—this to Byles— "instead of setting an example to the laddies under your charge, should be accused of a mean and cunning offence against the laws of the land, and I cannot look at your face without having grave doubts. And to think that the sons of a respected minister of the kirk should be found in such company, and with all the appearance of vagrants, must be a great trial to their father, and I am sure he has the sympathy of Muirtown. As for you, Cosh, I never expected to see the son of a brother Bailie in such a position. All I can hope is that this will be a lesson to you to keep clear of evil companions and evil ways, and that you may live to be a respectable citizen. But do not presume on your escape to-day —that is all I have to say."

Outside the court-room the head keeper caught Speug and gave him his mind.

"Ye're a limb o' Satan, Peter McGuffie, and that English-speakin' imp is little better. My belief is that this has been a pliskie (trick) o' yours frae beginning to end, and I just give ye one word o' advice—don't let me catch you in Kilspindie Woods, or it will be the worse for you."

VII

THE COUNT

IF you excluded two or three Englishmen who
spoke with an accent suggestive of an effeminate
character, and had a fearsome habit of walking on
the Sabbath, and poor " Moossy," the French master
at the Seminary, who was a quantity not worth considering, the foreign element in Muirtown during the
classical days consisted of the Count. He never
claimed to be a Count, and used at first to deprecate
the title, but he declined the honour of our title with
so much dignity that it seemed only to prove his
right, and by and by he answered to the name with
simply a slight wave of his hand which he meant for
deprecation, but which came to be considered a
polite acknowledgement. His real name was not
known in Muirtown—not because he had not given
it, but because it could not be pronounced, being
largely composed of x's and k's, with an irritating
parsimony of vowels. We had every opportunity of
learning to spell it, if we could not pronounce it, for
it was one of the Count's foreign ways to carry a

card-case in his ticket-pocket, and on being introduced to an inhabitant of Muirtown to offer his card
with the right hand while he took off his hat with
the left, and bowed almost to a right angle. Upon
those occasions a solid man like Bailie MacFarlane
would take hold of the card cautiously, not knowing
whether so unholy a name might not go off and
shatter his hand ; and during the Count's obeisance
which lasted for several seconds, the Bailie regarded
him with grave disapproval. The mind of Muirtown,
during this performance of the Count's, used to be
divided between regret that any human being should
condescend to such tricks, and profound thankfulness
that Muirtown was not part of a foreign country
where people were brought up with the manners of
poodles. Our pity for foreigners was nourished by
the manner of the Count's dress, which would have
been a commonplace on a *boulevard*, but astounded
Muirtown on its first appearance, and always lent an
element of piquant interest to our streets. His
perfectly brushed hat, broadish in the brim and
curled at the sides, which he wore at the faintest
possible angle, down to his patent leather boots,
which it was supposed he obtained in Paris, and
wore out at the rate of a pair a month—all was
unique and wonderful, but it was his frock-coat which
stimulated conversation. It was so tight and fitted
so perfectly, revealing the outlines of his slender
form, and there was such an indecent absence of

waist—waist was a strong point with Muirtown men,
and in the case of persons who had risen to office,
like the Provost, used to run to fifty inches—that a
report went round the town that the Count was a
woman. This speculation was confirmed rather than
refuted by the fact that the Count smoked cigarettes,
which he made with Satanic ingenuity while you
were looking at him, and that he gave a display of
fencing with the best swordsman of a Dragoon regiment in the barracks, for it was shrewdly pointed out
that those were just the very accomplishments of
French "Cutties." This scandal might indeed have
crystallised into an accepted fact, and the Provost
been obliged to command the Count's departure, had
it not been for the shrewdness and good nature of
the "Fair Maid of Muirtown." There always was a
fair maid in Muirtown—and in those days she was
fairest of her succession : let this flower lie on her
grave. She declared to her friends that she had
watched the Count closely and had never once seen
him examine a woman's dress when the woman
wasn't looking ; and after that no person of discern-
ment in Muirtown had any doubt about the Count's
sex. It was, however, freely said—and that story
was never contradicted—that he wore stays, and
every effort was made to obtain the evidence of his
landlady. Her gossips tried Mistress Jamieson with
every wile of conversation, and even lawyer's wives,
pretending to inquire for rooms for a friend, used to

lead the talk round to the Count's habits; but that worthy matron was loyal to her lodger, and was not quite insensible to the dignity of a mystery.

"Na, na, Mistress Lunan, I see what you're after; but beggin' your pardon, a landlady's a landlady, and my mouth's closed. The Count disna ken the difference atween Saturday and Sabbath, and the money he wastes on tobacco juist goes to ma heart; but he never had the blessin' of a Gospel ministry nor the privileges of Muirtown when he was young. As regards stays, whether he wears them or disna wear them I'm no prepared to say, for I thank goodness that I've never yet opened a lodger's boxes nor entered a lodger's room when he was dressin'. The Count pays his rent in advance every Monday morning; he wanted to pay on Sabbath, but I told him it was not a lawful day. He gives no trouble in the house, and if his doctor ordered him to wear stays to support his spine, which I'm no sayin' he did, Mistress Lunan, it's no concern o' mine, and the weather is inclining to snow."

His dress was a perfect fabric of art, however it may have been constructed; and it was a pleasant sight to see the Count go down our main street on a summer afternoon, approving himself with a side glance in the mirrors of the larger shops, striking an attitude at our bookseller's when a new print was exposed in the window, waving his cigarette and blowing the smoke through his nostrils, which was considered a "tempting of Providence," making his respectful salutations to every lady whom he knew, and responding with "Celestial, my friend!" to Bailie MacFarlane's greeting of "Fine growing weather." When he sailed past McGuffie's stable-yard, like Solomon in all his glory, that great man, who always persisted in regarding the Count as a sporting character, would touch the rim of his hat with his forefinger—an honour he paid to few—and, after the Count had disappeared, would say "Gosh!" with much relish. This astounding spectacle very early attracted the attention of the Seminary boys, and during his first summer in Muirtown it was agreed that he would make an excellent target for snowball practice during next winter. The temptation was not one which could have been resisted, and it is to be feared that the Count would have been confined to the house when the snow was on the ground had it not been for an incident which showed him in a new light, and established him, stays or no stays, in the respect of the Seminary for ever. There had been a glorious fight on the first day of the war with the "Pennies," and when they were beaten, a dozen of them, making a brave rearguard fight, took up their position with the Count's windows as their background. There were limits to license even in those brave old days, and it was understood that the windows of houses, especially private houses, and still more especially in the vicinity of the Seminary, should not be broken, and if they were broken the culprits were hunted down and interviewed by " Bulldog " at length. When the " Pennies " placed themselves under the protection of the Count's glass, which was really an unconscious act of meanness on their part, the Seminary distinctly hesitated ; but Speug was in command, and he knew no scruples as he knew no fear.

" Dash the windows ! " cried the Seminary captain ; and when the " Pennies " were driven along the street, the windows had been so effectually dashed that there was not a sound pane of glass in the Count's sitting-room. As the victorious army returned to their capital, and the heat of battle died down, some anxiety about tomorrow arose even in minds not given to care, for Mistress Jamieson was not the woman to have her glass broken for nothing, and it was shrewdly suspected that the Count, with all his dandyism, would not take this affront lightly. As a matter of fact, Mistress Jamieson made a personal call upon the Rector that evening, and explained with much eloquence to that timid, harassed scholar that, unless his boys were kept in better order, Muirtown would not be a place for human habitation ; and before she left she demanded the blood of the offenders ; she also compared Muirtown in its present condition to Sodom and Gomorrah. As the Rector was always willing to leave discipline in the capable hands of Bulldog, and as the chief sinners would almost certainly be in his class in the forenoon, the Count, who had witnessed the whole battle from a secure corner in his sitting-room, and had afterwards helped Mistress Jamieson to clear away the *débris*, went to give his evidence and identify the culprit. He felt it to be a dramatic occasion, and he rose to its height ; and the school retained a grateful recollection of Bulldog and the Count side by side—the Count carrying himself with all the grace and dignity of a foreign ambassador come to settle an international dispute, and Bulldog more austere than ever, because he hated a " tell-pyet," and yet knew that discipline must be maintained.

The Count explained with many flourishes that he was desolated to come for the first time to this so distinguished a Gymnasium upon an errand so distasteful, but that a lady had laid her commands on him (" Dis the body mean Lucky Jamieson ? " whispered Speug to a neighbour), and he had ever been a slave of the sex (Bulldog at this point regarded him with a disdain beyond words). The Rector of this place of learning had also done him, an obscure person, the honour of an invitation to come and assist at this function of justice ; and although, as the Count explained, he was no longer a soldier, obedience was still the breath of his nostrils. Behold him, therefore, the servant of justice, ready to be questioned or to lay down his life for law ; and the

Count bowed again to Bulldog, placing his hand
upon his heart, and then leant in a becoming attitude
against the desk, tapping his shining boots with his
cane, and feeling that he had acquitted himself with
credit.

"We're sorry to bring ye out on such a day, sir,"
and Bulldog's glance conveyed that such a figure as
the Count's ought not to be exposed in snowtime;
"but we'll not keep ye long, and I'll juist state the
circumstances with convenient brevity. The boys of
the Seminary are allowed to exercise themselves in
the snowtime within limits. If they fight wi' neighbouring schools, it's a maitter of regret; but if they
break windows, they're liable to the maist extreme
penalty. Now, I'm informed that some of the young
scoundrels—and I believe the very laddies are in this
class-room at this meenut" (Speug made no effort to
catch Bulldog's eye, and Howieson's attention was
entirely occupied with mathematical figures)—" have
committed a breach of the peace at Mistress Jamieson's
house. What I ask you, sir, to do"—and Bulldog
regarded the Count with increasing disfavour, as he
thought of such a popinjay giving evidence against
his laddies—" is, to look round this class-room and
point out, so far as ye may be able, any boy or boys
who drove a snowball or snowballs through the
windows of your residence."

During this judicial utterance the eyes of the Count
wandered over the school with the most provoking

intelligence, and conveyed even to the dullest, with a vivacity of countenance of which Muirtown was not capable, that Bulldog was a tiresome old gentleman, that the boys were a set of sad dogs, capable of any mischief, that some of them were bound to get a first-class thrashing, and worst of all that he, the Count, knew who would get it, and that he was about to give evidence in an instant with the utmost candour and elegance of manner. When his glance lighted on Speug it was with such a cheerful and unhesitating recognition that Speug was almost abashed, and knew for certain that for him, at least, there could be no escape ; while Howieson, plunging into arithmetic of his own accord for once, calculated rapidly what would be his share of the broken glass, Neither of them would have denied what he did to save himself twenty thrashings ; but they shared Bulldog's disgust that a free-born Scot should be convicted on the evidence of a foreigner, whom they always associated in his intellectual gifts and tricks of speech with the monkey which used to go round seated on the top of our solitary barrel-organ.

" When it is your pleasure, sir," said Bulldog sternly ; and there was a silence that could be felt, whilst Speug already saw himself pointed out with the Count's cane.

The shutters went suddenly down on the Count's face ; he became grave and anxious, and changed from a man of the world, who had been exchanging

a jest with a few gay Bohemians, into a witness in
the Court of Justice.

"Assuredly, monsieur, I will testify upon what you
call my soul and conscience," and the Count indicated
with his hand where both those faculties were contained. "I will select the boy who had audacity, I
will say profanity, to break the windows of my good
friend and hostess, Madame Jamieson."

The Count gave himself to the work of selection,
but there was no longer a ray of intelligence in his
face. He was confused and perplexed, he looked
here and he looked there, he made little impatient
gestures, he said a bad French word, he flung up a
hand in despair, he turned to Bulldog with a frantic
gesture, as of a man who thought he could have done
something at once, and found he could not do it at
all. Once more he faced the school, and then Speug,
with that instinct of acute observation which belongs
to a savage, began to understand, and gave Howieson
a suggestive kick.

"As a man of honour," said the Count with much
solemnity, "I give my testimony, and I declare that I
do not see one of the boys who did forget themselves
yesterday and did offer the insult of an assault to
Madame's domicile."

And it would have been curious if he had seen the
boys, for the Count was looking over their heads, and
studying the distant view of the meadow and the
River Tay with evident interest and appreciation.

The mind of Speug was now clear upon the Count, and Bulldog also understood, and in two seconds, so quick is the flash of sympathy through a mass of boy life, the youngest laddie in the mathematical class-room knew that, although the Court might have had the misfortune to be born in foreign parts, and did allow himself to dress like a dancing-master, inside that coat, and the stays too, if he had them on, there was the heart of a man who would not tell tales on any fellow, and who also liked his bit of fun.

"It's a peety, Count," said Bulldog, with poorly concealed satisfaction, "that ye're no· in a poseetion to recognise the culprits, for if they're no' here my conviction is they're no' to be found in Muirtown. We can ask no more of ye, sir, and we're much obleeged for yir attendance."

"It is a felicitous affair," said the Count, "which has the fortune to introduce me to this charming company," and the Count bowed first to Bulldog and then to the school with such a marked indication in one direction that Speug almost blushed. "My sorrow is to be so stupid a witness; but, monsieur, you will allow me to pay the penalty of my poor eyesight. It will be my pleasure," and again the Count bowed in all directions, "to replace the glass in Madame's house, and the incident, pouf! it is forgotten."

There was a swift glance from all parts of the

class-room, and permission was read in Bulldog's face. Next instant the mathematical class-room was rent with applause, such as could only be given when fifty such lads wanted to express their feelings, and Speug led the circus.

"Ye will allow me to say, sir," and now Bulldog came as near as possible to a bow, "that ye have acted this day as a gentleman, and so far as the boys of Muirtown Seminary are concerned ye're free to come and go among us as ye please."

The departure of the Count, still bowing, with Bulldog attending him to the door and offering him overshoes to cover the polished leather boots, was a sight to behold, and the work done for the rest of the morning was not worth mentioning.

During the lunch hour the school was harangued in short, pithy terms by Speug, and in obedience to his invitation Muirtown Seminary proceeded in a solid mass to the Count's residence, where they gave a volley of cheers. The Count was more gratified than by anything that had happened to him since he came to Muirtown; and throwing up one of the newly repaired windows he made an eloquent speech, in which he referred to Sir Walter Scott and Queen Mary and the Fair Maid of Perth, among other romantic trifles; declared that the fight between the "Pennies" and the Seminary was worthy of the great Napoleon; pronounced Speug to be *un brave garçon*; expressed his regret that he could not receive the school in his limited apartments, but invited them to cross with him to the Seminary tuckshop, where he entertained the whole set to Mistress MacWhae's best home-made ginger-beer. He also desired that Mistress Jamieson should come forward to the window with him and bow to the school, while he held her hand—which the Count felt would have been a really interesting tableau. It certainly would have been, but Mistress Jamieson refused to assist in the most decided terms.

" Me stand wi' the Count at an open window, hand in hand wi' him, and bowin', if ye please, to thae blackguard laddies? Na, na; I'm a widow o' good character and a member o' the Free Kirk, and it would ill set me to play such tricks. But I'll say this for the Count—he behaved handsome; and I'm judgin' the'll no be another pane o' glass broken in my house so long as the Count is in it." And there never was.

It were not possible to imagine anything more different than a Muirtown boy and the Count; but boys judge by an instinct which never fails within its own range, and Muirtown Seminary knew that, with all his foreign ways, the Count was a man. Legends gathered around him and flourished exceedingly, being largely invented by Nestie, and offered for consumption at the mouth of the pistol by Speug, who let it be understood that to deny or even to smile at Nestie's most incredible invention would be a ground

of personal offence.   The Count was in turn a foreign
nobleman, who had fallen in love with the Emperor
of Austria's daughter and had been exiled by the
imperial parent, but that the Princess was true to the
Count, and that any day he might be called from
Mistress Jamieson's lodgings to the palace of Vienna ;
that he was himself a king of some mysterious
European State, who had been driven out by conspirators, but whose people were going to restore
him, and that some day Speug would be staying with
the Count in his royal abode and possibly sitting
beside him on the throne.   During this romance
Speug felt it right to assume an air of demure
modesty, which was quite consistent with keeping a
watchful eye on any impertinent young rascal who
might venture to jeer, when Speug would politely ask
him what he was laughing at, and offer to give him
something to laugh for.   That the Count was himself
a conspirator, and the head of a secret society which
extended all over Europe, with signs and passwords,
and that whenever any tyrant became intolerable,
the warrant for his death was sent from Mistress
Jamieson's.   Whenever one fable grew hackneyed
Nestie produced another, and it was no longer
necessary in Muirtown Seminary to buy Indian tales
or detective stories, for the whole library of fiction
was now bound up and walking about in the
Count.

Between him and the boys there grew up a fast

friendship, and he was never thoroughly happy now
unless he was with his "jolly dogs." He attended
every cricket match, and at last, after he had learned
how, kept the score, giving a cheer at every new run
and tearing his hair when any of his boys were
bowled out. He rushed round the football field
without his cane, and generally without his hat; and
high above all cheers could be heard his "Bravo—
bravo, forwards! Speug!" as that enterprising player
cleft his way through the opponent's ranks. It
mattered nothing to the Count that his boots were
ruined, and his speckless clothes soiled, he would not
have cared though he had burst his stays, so long as
the "dogs" won, and he could go up in glory with
them to Janet MacWhae's and drink to their health
in flowing ginger-beer. During the play hour his
walk seemed ever to bring him to the North Meadow,
and if a ball by accident, for none would have done
it by intention, knocked off the Count's hat, he cried
" Hoor-r-rah!" in his own pronunciation and bowed
in response to this mark of attention. It was a pretty
sight to see him bending forward, his hands resting
on his knees, watching a battle royal between the
tops of Speug and Howieson; and if anything could
be better it was to see the Count trying to spin a top
himself, and expostulating with it in unknown
tongues.

As the boys came to the school in the morning
and went home in the evening up Breadalbane

Street, the Count was always sitting at one of the
windows which had been broken, ready to wave
his hand to any one who saluted him, and in the
afternoon he would often open the window to get the
school news and to learn whether there would be a
match on Saturday. As time went on this alliance
told upon the Count's outer man ; he never lost his
gay manner, nor his pretty little waist, nor could he
ever have been taken for a Scot, nor ever, if he had
lived to the age of Methuselah, have been made an
elder of the Kirk ; but his boots grew thicker, though
they were always neat, and his clothes grew rougher,
though they were always well made, and his ties
became quieter, and his week-day hat was like that
of other men, and, except on Sundays, Muirtown
never saw the glory of the former days. With his
new interest in life, every one noticed that the Count
had grown simpler and kindlier, and Muirtown folk,
who used to laugh at him with a flavour of contempt, began to love him through their boys. He
would walk home with Bulldog on a summer evening,
the strangest pair that ever went together ; and it
was said that many little improvements for the
comfort of the lads, and many little schemes for their
happiness at Muirtown Seminary, were due to the
Count. It was believed that the time did come when
he could have returned to his own land, but that he
did not go because he was a lonely man and had
found his friends in Muirtown ; and when he died,

now many years ago, he left his little all for the benefit of his "jolly dogs," and the Count, who had no mourners of his blood, was followed to his grave by every boy at Muirtown Seminary.

VIII

A TOURNAMENT

SINCE the day when Speug and a few young
friends had broken every pane of glass in the
Count's windows, and the Count had paid for the
damage like a gentleman, that excellent foreigner
had spent all his spare cash—which we thought
afterwards was not very much — in encouraging
athletic exercises among the Seminary lads. His
zeal, like that of every other convert, was much
greater than his knowledge, and left to his own
devices he would certainly have gone far astray ; but
with the able assistance of Speug, with whom he took
intimate counsel, it was astonishing what a variety
could be infused into the sports. When every ordinary competition had been held, and champions had
been declared (and this had never been done before
in the history of the school) for the hundred yards,
the quarter, and the mile (the ten miles down the
Carse and over the top of Kinnoul Hill had been
stopped by an impromptu meeting of parents), for
broad jumping and high jumping, for throwing the

cricket ball and kicking the football, Speug came out
with a quite new programme which was rapturously
received, and had it not met with a cross-providence
would have lasted over four happy Saturdays and
considerably reduced the attendance at the Seminary.
The first item was a swimming match across the
Tay, a river not to be trifled with, and four boys
were saved from death by a salmon cobble, whose
owner fortunately turned up to watch the sport.
The Count was so excited by this event that he not
only lost his hat in the river, but being prevented
from going in to help, for the very good reason that he
could not swim a stroke, he took off and flung the
coat, which was the marvel of Muirtown, into the river,
in the hope that it might serve as a lifebelt.   The
second item, upon which Speug prided himself very
much, was a climbing match, and for this he had
selected a tree which seemed to be designed for the
purpose, since it had a rook's nest on its highest
branch, and no branches at all for the first twenty
feet.   The conditions were, that every boy above
twelve should have his chance, and the boy who
climbed to the top, put his hand into the rook's nest,
and came down in the shortest time, should get the
prize.   The Seminary above twelve were going up
and down that tree a whole Saturday morning, and
in one kirk next day thanks were offered in the first
prayer in peculiarly dignified and guarded terms that
half the families of Muirtown had not been bereaved.

As a matter of fact, nobody was killed, and no limbs were broken, but Speug, who was not allowed to enter for this competition, but acted as judge, with his tongue out all the time at the sight of the sport, had to go up twice on errands of mercy, once to release his friend Howieson, who had missed a branch and was hanging by his feet, and the second time to succour Pat Ritchie, who was suspended by the seat of his trousers, swaying to and fro like a gigantic apple on the branch. It was understood that the Seminary had never enjoyed themselves so entirely to their heart's content, but the Count's moral courage failed during the performance, and at the most critical moment he was afraid to look. When Muirtown got wind of this last achievement of Speug's, indignation meetings were held at church-doors and street corners, and it was conveyed to the Rector—who knew nothing about the matter, and was so absent-minded that if he had passed would never have seen what was going on—that if Providence was going to be tempted in this fashion again, the matter would he brought before the Town Council. The Count himself would have been faithfully dealt with had he not been considered a helpless tool in the hands of Speug, who was now understood to have filled the cup of his sins up to the brim. He might indeed have been at last expelled from the Seminary, of which he was the chief ornament, had it not been that the Count went to the Rector and explained that the idea had been his from beginning to end, and that it was with the utmost difficulty he could induce Speug even to be present. For, as I said, the Count was a perfect gentleman, and always stood by his friends through thick and thin ; but the thrashing which Speug got from Bulldog was monumental, and in preparation for it that ingenious youth put on three folds of underclothing.

What Speug bitterly regretted, however, was not the punishment, which was cheap at the money, but the loss of the next two items in his programme. He had planned a boxing competition, in which the main feature was to be a regular set-to between Dunc Robertson and himself, to decide finally which was the better man, for they had fought six times and the issue was still doubtful ; and Speug, who had a profligate genius outside the class-rooms, had also imagined a pony race with hurdles ; and as about twenty fellows, farmers' sons and others, had ponies, of which they were always bragging, and Speug had the pick of his father's stables, he modestly believed that the affair would be worth seeing. When the hurdle race was forbidden, for which Speug had already begun to make entries and to arrange weights with his father's valuable assistance, he took the matter so much to heart that his health gave way, and Mr. McGuffie senior had to take him to recruit at the Kilmarnock Races, from which he returned in the highest spirits and full of stories.

For some time after this painful incident the Count lay low and adopted a deprecating manner when he met the fathers and mothers of Muirtown ; but he gave his friends to understand that his resources were not at an end, and that he had a surprise in store for the Seminary. Speug ran over every form of sport in casual conversation to discover what was in the Count's mind, but he would not be drawn and grew more mysterious every day. One Saturday evening in midsummer he took Speug and Nestie into his confidence, explaining that his idea would be announced to the assembled school by himself next Wednesday, and that it had nothing to do, as Speug had hinted in turn, with rats, or rabbits, or fencing, or the sword dance. With their permission he would say one word which would be enough for persons of so distinguished an imagination, and that word was "Tournament" ; and then he would speak of nothing else except the beauty of the evening light upon the river, which he declared to be "ravishing," and the excellence of a certain kind of chocolate which he carried in his pocket, and shared generously with his "dogs." As he parted with his friends the Count tapped his nose and winked at them—"Tournament — great, magnificent, you will see, ha, ha ! you will see" ; and Speug went home in a state of utter confusion, coming finally to the conclusion that the Count intended to introduce some French game, and in that case it would be his painful duty to oppose the Count tooth and nail, for everybody knew that French games were only for girls, and would bring endless disgrace upon Muirtown Seminary. During Sunday Nestie had turned the matter over in his mind, and being full of Scott's novels he was able on Monday to give the astonished school a full programme with the most minute particulars. The tournament was to be held in the North Meadow ; the judge was to be the Commander of the cavalry at the barracks ; John Chalmers, the town's bellman, was to be herald ; the Fair Maid of Perth was to be the Queen of Beauty ; and the combatants were to be such knights as Robertson, Howieson, and of course Speug. Each knight was to be in armour, and Nestie freely suggested dish-covers would be useful as breastplates, broom-handles would come in conveniently for lances, and as ponies were now forbidden, sturdy boys of the lower forms would be used instead. The two knights who challenged one another would rush from opposite ends of the lists, meet in the centre, lance upon breastplate, horse to horse, and man to man, and the one that overthrew the other would receive the prize ; and at the thought of such a meeting between Speug and Dunc Robertson, each in full armour, the delighted school smacked their lips.

"Muirtown Races 'ill be nothing to it," said Ritchie. "I'll lay anybody a shilling that Speug coups (capsizes) Dunc the first meeting ; but "—feeling as if it were almost too good to be true—" I dinna believe a word

o't. Nestie is a fearsome liar." And after the school
had spoken of nothing else for a day, Dunc Robertson
asked the Count boldly whether such things were
true.

" *Mon ami*," said the Count, who had tasted Nestie's
romance with much relish, " you will pardon me, but
it is a *banalité*, that is what you call a stupidity, to
ask whether so good a *jeu d'esprit* is true. True ?
Truth is a dull quality, it belongs to facts ; but Nestie,
he does not live among facts, he flies in the air, in the
atmosphere of poetry. He is a *raconteur*. A tournament with knights on the North Meadow—good !
Our little Nestie, he has been reading *Ivanhoe* and
he is a troubadour." And the Count took off his hat
in homage to Nestie's remarkable powers as an author
of fiction.

" But yes, it will be a tournament ; but not for the
body, for the mind. My dogs are jolly dogs ; they
can run, they can leap, they can swim, they can kick
the ball ; now they must think, ah ! so deep. They
must write their very best words, they must show that
they have beautiful minds ; and they will do so, I
swear they will, in the tournament, which will not be
on the meadow—no ; too many cows there, and too
many washers of clothes—but in seclusion, in the
class-room of that brave man called the Bulldog. It
will be a battle," concluded the Count with enthusiasm,
" of heads : and the best head, that head will have the
prize, *voilà*."

"Silence!" and Bulldog brought his cane down upon his desk that Wednesday afternoon when the whole upper school was gathered in his class-room, bursting with curiosity. "The Count has a proposeetion to lay before you which he will explain in his own words and which has the sanction of the Rector. Ye will be pleased to give the Count a respectful hearing, as he deserves at yir hands." And Bulldog was there to see that the Count's deserts and his treatment strictly corresponded.

"Monsieur," and the Count bowed to Bulldog, "and you," and now he bowed to the boys, "all my friends of the Seminary, I have the honour to ask a favour which your politeness will not allow you to refuse. Next Saturday I will dare to hold a reception in this place, with the permission of the good Bull—— I do forgot myself—I mean the distinguished master. And when you come, I promise you that I will not offer you coffee—pouf! it is not for the brave boys I see before me, *non*," and the Count became very roguish. "I will put a leetle, very leetle sentence on the——" ("Blackboard," suggested Bulldog). "*Merci*, yes, the blackboard; no, the honourable master he will have the goodness to write it in his so beautiful characters. One sentence, that is all, and you will sit for one hour in this room where you make your studies, and you will write all the beautiful things which come into your heads about that sentence. You will then do me the pleasure of letting me carry home all those beautiful things, and I will read them ; and the writer who affects me most, I will ask him to accept a book of many volumes, and the Lor' Mayor " (" Provost," interpolated Bulldog) " will present it on the great day in the Town Hall.

" No one, not even the honourable master himself, will know that leetle sentence till it be written on the—the——" (" Blackboard," said Bulldog, with asperity), " and every boy will be able to write many things about that sentence. The scholars upon whom I do felicitate the honourable master will write much learning," and the Count made a graceful inclination in the direction of the two Dowbiggins ; " and the brave boys who love the sport, they will also write, ah ! ah ! "—and the Count nodded cheerfully in the direction of Speug—" such wonderful things. There will be no books ; no, you will have your heads, and and so it will be the fair play, as you say," repeated the Count with much satisfaction, " the fair play."

Bulldog dismissed the school after he had explained that no one need come unless he wished, but that any one who didn't come was missing the opportunity of securing an honourable distinction, and would also show himself to be an ungrateful little scoundrel for all that the Count had done for the Seminary.

" Dod," said Jock Howieson, with much native shrewdness, " aifter all his palaver it's naething but anither confounded exercise," for that worthy had

suffered much through impositions, and had never
been able to connect one sentence with another in an
intelligent manner. " The Dowbiggins can go if they
want, and they're welcome to the books. I'm going
next Saturday to Woody Island—will you come,
Speug ? " And it hung in the balance whether or not
the Count would be openly affronted next Saturday
when he found himself in the company of half a
dozen "swats," while his "jolly dogs " were off in a
pack to their island of romance.

Speug could not imagine himself sitting in a class-
room on Saturday afternoon, except under brute force,
and yet he felt it would be ungrateful after all his
kindness to leave the Count in the company of such
cheerless objects as the Dowbiggins. The remembrance of all the sporting prizes he had won at the
Count's hands, and the sight of the Count cheering
at the sports, came over his ingenuous heart and moved
him to the most unselfish act of his life. " Jock
Howieson," said Speug, with considerable dignity,
" ye may go to Woody Island if ye like, but it 'ill be
the dirtiest trick ye ever played, and I'll black both
yir een for ye on Monday. Have we ever had a
match, cricket or football, the last four years, and the
Count hesna been there ? Who got up the sports
and gave the prizes ? Tell me that, Jock ? Who
stands gingerbeer at Lucky MacWhae's, answer me
that, Jock, ye meeserable wretch ? " and then clinch-
ing every argument on " Who paid for the broken

glass? I'm doon richt ashamed o' ye, Jock Howie-son."

"Will ye go yourself, Speug?" demanded Jock, writhing under this torrent of reproach. "I think I see ye writin' an essay on the history o' the Romans, or sic like trash. Ye 'ill hunt us into Bulldog's class-room, and then go off yirsel to shoot rabbits; but ye 'ill no play ony tricks on me, Peter McGuffie."

"I will go," said Speug, manfully, "though I'll no promise to write."

"Say as sure's death," said Jock, knowing Speug's wiles.

"Sure as death," said Speug, and then the school knew, not only that he would go, though he had to sit six hours instead of one, but also that every self-respecting boy in the Seminary must also put in an appearance at the Count's reception.

"Best thing you ever did, Speug," said Nestie on the way home, "since you p-pulled me out of the Tay, and I should say that you have a good chance of the prize. What the Count wants is ori-gin-ginality, and I never heard a chap with so much original talk as you've got, Speug. Just you put some of it down, like what you give to the P-pennies, and you'll come out first, and it'll be the first prize you ever won."

"If there was a prize for impidence, and the entries were open to all Scotland," said Speug, "ye would pass the post first and trottin'."

"How I Spent My Saturday,"

was what the school saw on the board when the Count removed the white cloth, and then he gave a brief exposition of his desires.

"Have the goodness, if you please, to write, not what you ought, but what you want. Were you at the cricket match, you will tell me of the capture of the wickets ; or you were in the country, I will hear of the woods and the beautiful pheasants" (this delicate allusion to Mr. Byles' poaching experiences was much appreciated) ; "or you were among the books, then you will describe what you love in them ; or you were looking at a horse, I expect to hear about that horse"; and the whole school understood that this was a direct invitation to Speug, to give an exact picture of an Irish mare that his father had just bought. "The subject, ah!" said the Count, "that does not matter ; it is the manner, the style, the *esprit*, that is what I shall value. I wish you all the good success, and I will go a walk in the meadow till you have finished."

"Do yir best, laddies," said Bulldog, "for the credit of the school and to please the Count. If I see ony laddie playing tricks I'll do my part to teach him sobriety, and if I see one copying from another, out he goes. Ye have one hour from this meenut, make the most o't," and the tournament was open.

Bulldog, apparently reading his morning paper, and only giving a casual glance to see that no one took advantage of the strange circumstances, was really watching his flock very closely, and checking his judgement of each one by this new test. Dull, conscientious lads like the Dowbiggins began at once, in order that they might not lose a moment of time, but might put as much written stuff upon the paper as possible; yet now and again they stopped and looked round helplessly because they had no books and no tutor to assist them, and they realized for the first time how little they had in their own heads.

"Ha! ha!" said Bulldog to himself, "I kent ye were naithing but a painted show, and it 'ill do ye good to find that out for yirselves."

Jock Howieson and his kind regarded the whole matter as a new form of entertainment, and as he could not have put into anything approaching connected words the experiences of his last Saturday, he employed the time in cutting up his unwritten paper into squares of an inch, and making them into pellets with which he prevented the Dowbiggin mind from being too much absorbed in study. He did this once too often, and Bulldog went down to call upon him with a cane and with plain, simple words.

"His head is an inch thick," said Bulldog, as he went back to his desk, "but there's the making of a man in Jock, though he 'ill never be able to write a decent letter to save his life. He would suit the Scots Greys down to the ground."

Speug had given a solemn promise to Nestie, under the customary form of oath, that he would write something, and whatever he wrote he would hand in, though it was only twenty words, and Speug never went back from his oath. When Howieson caught the Dowbiggin ear with a pellet there is no doubt that a joyful light came into Speug's eyes, and he struggled with strong temptation, and when old friends made facetious signs to him he hesitated more than once, but in the end assumed an air of dignified amazement, explaining, as it were, that his whole mind was devoted to literary composition, and that he did not know what they meant by this impertinent intrusion upon a student's privacy. Cosh certainly jumped once in his seat as if he had been stung by a wasp, and it is certainly true that at that moment there was a piece of elastic on the thumb and first finger of Speug's left hand, but his right hand was devoted to literature. The language which Cosh allowed himself to use in the heat of the moment was so unvarnished that it came under Bulldog's attention, who told him that if he wanted to say anything like that again he must say it in Latin, and that he ought to take notice of the excellent conduct of Peter McGuffie, who, Bulldog declared, was not at all unlikely to win the prize. And as the master returned to his seat his back was seen to shake, and the wink with which Speug favoured the class, in a brief rest from labour, was a reward for an hour's drudgery. Bulldog knew everybody up and down, out and in—what a poor creature Cosh was, and what good stuff could be found in Speug ; and he also knew everything that was done—why Cosh had said what he said, and why Speug at that moment was lost in study. Bulldog was not disappointed when Nestie's face lighted up at the title of the essay, and he knew why his favourite little lad did not write anything for fifteen minutes, but looked steadily out at the window and across the North Meadow, and he returned to his paper with a sense of keen satisfaction when Nestie at last settled down to work and wrote without ceasing, except when now and again he hesitated as for a word, or tried a sentence upon his ear to know how it sounded. For the desire of Bulldog's heart was that Nestie should win, and if— though that, of course, was too absurd—Speug by the help of the favouring gods should come in second, Bulldog would feel that he had not lived in vain.

"Ye have three meenuts to dot your i's and stroke your t's," said Bulldog, "and the Count will tell ye how ye're to sign yir names," and then the Count, who had come in from his walk, much refreshed, advanced again to the desk.

"It would be one great joy to have your autographs," said the Count, "and I would place them in

a book and say, 'My friends'; but honour forbids.
As I shall have the too great responsibility of judging,
it is necessary that I be—ah! I have forgotten the
word—yes! show the fair play. No, I must not
know the names; for if I read the name of my
friend the ever active, the ever brave, the ever interesting Speug" (at this indecent allusion Speug grew
purple and gave the bench in front of him to understand by well known signs that if they looked at him
again he might give them something to look for
outside), "I would say that Speug is a sportsman
but he is not a *littérateur*, and I might not do my
comrade the full justice. And if I read the name of
the composed, the studious, the profound young
gentlemen who are before me" (and it was fortunate
the Dowbiggins had their backs to the school), "I
would know that it must be the best before I read it,
and that would not be the fair play.

"No! you will write on your admirable essay a
motto—what you please—and your name you will
put in an envelope, so," and the Count wrote his own
name in the most dashing manner, and in an awful
silence, on a piece of paper, and closed the envelope
with a graceful flourish : "and outside you will put
your motto, so it will be all the fair play, and in the
Town Hall next Saturday I shall have the felicity to
declare the result. *Voilà!* Has my plan your
distinguished approbation?" and the Count made a
respectful appeal to Bulldog. "Nothing could be

fairer, you say? Then it is agreed, and I allow myself to wish you adieu for this day."

When the school assembled for conference among the Russian guns, their minds were divided between two subjects. The first was what Speug had written, on which that strenuous student would give no information, resenting the inquiry both as an insult to his abilities and an illustration of vain curiosity on the part of the school. Nestie, however, volunteered the trustworthy information that Speug had spent his whole time explaining the good which he had got from being kept in one Saturday forenoon and doing mathematical problems under the eye of Bulldog. And Nestie added that he thought it mean of Peter to "suck up" to the master in this disgraceful fashion just for the sake of getting a prize. Peter confided to Nestie afterwards that he had really done his best to describe a close race for the Kilmarnock Cup, but that he didn't think there were six words properly spelt from beginning to end, and that if he escaped without a thrashing he would treat Nestie to half a dozen bottles of ginger-beer.

Regarding the winner—for that was the other subject—there was a unanimous and sad judgement : that Dunc Robertson might have a chance, but that Thomas John, the head of the Dowbiggins, would carry off the prize, as he had carried off all the other prizes ; and that, if so, they would let him know how they all loved him at the Town Hall, and that it

would be wise for him to go home with the Count's
prize and all the other prizes in a cab, with the windows up.

The prize-giving in the Town Hall was one of the
great events in the Muirtown year, and to it the
memory of a Seminary lad goes back with keen
interest. All the forenoon the Provost and the
bailies had been sitting in the classroom of the
Seminary, holding Latin books in their hands, which
they opened anywhere, and wagging their heads in
solemn approval over the translation by Thomas
John and other chosen worthies, while the parents
wandered from place to place and identified their
sons, who refused to take any notice of them unless
nobody was looking. What mothers endured cannot
be put into words, when they saw their darling boys
(whom they had seen dressed that morning in their
Sunday clothes, and sent away in perfect array, with
directions that they were not to break their collars,
nor soil their jackets, nor disarrange their hair the
whole day, or they need not come home in the evening) turn up in a class-room before the respectables
of Muirtown as if their heads had not known a brush
for six months, with Speug's autograph upon their
white collar, a button gone from their waistcoat, and
an ounce of flour in a prominent place on their once
speckless jacket.

"Yes," said one matron to another, with the calmness of despair, " that is my Jimmy, I canna deny it ;

but ye may well ask, for he's more like a street waufie than onything else. On a day like this, and when I see what a sight he's made of himself in two hours I could almost wish he had been born a girl."

"Losh keep us, Mistress Chalmers, ye maunna speak like that, for it's no chancy, he micht be taken away sudden, and ye would have regrets; forbye your laddie's naithing to my Archie, for the last time I saw him, as I'm a livin' woman, there wasna more than two inches of his necktie left, and he was fishing his new Balmoral bonnet out of the water-barrel in the playground. Ye needna expect peace if the Almichty give ye laddies, but I wouldna change them for lassies—na, na, I'll no' go that length."

And the two matrons sustained themselves with the thought that if their boys were only a mere wreck of what they had been in the morning, other people's boys were no better, and some of them were worse, for one of them had inflicted such damages on his trousers that, although he was able to face the public, he had to retire as from the royal presence; nor was it at all unlike the motherly mind to conceive a malignant dislike to the few boys who were spick and span, and to have a certain secret pride even in their boys' disorder, which at any rate showed that they were far removed from the low estate of lassies.

The great function of the day came off at two o'clock, and before the hour the hall was packed with fathers, mothers, sisters, elder brothers, uncles, aunts, cousins and distant relatives of the boys, while the boys themselves, beyond all control and more dishevelled than ever, were scattered throughout the crowd. Some were sitting with their parents and enduring a rapid toilet at the hands of their mothers; others were gathered in clumps and arranging a reception for the more unpopular prize-winners; others were prowling up and down the passages, exchanging sweetmeats and responding (very coldly) to the greeting of relatives in the seats, for the black terror that hung over every Seminary lad was that he would be kissed publicly by a maiden aunt. Mr. Peter McGuffie senior came in with the general attention of the audience, and seated himself in a prominent place with Speug beside him. Not that Mr. McGuffie took any special interest in prize-givings, and certainly not because Speug had ever appeared in the character of a prize-winner. Mr. McGuffie's patronage was due to his respect for the Count and his high appreciation of what he considered the Count's sporting offer, and Mr. McGuffie was so anxious to sustain the interest of the proceedings that he was willing, although he admitted that he had no tip, to have a bet with any one in his vicinity on the winning horse. He also astonished his son by offering to lay a sovereign on Nestie coming in first and half a length ahead, which was not so much based upon any knowledge of Nestie's literary qualifications as on the strange friendship between Nestie and his promising son. As the respectable Free Kirk elder who sat next Mr. McGuffie did not respond to this friendly offer, Mr. McGuffie put a straw in his mouth and timed the arrival of the Provost.

When that great dignitary, attended by the bailies and masters, together with the notables of Muirtown, appeared on the platform, the boys availed themselves of the licence of the day, shouting, cheering, yelling, whistling and bombarding all and sundry with pellets of paper shot with extraordinary dexterity from little elastic catapults, till at last Bulldog, who in the helplessness of the Rector always conducted the proceedings, rose and demanded silence for the Provost, who explained at wide intervals that he was glad to see his young friends (howls from the boys) and also their respected parents (fresh howls, but not from the parents) ; that he was sure the fathers and mothers were proud of their boys to-day (climax of howls) ; that he had once been a boy himself (unanimous shout of " No " from the boys) ; that he had even fought in a snowball fight (loud expressions of horror) ; that he was glad the Seminary was flourishing (terrific outburst, during which the Provost's speech came to an end, and Bulldog rose to keep order).

One by one the prize-winners were called up from the side of their proud parents, and if they were liked and had won their prizes with the goodwill of their fellows, each one received an honest cheer which was heartier and braver than any other cheer of the day, and loud above it sounded the voice of Speug, who, though he had never received a prize in his life, and never would, rejoiced when a decent fellow like Dunc Robertson, the wicket-keeper of the eleven and the half-back of the fifteen, showed that he had a head as well as hands. When a prig got too many prizes there was an eloquent silence in the hall, till at last a loud, accurate and suggestive "Ma-a-a-a!" from Speug relieved the feelings of the delighted school, and the unpopular prize-winner left the platform amid the chorus of the farmyard—cows, sheep, horses, dogs, cats and a triumphant ass all uniting to do him honour. It was their day, and Bulldog gave them their rights, provided they did not continue too long, and every boy believed that Bulldog had the same judgement as themselves.

To-day, however, the whole gathering was hungering and thirsting for the declaration of the Count's prize, because there never had been such a competition in Muirtown before, and the Count was one of our characters. When he came forward, wonderfully dressed, with a rose in his buttonhole and waving a scented handkerchief, and bowed to everybody in turn, from the Provost to Mr. McGuffie, his reception was monumental and was crowned by the stentorian approbation of Speug's father. Having thanked the company for their reception, with his hand upon his heart, and having assured the charming mothers of his young friends of his (the Count's) most respectful devotion, and declared himself the slave of their sisters, and having expressed his profound reverence for the magistrates (at which several bailies tried to look as if they were only men, but failed), the Count approached the great moment of the day.

The papers, he explained upon his honour, were all remarkable, and it had been impossible for him to sleep, because he could not tear himself away from the charming reflections of his young friends. (As the boys recognized this to be only a just compliment to their thoughtful disposition and literary genius, Bulldog had at last to arise and quell the storm.) There was one paper, however, which the Count compared to Mont Blanc, because it rose above all the others. It was "ravishing," the Count asserted, "superb"; it was, he added, the work of "genius." The river, the woods, the flowers, the hills, the beautiful young women, it was all one poem. And as the whole hall waited, refusing to breathe, the Count enjoyed a great moment. "The writer of this distinguished poem—for it is not prose, it is poetry—I will read his motto." Then the Count read, "Faint Heart never Won Fair Lady," and turning to the Provost, "I do myself the honour of asking your Excellency to open this envelope and to read the name to this distinguished audience." Before the Provost could get the piece of paper out of the envelope, Speug, who was in the secret of the motto, jumped up on his seat and, turning with his face to the audience, shouted at the pitch of his voice through the stillness of the hall, " Nestie Molyneux." And above the great shout that went up from the throat of the Seminary could be heard, full and clear, the view-hallo of Mr. McGuffie senior, who had guessed the winner without ever seeing the paper.

IX

MOOSSY

IF the eyes of an old boy do not light up at the mention of "Moossy," then it is no use his pleading the years which have passed and the great affairs which have filled his life; you know at once that he is an impostor and has never had the privilege of passing through Muirtown Seminary. Upon the genuine boy—fifty years old now, but green at heart —the word is a very talisman, for at the sound of it the worries of life and the years that have gone are forgotten, and the eyes light up and the face relaxes, and the middle-aged man lies back in his chair for the full enjoyment of the past. It was a rough life in the Seminary, with plain food and strenuous games; with well-worn and well-torn clothes; where little trouble was taken to give interest to your work, and little praise awarded when you did it well; where you were bullied by the stronger fellows without redress, and thrashed for very little reason; where there were also many coarsenesses which were sickening at the time to any lad with a sense of decency, and which he is glad, if he can, to forget; but, at least, there was one oasis in the wilderness where there was nothing but enjoyment for the boys, and that was the " Department of Modern Languages," over which Moossy was supposed to preside.

Things have changed since Moossy's day, and now there is a graduate of the University of Paris and a fearful martinet to teach young Muirtown French, and a Heidelberg man with several degrees and four swordcuts on his face to explain to Muirtown the mysteries of the German sentence. Indignant boys, who have heard appetising tales of the days which are gone, are compelled to "swat" at Continental tongues as if they were serious languages like Latin and Greek, and are actually kept in if they have not done a French verb. They are required to write an account of their holidays in German, and are directed to enlarge their vocabulary by speaking in foreign tongues among themselves. Things have come to such a pass it is said—but I do not believe one word of this—that the modern Speug, before he pulls off the modern Dowbiggin's bonnet and flings it into the lade, which still runs as it used to do, will be careful to say " *Erlauben Sie mir*," and that the modern Dowbiggin, before rescuing his bonnet, will turn and inquire with mild surprise, " *Was wollen Sie, mein Freund ?* " and precocious lads will delight their parents at the breakfast-table by asking for their daily

bread in the language and accent of Paris, because
for the moment they have forgotten English. It is
my own firm conviction, and nothing can shake it,
that Muirtown lads are just as incapable of explaining
their necessary wants in any speech except their own
as they were in the days of our fathers, and that if a
Seminary boy were landed in Calais to-day, he would
get his food at the buffet by making signs with his
fingers, as his father had done before him and as
becomes a young barbarian. He would also take
care, as his fathers did, that he would not be cheated
in his change nor be put upon by any "Frenchy."
Foreign graduates may do their best with Seminary
lads—and their kind elsewhere—but they will not
find it easy to shape their unruly tongues; for the
Briton is fully persuaded in the background of his
mind that he belongs to an imperial race and is born
to be a ruler, that every man will sooner or later have
to speak his language, and that it is undignified to
condescend to French. The Briton is pleased to
know that foreign nations have some means of communication between themselves—as, indeed, the lower
animals have, if you go into the matter; but since
the Almighty has put an English (or Scots) tongue
in his mouth, it would be flying in the face of
Providence not to use it. It is, however, an excellent
thing to have the graduates, and the trim class-room,
and the tables of the foreign verbs upon the wall, and
the conversation classes—Speug at a conversation

class!—and all the rest of it; but, oh! the days of long ago—and Moossy!

Like our only other foreigner, the Count, Moossy was a nameless man, for although it must have been printed on the board in the vestibule of the school, which had a list of masters and of classes, no one can now hint at Moossy's baptismal name, nor even suggest his surname. The name of the Count had been sunk in the nobility which we conferred upon him, and which was the tribute of our respectful admiration, but "Moossy" was a term of good-humoured contempt. We were only Scots lads of a provincial town, and knew nothing of the outside world; but yet, with the instincts of a race of Chieftains and Clansmen, we distinguished in our minds between our two foreigners and placed them far apart. No doubt the Count was womanish in his dress, and had fantastic manners, but we knew he was a gallant gentleman, who was afraid of nobody and was always ready to serve his friends; he was *débonnaire*, and counted himself the equal of any one in Muirtown, but Moossy was little better than an abject. He was a little man, to begin with, and had made himself smaller by stooping till his head had sunk upon his chest and his shoulders had risen to his ears; his hair fell over the collar of his coat behind, and his ill-dressed beard hid any shirt he wore; his hands and face showed only the slightest acquaintance with soap and water, and although Speug was not always

careful in his own personal ablutions, and more than
once had been sent down to the lade by Bulldog to
wash himself, yet Speug had a healthy contempt
for a dirty master. Moossy's clothes, it was believed,
had not been renewed since he came to the Seminary,
and the cloak which he wore on a winter day was a
scandal to the town. His feet were large and flat,
and his knees touched as the one passed the other,
and the Seminary was honestly ashamed at the sight
of him shambling across the North Meadow. He
looked so mean, so ill put together, so shabby, so
dirty, that the very "Pennies" hooted at him and
flung him in our faces. The Rector was also careless
of his dress, and mooned along the road, but then
everybody knew that he was a mighty scholar, and
that if you woke him from his meditation he would
answer you in Greek ; but even Speug understood
that Moossy was not a scholar. The story drifted
about through Muirtown, and filtered down to the
boys, that he was a bankrupt tradesman who had
fled from some little German town and landed in
Muirtown, and that because he could speak a little
English, and a little French, as German tradesmen
can, he had been appointed by an undiscriminating
Town Council to teach foreign tongues at the
Seminary. It is certain he had very little education
and no confidence in himself, and so he was ever
cringing to the bailies, which did him no injury,
for these great men regarded themselves as beings

bordering on the supernatural; and he was ever deferring and giving in to the boys, which was the maddest thing that any master could do, and only confirmed every boy in his judgement that Moossy was one of the most miserable of God's creatures.

His classes met in the afternoon, and were regarded as a pleasant relaxation after the labours of the day, and to escape from the government of Bulldog to the genial freedom of Moossy's room proved, as we felt in a vague way, that Providence had a tender heart towards the wants and enjoyments of boys. It goes without saying that no work was done, for there were only half a dozen who had any desire to work, and they were not allowed, in justice to themselves and to their fellows, to waste the mercies which had been provided. Upon Bulldog's suggestion, Moossy once provided himself with a cane, but it failed in his hands the first time he tried to use it, which was not at all wonderful, as Jock Howieson, who did not approve of canes, and regarded them as an invention of the Evil One, had doctored Moossy's cane with a horse-hair, so that it split into two at a stroke, and one piece flying back struck Moossy on the face.

"That'll learn him to be meddling with canes. It's plenty that Bulldog has a cane, without yon meeserable wretch"; and that was the last effort which Moossy made to exercise discipline.

Every afternoon he made a pitiable appeal that the boys would behave and learn their verbs. For about ten minutes there was quietness, and then, at the sight of Thomas John, sitting at the head of his form and working diligently upon a French translation, which he could do better than Moossy himself, Speug would make a signal to the form, and, leading off from the foot himself, the form would give one quick, unanimous, and masterful push, and Thomas John next instant was sitting on the floor; while if, by any possibility, they could land all his books on him as he lay, and baptize him out of his own ink-bottle, the form was happy and called in their friends of other forms to rejoice with them. Moossy, at the noise of Thomas John's falling, would hurry over and inquire the cause, that a boy so exemplary and diligent should be sitting on the floor with the remains of his work around him; and as Thomas John knew that it would be worth his life to tell the reason, Moossy and he pretended to regard it as one of the unavoidable accidents of life, and after Thomas John had been restored to his place, and the ink wiped off his clothes, Moossy exhorted the form to quietness and diligence. He knew what had happened, and would have been fit for a lunatic asylum if he had not; and we knew that he knew, and we all despised him for his cowardice. Had there been enough spirit in Moossy to go for Speug (just as Bulldog would have done), and thrash him there and

then as he sat in his seat, brazen and unashamed, we
would all have respected Moossy, and no one more
than Speug, to whom all fresh exploits would have
had a new relish.   But Moossy was a broken-spirited
man, in whom there was no fight, who held a post he
was not fit for, and held it to get a poor living for
himself and one who was dearer to him than his own
life.   So helpless was he, and so timid, that there
were times when the boys grew weary of their teasing
and disorder, and condescended to repeat a verb in
order to pass the time.

When the spring was in their blood—for, like all
young animals, they felt its stirring—then there were
wonderful scenes in Moossy's class-room.   He dared
not stand in those days between two forms, with his
face to the one and his back to the other, because of
the elastic catapults and the sharp little paper bullets,
which, in spite of his long hair, would always find out
his ears ; and if he turned round to face the battery,
the other form promptly unmasked theirs, and
between the two he was driven to the end of the
room ; and then, in his very presence, without a pretence of concealment, the two forms would settle their
differences, while, in guttural and uncultured German,
Moossy prayed for peace.   Times there were, I am
sorry to say, when at the sting of the bullet Moossy
said bad words, and although they were in German,
the boys knew that it was swearing, and Speug's
voice would be loudest in horror.

" Mercy on us, lads ! this is awful language to hear in the Seminary ! If the Town Council gets word of this, there'll be a fine stramash. For masel'," Speug would conclude piously, " I'm perfectly ashamed." And as that accomplished young gentleman had acquired in the stables a wealth of profanity which was the amazement of the school, his protest had all the more weight. Poor Moossy would apologize for what he had said, and beseech the school neither to say it themselves nor to tell what they had heard ; and for days afterwards Speug would be warning Thomas John that if he, Speug—censor of morals— caught him cursing and swearing like Moossy, he would duck him in the lade, and afterwards bring him before the Lord Provost and magistrates.

There was no end to the devices of the Seminary for enjoying themselves and tormenting Moossy ; and had it not been for Nestie, who had some reserves of taste, the fun would have been much more curious. As it was, Moossy never knew when he might not light upon a frog, till it seemed as if the class-room for modern languages were the chosen home for the reptiles of the district. One morning, when he opened his desk, a lively young Scots terrier puppy sprang up to welcome him, and nearly frightened Moossy out of such wits as he possessed. He had learned to open the door of his class-room cautiously, not knowing whether a German Dictionary might not be ingeniously poised to fall upon his

head. His ink-bottle would be curiously attached to
his French Grammar, so that when he lifted the book
the bottle followed it and sent the spray of ink over
his person, adding a new distinction of dirtiness to
his coat.   Boys going up to write on the blackboard,
where they never wrote anything but nonsense, would
work symbols with light and rapid touch upon the
back of Moossy's coat as they returned ; and if one
after the other, adding to the work of art, could draw
what was supposed to be a human face upon Moossy,
the class was satisfied it had not lost the hour.
There were times when Moossy felt the hand even
on the looseness of that foolish coat, and turned
suddenly ; but there was no shaking the brazen
impudence of Muirtown, and Moossy, looking into
the stolid and unintelligent expression of Howieson's
face, thought that he had been mistaken.   If one boy
was set up to do a verb, the form, reading from their
books and pronouncing on a principle of their own,
would do the verb with him and continue in a loud
and sonorous song, till Moossy had to stop them one
by one, and then they were full of indignation at
being hindered in their studies of the German
language.

Moossy was afraid to complain to the Rector, lest
his own incompetence should be exposed and his
bread be taken from him ; and of this the boys, with
the unerring cunning of savages, were perfectly
aware, and the torture might have gone on for

years had it not been for the intervention of
Bulldog and a certain incident. As the French
class-room was above the mathematical, any special
disturbance could be heard in the quietness below ;
and whatever else they did, the students of foreign
languages were careful not to invite the attention
of Bulldog. Indeed, the one check upon the freedom of Moossy's room was the danger of Bulldog's
arrival, who was engaged that hour with the little
boys and had ample leisure of mind to take note
of any outrageous noise above, and for want of
occupation was itching to get at old friends like
Howieson. There are times, however, when even
a savage forgets himself, and one spring day the
saturnalia in Moossy's room reached an historical
height. It had been discovered that any dislike
which Moossy may have had to a puppy in his
desk, and a frog in his top-cloak pocket, was
nothing to the horror with which he regarded
mice. As soon as it was known that Moossy
would as soon have had a tiger in the French
class-room as a mouse upon the loose, it was felt
that the study of foreign languages should take a new
departure. One morning the boys came in with
such punctuality, and settled to their work with
such demure diligence, that even Moossy was suspicious and watched them anxiously. For ten
minutes there was nothing heard but the drone of
the class mangling German sentences, and then

Howieson cried aloud in consternation, ' A mouse ! "

"Vat ees that you say ? Ah ! mices ! vere ? " and Moossy was much shaken.

"Yonder," said Speug, pointing to where a mouse was just disappearing under the desk; "and there's another at the fireplace. Dod, the place is fair swarming, and, Moossy, there's one trying to run up your leg. Take care, man, for ony sake."

"A mices," cried Moossy, "vill up my legs go; I vill the desk ascend," and with the aid of a chair Moossy scrambled on to his desk, where he entrenched himself against attack, believing that at that height he would be safe from "mices."

Speug suggested that as this plague of mice had burst upon the French class-room the scholars should meet the calamity like men, and asked Moossy's permission to go out upon the chase. For once Moossy and his pupils had one mind, and the school gave itself to its heart's content, and without a thought of consequences, to a mouse hunt. Nothing is more difficult than to catch a mouse, and the difficulty is doubled when no one wishes to catch it; and so the school fell over benches, and over one another, and jumped over the desks and scrambled under them, ever pretending to have caught a mouse, and really succeeding once in smothering an unfortunate animal beneath the weight of half a dozen boys. Thomas

John was early smeared with ink from top to bottom by an accident in which Howieson took a leading part, and the German Dictionary intended for a mouse happened to take Cosh on the way, which led to an encounter between that indignant youth and Bauldie, in which mice were forgotten. The blackboard was brought down with a crash, and a form was securely planted on its ruins. High above the babel Moossy could be heard crying encouragement, and demanding whether the "mices" had been caught, but nothing would induce him to come down from his fastness. When things were at their highest, and gay spirits like Speug were beginning to conclude that even a big snow fight was nothing to a mouse hunt, and Howieson had been so lifted that he had mounted a desk, not to catch a mouse, but to give a cheer, and was standing there without collar or tie, dishevelled, triumphant, and raised above all the trials of life, the door opened and Bulldog entered. And it was a beautiful tribute to the personality of that excellent man, that the whole room crystallized in an instant, and every one remained motionless, frozen, as it were, in the act.

Bulldog looked round with that calm composure which sat so well upon him, taking in Moossy perched upon his desk, Howieson on his form, Speug sitting with easy dignity on the top of Thomas John, and half a dozen worthies still tied together in a scrimmage, as if this were a sight to which he was accustomed every day in Muirtown Seminary.

"Foreign languages," he began, after a pause of ten seconds, "is evidently a verra divertin' subject of study, and I wonder that any pupil is left in the department of mathematics. I was not aware, Jock, that ye needed to stand on a form before you could do your German, and I suppose that is the French class in the corner. I'm sorry to intrude, but I'm pleased to see a class in earnest about its work ; I really am."

"Mices!" remarked Bulldog in icy tones, as poor Moossy came down from his desk and began to explain. "My impression is that you are right, as far as I can judge—and I have some acquaintance with the circumstances. There are a considerable number of mices in this room, a good many more mices than were brought in somebody's pocket this morning. The mices I see were in my class-room this morning, and they were very quiet and peaceable mices, and they'll be the same in this class-room after this, or I'll know the reason why. If you'll excuse me," and Bulldog embraced the whole scene in a comprehensive farewell, " I'll leave the foreign class-room and go down and see what my laddies are doing with their writing"; and when Bulldog closed the door Howieson realized that he owed his escape to Bulldog's respect for another man's class-room, but that the joyful day in modern languages had come to an end. There would be no more "mices."

Next Saturday afternoon Speug and Nestie were out for a ramble in the country, and turning into a lane where the hedgerows were breaking into green and the primroses nestling at the roots of the bushes they came upon a sight which made them pause so that they could only stand and look. Down the lane a man was dragging an invalid-chair, a poor and broken thing which had seen its best days thirty years ago. In the chair a woman was sitting, or rather lying, very plainly but comfortably dressed, and carefully wrapped up, whose face showed that she had suffered much, but whose cheeks were responding to the breath of spring. As they stood, the man stopped and went to the bank and plucked a handful of primroses and gave them to the woman ; and as he bent over her, holding up the primroses before her eyes, and as they talked together, even the boys saw the grateful pleasure in her eyes. He adjusted the well-worn cloak and changed her position in the chair, and then went back to drag it, a heavy weight down the soft and yielding track ; and the boys stood and stared and looked at one another, for the man who was caring so gently for this invalid, and toiling so manfully with the lumbering chair, was Moossy.

"C-cut away, Speug," said Nestie ; "he wouldn't

like us to see him. I say, he ain't a bad sort—
Moossy—after all. Bet you a bottle of g-ginger-beer
that's Moossy's wife, and that's why he's so poor."

They were leaving the lane when they heard an
exclamation, and going back they found that the
miserable machine had slipped into the ditch and
there stuck fast beyond poor Moossy's power of
recovery. With many an " Ach ! " and other words,
too, he was bewailing the situation and hanging over
his invalid, while she seemed to be cheering him and
trying if she could so lie in the chair as to lessen the
weight upon the lower side, while every minute the
wheel sank deeper in the soft earth.

"What are you st-staring at, you idle, worthless
v-vagabond?" said Nestie to Speug. "Come along
and give a hand to Moossy," who was so pleased to
get some help in the lonely place that he forgot
the revealing of his little secret. With Speug in the
shafts, who had the strength of a man in his compact
little body, and Moossy pulling on the other side,
the coach was soon upon the road again, amid a
torrent of gratitude from Moossy and his wife, partly
in English, but mostly in German, but all quite plain
to the boys, for gratitude is always understood in any
language. They came bravely along the lane, Speug
pulling, Moossy hanging over his wife to make sure
she had not been hurt, and Nestie plucking flowers
to make up a nosegay in memory of the lane, while
Moossy declared them to be *"Zwei herzliche Knaben."*

When they came to the main road, Speug would not give up his work, but brought the carriage manfully to the little cottage, hidden in a garden, where Moossy lodged. When she had been carried in— she was so light that Moossy could lift her himself— she compelled the boys to come in, too, and Moossy made fragrant coffee, and this they had with strange German cakes, which were not half bad, and to which they both did ample justice. Going home, Nestie looked at Speug, and Speug looked at Nestie, and though no words passed it was understood that the days of the troubles of Moossy in the Seminary of Muirtown were ended.

During the remaining year of Moossy's labours at the Seminary it would not be true to say that he became a good or useful master, for he had neither the knowledge nor the tact, or that the boys were always respectful and did their work, for they were very far removed from being angels ; but Moossy did pluck up some spirit, and Speug saw that he suffered no grievous wrong. He also took care that Moossy was not left to be his own horse from day to day, but that the stronger varlets of the Seminary should take some exercise in the shafts of Moossy's coach. Howieson was a young gentleman far removed from sentiment, and he gave it carefully to be understood that he only did the thing for a joke ; but there is no question that more than once Jock brought Moossy's carriage, with Moossy's wife in it, success-fully along that lane and other lanes, and it is a fact that, on a certain Saturday, Speug came out with one of his father's traps, and Mistress Moossy, as she was called, was driven far and wide about the country around Muirtown.

"You are what the papers call a ph-philanthropist, Speug," said Nestie, "and I expect to hear that you are opening an orphan asylum." And Speug promptly replied that, if he did, the first person to be admitted would be Nestie, and that he would teach him manners.

It was a fortunate thing for Moossy that some one died in Germany and left him a little money, so that he could give up the hopeless drudgery of the Seminary and go home to live in a little house upon the banks of the Rhine. His wife, who had been improving under Dr. Manley's care, began to brisk up at once, and was quite certain of recovery when one afternoon they left Muirtown Station. Some dozen boys were there to see them off, and it was Jock and Speug who helped Moossy to place her comfortably in the carriage. The gang had pooled their pocket-money—selling one or two treasures to swell the sum—that Moossy and his wife might go away laden with such dainties as schoolboys love, and Nestie had a bunch of flowers to place in her hands. They still called him Moossy, as they had done before, and he looked, to tell the truth, almost as shabby and his hair was as long as ever; but he

was in great spirits and much touched by the kindness of his tormentors.   As the English mail pulled
out of Muirtown Station with quickening speed, the
boys ran along the platform beside the carriage
shaking hands with Moossy through the open
window and passing in their gifts.

"Take care o' mices!" shouted Jock, with agreeable humour, but the last sight Moossy had of
Muirtown was Speug standing on a luggage-barrow
and waving farewell.

X

A LAST RESOURCE

THAT the Rector should be ill and absent from
his classes from time to time was quite in the
order of things, because he was a scholar and absent-
minded to a degree—going to bed in the morning,
and being got out of bed in rather less than time for
his work ; eating when it occurred to him, but pre-
ferring, on the whole, not to eat at all ; wearing very
much the same clothes summer and winter, and if he
added a heavy top-coat, more likely putting it on in
the height of summer and going without it when
there were ten degrees of frost. It was not for his
scholarship, but for his peculiarities that the school
loved him ; not because he edited a " Cæsar " and
compiled a set of Latin exercises, for which perfectly
unnecessary and disgusting labours the school hated
him, but because he used to arrive at ten minutes
past nine, and his form was able to jeer at Bulldog's
boys as they hastened into their class-room with
much discretion at one minute before the hour.
Because he used to be so much taken up with a

happy phrase in Horace that he would forget the
presence of his class, and walk up and down before
the fireplace, chortling aloud ; and because sometimes
he was so hoarse that he could only communicate
with the class by signs, which they unanimously
misunderstood. Because he would sometimes be
absent for a whole week, and his form was thrown
in with another, with the result of much enjoyable
friction, and an almost perfect neglect of work. He
was respected and never was annoyed, not even by
ruffians like Howieson, because every one knew that
the Rector was an honourable gentleman, with all
his eccentric ways, and the *Muirtown Advertiser* had
a leader every spring on the achievements of his
scholars. Edinburgh professors who came to examine the school used to fill up their speeches on the
prize-day with graceful compliments to the Rector,
supported by classical quotations, during which the
boys cheered rapturously and the Rector looked as
if he were going to be hung. He was one of the
recognized glories of Muirtown, and was freely
referred to at municipal banquets by bailies whose
hearts had grown merry within them drinking the
Queen's health, and was associated in the peroration
to the toast of "the Fair City" with the North
Meadow and the Fair Maid, and the River Tay and
the County Gaol.

Bulldog was of another breed. Whatever may
have been his negligences of dress and occupation

in private life—and on this subject Nestie and Speug told fearful lies—he exhibited the most exasperating regularity in public, from his copper-plate handwriting to his speckless dress, but especially by an inhuman and absolutely sinful punctuality. No one with a heart within him and some regard to the comfort of his fellow creatures, especially boys, had any right to observe times and seasons with such exactness. During all our time, except on the one great occasion I wish to record, he was never known to be ill, not even with a cold; and it was said that he never had been for a day off duty, even in the generation before us. His erect, spare frame, without an ounce of superfluous flesh, seemed impervious to disease, and there was a feeling in the background of our minds that for any illness to have attacked Bulldog would have been an act of impertinence which he would have known how to deal with. It was firmly believed that for the last fifty years—and some said eighty, but that was poetry—Bulldog had entered his class-room every morning, except on Saturdays, Sundays, and holidays, at 8.50, and was ready to begin work at the stroke of nine. There was a pleasant story that in the days of our fathers there had been such a fall of snow and so fierce a wind that the bridge had been drifted up, and no one could cross that morning from the other side. The boys from the south side of the town had brought news of the drift to the school, and the earlier arrivals, who had come in hope of a snow-fight, were so mightily taken with the news that they hurried to the Muirtown end of the bridge to look at the drift, and danced with joy at the thought that on the other side Bulldog was standing, for once helpless and dismayed. Speug's father, true ancestor of such a son, had shouted across the drift invitations for Bulldog to come over, secure in the fact that he could not be seen across its height, and in the hope that Bulldog would not know his voice. When they were weary celebrating the event, and after a pleasant encounter with a hastily organized regiment of message boys, the eager scholars sauntered along to the school, skirmishing as they went, just to be ready for the midday fight with the "Pennies." For the pure joy of it they opened the door of the mathematical class-room, merely to see how it looked when Bulldog was not there, and found that estimable teacher at his desk, waiting to receive them with bland courtesy. Some said that he had stayed in Muirtown all night, anticipating that drift, others that he had climbed over it in the early morning, before Muirtown was awake; but it was found out afterwards that he had induced old Duncan Rorison, the salmon fisher, to ferry him across the flooded river, that it took them an hour to reach the Muirtown side, and that they had both been nearly drowned in the adventure.

"Come in, my boys," was all that he said. "Ye're

a little late, but the roads are heavy this morning. Come to the fire and warm yir hands before ye begin yir work. It's a fine day for mathematics," and Mr. McGuffie senior used to tell his son with much relish that their hands were warmed. The school was profoundly convinced that if necessary Bulldog would be prepared to swim the river rather than miss a day in the mathematical class-room.

It was a pleasant spring morning, and the " marble " season had just begun, when Howieson, after a vicious and well-directed stroke which won him three " brownies," inquired casually whether anybody had seen Bulldog go in ; for, notwithstanding the years which came and went, his passing in was always an occasion. Every one then recollected that he had not been seen, but no one for a moment suggested that he had not arrived ; and even when the school trooped into the class-room and found Bulldog's desk empty, there was no exhilaration and no tendency to take advantage of the circumstances. No one knew where he might be lying in wait, and from what quarter he might suddenly appear ; and it was wonderful with what docility the boys began to work under the mild and beneficent reign of Mr. Byles, who had not at that time joined with the Dowbiggins in the unlawful pursuit of game. As the forenoon wore on there was certainly some curiosity, and Nestie was questioned as to Bulldog's whereabouts ; but it was understood to be a point of honour with Nestie, as a member of his household, to give no information about Bulldog's movements, and so the school were none the wiser. There was some wild talk during the hour, and a dozen stories were afloat by afternoon.   Next morning it was boldly said that Bulldog was ill, and some, who did not know what truth was, asserted that he was in bed, and challenged Nestie to deny the slander. That ingenious young gentleman replied vaguely but politely, and veiled the whole situation in such a mist of irrelevant detail that the school went in for the second day to the class-room rejoicing with trembling, and not at all sure whether Bulldog might not arrive in a carriage and pair, possibly with a large comforter round his throat, but otherwise full of spirits and perfectly fit for duty.   It was only after the twelve o'clock break and a searching cross-examination of Nestie that the school could believe in the goodness of Providence, and felt like the Children of Israel on the other bank of the Red Sea. Some were for celebrating their independence in the North Meadow and treating Mr. Byles with absolute contempt ; but there were others who judged with some acuteness that they could have the North Meadow any day, but they might never again have a full hour in the mathematical class-room without Bulldog.   There seemed a certain fitness in holding the celebration amid the scenes of labour and discipline, and the mathematical class went in to wait on Mr. Byles' instruction in high spirits and without one missing.   It is true that the

Dowbiggins showed for the first time some reluctance in attending to their studies, but it was pointed out to them in a very firm and persuasive way by Speug that it would be disgraceful for them to be absent when Bulldog was ill, and that the class could not allow such an act of treachery. Speug was so full of honest feeling that he saw Thomas John safely within the door, and, since he threatened an unreasonable delay, assisted him across the threshold from behind. There is no perfectly full and accurate account extant of what took place between twelve and one that day in the mathematical class-room, but what may be called contributions to history oozed out and were gratefully welcomed by the school. It was told how Bauldie, being summoned by Mr. Byles to work a problem on the board, instead of a triangle drew a fetching likeness of Mr. Byles himself, and being much encouraged by the applause of the class, and having an artist's love of his work, thrust a pipe into Mr. Byles' mouth (pictorially), and blacked one of Mr. Byles's eyes (also pictorially), and then went to his seat with a sense of modest worth. That Mr. Byles, through a want of artistic appreciation, resented this Bohemian likeness of himself, and, moved by a Philistine spirit, would have wiped it from the board ; but the senior members of the class would on no account allow any work by a young but promising master to be lost, and succeeded in the struggle in wiping Mr. Byles's own face with the chalky cloth.

That Mr. Byles, instead of entering into the spirit of the day, lost his temper and went to Bulldog's closet for a cane; whereupon Speug, seizing the opportunity so pleasantly afforded, locked Mr. Byles in that place of retirement, and so kept him out of any further mischief for the rest of the hour. That as Mr. Byles had been deposed from office on account of his incapacity, and the place of mathematical master was left vacant, Speug was unanimously elected to the position, and gave an address, from Bulldog's desk, replete with popular humour. That as Thomas John did not seem to be giving such attention to his studies as might have been expected, Speug ordered that he be brought up for punishment, which was promptly done by Bauldie and Howieson. That after a long review of Thomas John's iniquitous career, Speug gave him the tawse with much faithfulness, Bauldie seeing that Thomas John held out his hand in a becoming fashion; then that unhappy young gentleman was sent to his seat with a warning from Speug that this must never occur again. That Nestie, having stealthily left the room, gave such an accurate imitation of Bulldog's voice in the passage—" Pack of little fiddlers taking advantage of my absence; but I'll warm them "—that there was an instantaneous rush for the seats; and when the door opened and Nestie appeared, the mathematical class-room was as quiet as pussy, and Speug was ostentatiously working at a mathematical problem. There are men living who look back on that day with modest, thankful hearts, finding in its remembrance a solace in old age for the cares of life; and the scene on which they dwell most fondly is Nestie, whose face had been whitened for his abominable trick, standing on the top of Bulldog's desk, and singing a school song with the manner of the Count and the accent of Moossy, while Speug with a cane in his hand compelled Dowbiggin to join in the chorus, and Byles could be heard bleating from the closet. Ah, me! how soon we are spoiled by this sinful world, and lose the sweet innocence of our first years! how poor are the rewards of ambition compared with the simple pleasures of childhood!

It could not be expected that we should ever have another day as good again, but every one had a firm confidence in the originality of Speug when it was a question of mischief. We gathered hopefully round the Russian guns next morning—for, as I have said, the guns were our forum and place of public address —and, while affecting an attitude of studied indifference, we waited with desire to hear the plan of campaign from our leader's lips. But Speug, like all great generals, was full of surprises, and that morning he was silent and unapproachable. Various suggestions were made for brightening the mathematical labours and cheering up Mr. Byles, till at last Howieson, weary of their futility, proposed that the whole class should go up to the top of the North

Meadow and bathe in the river, and then Speug broke silence.

" Ye may go to bathe if ye like, Jock, and Cosh may go with ye, and if he's drowned it'll be no loss, nor, for that matter, if the half of ye are carried down the river.   For myself, I'm going to the mathematical class, and if onybody meddles wi' Byles I'll fight him in the back yard in the dinner-hour for half a dozen stone-gingers."

"Is there onything wrang with your head, Speug?" For the thought of Peter busy with a triangle under the care and pastoral oversight of Mr. Byles could only be explained in one way.

" No," replied Speug savagely, "nor with my fists, either. The fact is——"   And then Speug hesitated, realizing amid his many excellences a certain deficiency of speech for a delicate situation. " Nestie, what are ye glowering at? Get up on the gun and tell them aboot—what ye told me this meenut." And the school gathered in amazement round our pulpit, on which Nestie stood quite unconcerned.

" It was very good fun-n yesterday, boys, but it won't do to-t-to-day. Bully's very ill, and Doctor Manley is afraid that he may—d-die, and it would be beastly bad form-m to be having larks when Bulldog is—may be——"   And Nestie came down hurriedly from the gun and went behind the crowd, while Speug covered his retreat in an aggressive manner, all the more aggressive that he did not seem himself to be quite indifferent.

Manley said it. Then every boy knew it must be going hard with Bulldog ; for there was not in broad Scotland a cleverer, pluckier, cheerier soul in his great profession than John Manley, M.D., of Edinburgh, with half a dozen honours of Scotland, England, and France. He had an insight into cases that was almost supernatural, he gave prescriptions which nobody but his own chemist could make up, he had expedients of treatment that never occurred to any other man, and then he had a way with him that used to bring people up from the gates of death and fill despairing relatives with hope. His arrival in the sick room, a little man, with brusque, sharp, straightforward manner, seemed in itself to change the whole face of things and beat back the tides of disease. He would not hear that any disease was serious, but he treated it as if it were ; he would not allow a gloomy face in a sick room, and his language to women who began to whimper, when he got them outside the room, was such as tom cats would be ashamed of ; and he regarded the idea of any person below eighty dying on his hands as a piece of incredible impertinence. All over Perthshire country doctors in their hours of anxiety and perplexity sent for Manley ; and when two men like William McClure and John Manley took a job in hand together, Death might as well leave and go to another case, for he would not

have a look in with those champions in the doorway.
English sportsmen in lonely shooting-boxes sent for
the Muirtown crack in hours of sudden distress, and
then would go up to London and swear in the clubs
that there was a man down there in a country town
of Scotland who was cleverer than all the West End
swell doctors put together. He would not allow big
names of diseases to be used in his hearing, believing
that the shadow killed more people than the reality,
and fighting with all his might against the melan-
choly delight that Scots people have in serious sickness and other dreary dispensations. When Manley
returned one autumn from a week's holiday and
found the people of the North Free Kirk mourning
in the streets over their minister, because he was
dying of diphtheria, and his young wife asking grace
to give her husband up if it were the will of God
Manley went to the house in a whirlwind of indignation, declaring that to call a sore throat diphtheria
was a tempting of Providence, and that it was a mere
mercy that they hadn't got the real disease "just for
a judgement." It happened, however, that his treatment was exactly the same as that for diphtheria,
and although he remarked that he didn't know whether
it was necessary for him to come back again for such
an ordinary case, he did drop in by a series of accidents twice a day for more than a week; and although no one dared to whisper it in his presence, there
are people who think to this day that the minister

had diphtheria. As Manley, however, insisted that it was nothing but a sore throat, the minister felt bound to get better, and the whole congregation would have thanked Manley in a body had it not been that he would have laughed aloud. Many a boy remembered the day when he had been ill and sweating with terror lest he should die—although he wouldn't have said that to any living creature—and Manley had come in like a breeze of fresh air, and declared that he was nothing but a "skulking young dog," with nothing wrong about him, except the desire to escape for three days from Bulldog.

"Well, Jimmie, ye don't deserve it, for you're the most mischievous little rascal, except Peter McGuffie, in the whole of Muirtown ; but I'll give you three days in bed, and your mother will let you have something nice to eat, and then out you go and back to the Seminary," and going out of the door Manley would turn round and shake his fist at the bed, "just a trick, nothing else." It might be three weeks before the boy was out of bed, but he was never afraid again, and had some heart to fight his disease.

Boys are not fools, and the Seminary knew that, if Manley had allowed death to be even mentioned in connexion with Bulldog, it was more than likely that they would never see the master of the mathematical department again. And boys are a perfect absurdity, for—as sure as death—they were not glad. Bulldog had thrashed them all, or almost all, with

faithfulness and perseverance, and some of them he
had thrashed many times ; he had never petted any
of them, and never more than six times, perhaps, said
a kind word to them in public. But that morning, as
they stood, silent, awkward and angry, round the
guns, there is no doubt about it, the Seminary knew
that it loved Bulldog. Never to see his erect figure
and stern face come across the North Meadow, never
to hear him say again from the desk, " Attention to
your work, you little fiddlers " ; never to watch him
promenading down between the benches, overseeing
each boy's task and stimulating the negligent on
some tender part of their bodies ; never to be
thrashed by him again ! At the thought of this
calamity each boy felt bad in his clothes, and
Speug, resenting what he judged the impertinent
spying of Cosh, threatened to punch his head, and
" learn Cosh to be watching him." As everybody
knows, boys have no sentiment and no feeling, so the
collapse of that morning must be set down to pure
cussedness ; but the school was so low that Byles
ruled over them without resistance, and might have
thrashed them if he had so pleased and had not
ventured to use Bulldog's cane.

Had they not been boys, they would have called at
Bulldog's to learn how he was. Being boys, they
avoided his name and pretended they were indifferent ; but when they met Manley on the bridge that
afternoon, and judged he had come from Bulldog's,

they studied his face with the skill of wild animals, and concluded each one for himself that things were going badly with the master. They picked up every scrap of information from their fathers in the evening, although they fiercely resented the suggestion of their mothers that they would be concerned about " Mr. MacKinnon's illness "—as if they cared whether a master were ill or well, as if it were not better for them that he should be ill, especially such an old brute as Bulldog. And the average mother was very much disappointed by this lack of feeling, and said to her husband at night that she had expected better things from Archibald ; but if she had gone suddenly into Bauldie's room—for that was his real name, Archibald being only the thing given in baptism— she would have found that truculent worthy sobbing aloud and covering his head with the blankets, lest his elder brother, who slept in the same room, should hear him. You have no reason to believe me, and his mother would not have believed me, but—as sure as death—Bauldie was crying because Bulldog was sick unto death.

Next morning Speug and a couple of friends happened by the merest accident to be loitering at Bailie MacFarlane's shop window, and examining with interest the ancient furniture exposed, at the very time when that worthy magistrate came out and questioned Dr. Manley " How things were going up-bye wi' the maister ? "

"Not well, Bailie, not well at all. I don't like the case; it looks bad, very bad indeed, and I'm not a croaker. Disease is gone; and he's a strong man, not a stronger in Muirtown than MacKinnon; but he has lost interest in things, and isn't making an effort to get better; just lying quiet and looking at you—says he's taking a rest, and if we don't get him waked up, I tell you, Bailie, it will be a long one."

"Michty," said the Bailie, overcome with astonishment at the thought of Bulldog dying, as it were, of gentleness.

"Yes, yes," said Manley; "but that's just the way with those strong, healthy men, who have never known a day's sickness till they are old; they break up suddenly. And he'll be missed. Bailie, Bulldog didn't thrash you and me, else we would have been better men; but he has attended to our boys."

"He has been verra conscientious," and the Bailie shook his head, sadly mourning over a man who had laid down his life in discharge of discipline. But the boys departed without remark, and Speug loosened the strap of Bauldie's books, so that they fell in a heap upon the street, whereat there was a brisk interchange of ideas, and then the company went on its way rejoicing. So callous is a boy.

Nestie was not at school that day, and perhaps that was the reason that Speug grew sulky and illtempered, taking offence if any one looked at him, and picking quarrels in the corridors, and finally disappearing during the dinner-hour. It was supposed that he had broken bounds and gone to Woody Island, that forbidden Paradise of the Seminary, and that while the class was wasting its time with Byles, Peter was playing the Red Indian. He did not deny the charge next day, and took an hour's detention in the afternoon with great equanimity, but at the time, he was supposed to be stalking Indians behind the trees, and shooting them as they floated down the river on a log, he was lying among the hay in his father's stable, hidden from sight, and—as sure as death—Speug was trying to pray for Bulldog.

The virtues of Mr. McGuffie senior were those of the natural man, and Mr. McGuffie junior had never been present at any form of family prayers, nor had he attended a Sunday-school, nor had he sat under any minister in particular. He had had no training in devotional exercises, although he had enjoyed an elaborate education in profanity under his father and the grooms, and so his form of prayer was entirely his own.

"God, I dinna ken how to call You, but they say Ye hear onybody. I'm Peter McGuffie, but mebbe Ye will ken me better by Speug. I'm no a good laddie like Nestie, and I'm aye gettin' the tawse, but I'm awful fond of Bulldog. Dinna kill Bulldog, God; dinna kill Bulldog! If Ye let him aff this time I'll never say any bad words again—as sure as death— and I'll never play truant, and I'll never slap Dowbiggin's face, and I'll never steal birds' eggs, and I'll never set the terrier on the cats. I'll wash my face, and—my hands, too, and I'll go to the Sabbath-schule, and I'll do onything Ye ask me if Ye'll let off Bulldog. For ony sake, dinna kill Bulldog."

When Dr. Manley came out from the master's garden door that evening he stumbled upon Speug, who was looking very miserable, but began to whistle violently the moment he was detected, and denied that he had come to ask for news.

"You did, you young limmer, and you needn't tell me lies, for I know you, Speug, and your father before you. I wish I'd good news to give you, but I haven't. I fear you've had your last thrashing from Bulldog."

For a moment Speug kicked at a stone on the road and thrust his hands deep into his pockets; then the corners of his mouth began to twitch, and turning round he hid his face upon the wall, while his tough little body that had stood many a fight shook all over. Doctor Manley was the first person that had seen Speug cry, and he stood over him to protect him from the gaze of any wandering message boys who might come along the lane. By and by Speug began to speak between his sobs.

"It was a lee, Doctor, for I did come up to ask, but I didna like to let on. . . . I heard ye say that ye couldna rouse Bulldog to take an interest in onything, and I thought o' something."

" What was it, Speug?" and the doctor laid his hands on the boy's shoulder and encouraged him to proceed. " I'll never tell, you may trust me."

" Naething pleased Bulldog sae weel as givin' us a lickin; if he juist had a cane in his hands and a laddie afore him, Bulldog would sune be himsel' again, and—there's no a laddie in schule he's licked as often as me. And I cam up——" and Speug stuck.

" To offer yourself for a thrashing, you mean. You've mentioned the medicine ; 'pon my word, I believe it's just the very thing that will do the trick. Confound you, Speug ! if you haven't found out what I was seeking after, and I've been doctoring those Muirtown sinners for more than thirty years. Come along, laddie ; we've had our consultation, and we'll go to the patient." And Manley hurried Speug through the garden and into the house. " Wait a minute here," said the doctor, "and I'll come back to you." And in a little while Nestie came downstairs and found his friend in the lobby, confused and frightened for the first time in his life, and Nestie saw the marks of distress upon his face. " Doctor M-Manley told me, Speug, and " (putting an arm round his neck) " you're the g-goodest chap in Muirtown. It's awfully d-decent of you, and it 'ill p-please Bully tremendous." And then Speug went up as consulting physician to visit Bulldog. Nestie brought him forward to the bedside, and at last he had courage to look, and it took him all his time to play the man when he saw Bulldog so thin, so quiet, so gentle, with his face almost as white as the pillow, and his hands upon the bedclothes wasted like to the hands of a skeleton. The master smiled faintly, and seemed to be glad to see the worst of all his scholars, but he did not say anything. Dr. Manley kept in the background and allowed the boys to manage their own business, being the wisest of men as well as the kindliest. Although Nestie made signs to Speug and gave him every encouragement, Peter could not find a word, but stood helpless, biting his lip and looking the very picture of abject misery.

" Peter has come, sir," said Nestie, " to ask for you. He is very sorry that you are ill, and so are all the boys. Peter thought you might be wearying to—to use the c-cane, and Peter is wearying, too. Just a little one, sir, to p-please Speug," and Nestie laid an old cane he had hunted up, a cane retired from service, upon the bed within reach of Bulldog's hand. A twinkle of amusement came into the master's eye, the first expression of interest he had shown during his illness. He turned his head and looked at Peter, the figure of chastened mischief. The remembrance of the past—the mathematical class-room, the black-board with its figures, the tricks of the boys, the scratching of the pens, came up to him, and his soul was stirred within him. His hand closed again upon the sceptre of authority, and Peter laid a grimy paw open upon the bedclothes. The master gave it one little stroke with all the strength he had. "The fiddlers," he said softly, "the little fiddlers can't do without me, after all." A tear gathered in his eye and overflowed and rolled down Bulldog's cheek. Manley hurried the boys out of the room, who went into the garden, and, being joined by the master's dog, the three together played every monkey trick they knew, while upstairs in the sick-room Manley declared that Bulldog had turned the corner and would soon be back again among his "fiddlers."

The doctor insisted upon driving Peter home to his native stable-yard, for this was only proper courtesy to a consulting physician. He called him "Doctor" and "Sir Peter" and such like names all the way, whereat Peter was so abashed that friends seeing him sitting in Manley's phaeton, with such an expression on his face, spread abroad the tale that the doctor was bringing him home with two broken legs as the result of riding a strange horse. The doctor bade him good-bye in the presence of his father, tipping him ten shillings to treat the school on the news of Bulldog's convalescence, and next day stone-ginger was flowing like water down the throats of the Seminary.

XI

A PLEASANT SIN

CAPTIOUS people, such as ministers of religion and old maids of the precise kind, considered that the Seminary were guilty of many sins and mentioned them freely; but those excellent people erred through lack of vision. Hunting mice in Moossy's class-room, putting the Dowbiggin's clothes into a state of thorough repair, raiding the territory of the " Pennies," having a stand-up fight between two well-matched champions, say, once a month, and "ragging " Mr. Byles, might have an appearance of evil, but were in reality disguised virtues, feeding the high spirit of those who were active, and teaching the Christian grace of meekness to those who were passive. There was only one act which the Seminary knew it ought not to do, and which all the boys wanted to do, which they enjoyed very much in doing, and were quite willing to be punished for doing. The besetting sin of a school—a country school—which will remain its sin until the days of the millennium have fairly set in, was playing truant.

This crime was equivalent to high treason in the State, and consisted in a boy absenting himself from school without the knowledge of his parents, and without the consent of his master, for a day or half of a day. The boy did not disappear because he was ill, for he was on such occasions outrageously well ; nor because he was overburdened by work, for the truants always guarded themselves against brain fag ; nor because he wanted to hang about the streets, or smoke in secret places. He was simply seized with the passion of the open air and of the country. To tramp through the bosky woods, hunting for birds' eggs and watching the ways of wild animals ; to guddle for trout under the stones of some clear running mountain burn, or to swim in the cool water on a summer day, or to join the haymakers on a farm, and do a full day's work, as long as lesson time and harder. There was a joy in escaping from bounds, as if an animal had broken out from a menagerie ; there was joy in thinking, as you lay beside your burn or under the shadow of a tree, of the fellows mewed up in the hot class-room and swatting at their sums, under Bulldog's eye ; and joy in coming home in the evening, tired, but satisfied, and passing the empty Seminary with defiance. There is no joy— I mean sin—but has its drawbacks, and there were

clouds in the truant's sky. Country folk had their
own suspicions when they came on a couple of boys
going at large on a working day, when the school
was in session, as one might have a shrewd guess
if he came upon two convicts in their professional
dress fishing in some lonely spot on Dartmoor. But
there is a charitable sympathy with all animals who
have escaped from a cage, unless it be a tigress
looking for her dinner, and no one would have
thought of informing on the boys, except one bad
man ; and Providence, using Speug as an instrument,
punished him for his evil doings—as I shall tell.

"Well, laddies," some honest farmer would say,
as he came upon them sitting by the burnside eating
bread and cheese and counting up their trout, " I'm
judgin' it will be a holiday at the Seminary the
now, or mebbe the maister's given ye a day's
leave for yir health. Or is this the reward for
doing yir work so well ? Ye have all the appearance of scholars." And then the good man would
laugh at the simple raillery and the confusion of
the boys.

"Dinna answer, laddies; for least said soonest
mended, and ye mind where leears go to. But
I'm thinkin' ye wadna be the worse for a jug of
milk to wash down your dinner, and there's some
strawberries in the garden up by, just about ripe."

So they all went up to the farm kitchen and
had a glorious tuck in, and were afterwards turned

loose among the strawberries, while the farmer watched them with keen delight and a remembrance of past days. Whose place in heaven for such deeds of charity is already secure.

The authorities at home were not so lenient, and the experienced truant was careful, when he could, to time his arrival home about five o'clock in the afternoon, which allowed for the school hours and one hour more of special confinement. According to the truant's code he was not allowed to tell a lie about his escapade, either at home or at school but he was not obliged to offer a full and detailed statement of the truth. If his father charged him with being kept in at school for not having done his work, and rebuked him for his laziness, he allowed it to go at that, and did not accuse his father of inaccuracy. When, however, a boy was by habit and repute a truant, his father learned by experience and was apt to watch him narrowly. If the boy had an extra touch of the sun on his face, and his clothing was disorderly beyond usual, and his manner was especially unobtrusive, and his anxiety to please every person quite remarkable, and if in moments of unconsciousness he seemed to be chewing the cud of some recent pleasure, the father was apt to subject him to a searching cross-examination. And his mother had to beg the boy off with many a plea, such as mothers know how to use ; and if the others did not succeed, and the appeal to the heart was in vain, she could always send the good man back upon his memory, and put it to his conscience whether he ought to visit too severely upon his son, the sin the boy had inherited from himself.

It was next morning that the truant really paid for his pleasure; and the price was sharp, for there was no caning to be compared with that which followed a day in the country. It was a point of honour that no boy should show distress; but even veterans bit their lips as the cane fell first on the right hand and then on the left, and right across the palm, and sometimes doubling on the back of the hand, if the cane was young and flexible. Speug, though a man of war and able to endure anything, used to warm his hands at the fire, if the weather was cold, before going in to the inquisition, and after he had received a switching of the first order he would go down to the lade and cool his hands in the running water. It was an interesting spectacle to see four able-bodied sinners, who yesterday had given themselves to the study of Nature, now kneeling together, to efface their penalty in our waters of Lethe; but you must remember that they made no moan before the boys, and no complaint against the master. The school received them with respect when they came out, and Speug would indicate with a wink and a jerk of his head that Bulldog had exceeded himself; but he was not to

be trifled with for an hour or two, and if any
ill-mannered cub ventured to come too near when
Peter was giving his hands a cold bath, the chances
are that Peter gave the cub a bath, too, "just to
teach him to be looking where he had no business."

Possibly fear of consequences might hinder some
weak-hearted boys, but it never prevented any of the
hardy ruffians from having their day out when the
fever seized them. Playing truant was the same
thing for a boy as bolting for a high-spirited horse ;
done once, the animal is bound to try it again, and to
both, the joy of their respective sins must be very
much the same. Boys did not plan a week ahead
and then go astray in cold blood, because this sin was
not an act of malice aforethought—it was a sudden
impulse, not a matter of the will so much as of the
blood. Had one determined on Tuesday night to
take Wednesday, it might have turned out in our
fickle climate a cheerless day, when a boy would as
soon be playing marbles in the breaks, or cricket in
the dinner-hour, or, for that matter, amusing himself
in Moossy's class. No ; a boy rose in the morning
ready to go to school, without a thought of wood or
water—arranging his marbles, in fact, for the day, and
planning how to escape a lesson he had not prepared ;
but he was helpless against Nature if she set herself
to tempt him. No sooner had he put his nose outside
the door than the summer air, sweet and fresh, began

to play upon his face and reminded him of a certain wood. As he went through the streets of the town, a glimpse of the river, steely blue that morning in the sunshine, brought up a pool where a fat trout was sure to be lying. As he crossed the North Meadow, the wind was blowing free from the Highlands, and was laden with the scent of hay and flowers, and sent his blood a-tingling. The books upon his back grew woefully heavy, and the Seminary reminded him of the city gaol frowning out on the fields with its stately and unrelenting face. He loitered by the lade and saw the clear water running briskly, and across the meadow he could catch a glimpse of the river, and in the distance the Kilspindie Woods with their mysterious depths, and rising high above the houses on the other side of the river was the hill where he spent last Saturday. The bell rings and he goes in, but not to work ; the river is running through his heart, and the greenery is before his eyes, and the wind coming in puffs through the open window awakens the instinct of the wild animal in his breast and invites him to be free. Speug has a slate before him, but he is not pretending to do anything, he is looking out on the Meadow, and sniffing the air, just like a horse about to make its bolt. He catches Howieson's eye and reads that Jock is ready. Howieson inquires by signal of Bauldie whether he prefers compound fractions to a swim, and Bauldie explains, also by signal, that, much as he loves fractions, he will be

obliging that afternoon and join them in their swim.
A fourth would complete the party ; and when Speug
lifts his eyebrows with great dramatic art to " Piggie"
Mitchell, three desks off, " Piggie," like the gallant
spirit that he was, answers with a nod that he will
not be found wanting. Not a word has been said,
and no one will say " Truant " at any time, but at the
next break the four separate themselves quietly and
unobtrusively from their fellows, and by the time the
last boy has gone through the door, they are scudding
across the meadow to Speug's stable-yard, where they
will make their preparations. Sometimes nothing
more is needed than a hunch of bread and some fish-
hooks ; but as they ran Speug had dropped the word
Woody Island, and a day on Woody Island was a
work of art. It lay a couple of miles above the town,
long and narrow, formed with a division of the river
into its main current and a sluggish backwater. It
was covered with dense brushwood, except where
here and there a patch of green turf was left bare, and
the island was indented with little bays where the
river rippled on clean sand and gravel. It was only
a little island, but yet you could lose yourself in it, so
thick was the wood and so mazy, and then you had
to find your comrades by signal ; and it had little
tracks through it, and there was one place where you
could imagine a hole in the bank to be a cave, and
where certainly two boys could get out of sight if
they lay very close together and did not mind being

half smothered. When you went to Woody Island, and left the mainland, you were understood to blot out the Seminary and Muirtown and Scotland and civilization. Woody Island was somewhere in the wild West, and was still in the possession of the children of the forest; the ashes of their fires could be seen any day there, and you could come upon their wigwams in one of the open spots. There was a place where they had massacred three trappers and taken their scalps, and in that cave "Bull's-eye Charlie," the famous Indian scout, lying curled up like a ball, and with only the mouth of his rifle peeping out, had held twenty of the red-skinned braves at bay for a whole day. It was a fairy world in which our Indian tales could be reproduced upon the stage, and we ourselves could be the heroes we had so often admired. The equipment for the day consisted of four tomahawks (three axes out of small tool chests and one axe for breaking coals which "Piggie" used to steal for the day) two pistols (one belonging to Speug and the other to Bauldie); a couple of toy rifles—not things for kids, mark you, but long rifles with bayonets, and which could fire caps; a tent, which was in reality an old carriage cloth from Peter's yard; and a kettle for boiling water—I mean cooking the game—which Jock Howieson abstracted from his kitchen. Each boy had to visit his home on pretence of returning for a book, and bring away the necessary articles of war and as much food as he could steal from the pantry ; and then everything, axes included, and, if possible, the rifles, had to be hidden away about their persons until the four, skulking by back lanes, and separating from one another, reached the top of the North Meadow, after which they went up the bank of the river, none daring to make them afraid. They were out of bounds now, and the day was before them for weal or woe, and already Speug was changing into an Indian trapper, and giving directions about how they must deal with the Seminoles (see Mayne Reid), while Howieson had begun to speculate whether they would have a chance of meeting with the famous chief, Oceola. " Piggie " might want to try a cap on his rifle, but Speug would not allow him, because, although they had not yet entered the Indian territory, the crafty foe might have scouts out on this side of the river, and in that case there was no hope of Woody Island. The Indians would be in ambush among the trees on the bank, and the four would be shot down as they crossed.

Their first enemy, however, was not Oceola's Indians, but a white man—a renegade—who, to his shame, was in alliance with the Indians and was always ready to betray the trappers into their hands. This miscreant was a farmer on the mainland, who was the tenant of Woody Island, and had a deter-mined objection to any boys, or other savages, except, as I have said, the Seminole tribe living on the island, and who used to threaten pains and

penalties against any one whom he caught on his
land. One never knew when he might be about, and
it was absolutely necessary to reach the island without
his notice. There was a day in the past when Speug
used to watch till the farmer had gone into his midday dinner, and then creep along the bank of the
river and ferry himself across with the other trappers
in the farmer's boat, which he then worked round to
the other side of the island and kept there for the
return voyage in the evening, so that the farmer was
helpless to reach the island, and could only address
the unseen trespassers in opprobrious language from
the bank, which was sent back to him in faithful
echo. This forenoon the farmer happened to be
hoeing turnips with his people in a field opposite the
island, and Speug was delighted beyond measure, for
now the four had to drop down and crawl along
through the thick grass by the river's edge, availing
themselves of every bush and little knoll till they lay,
with all their arms, the tent, and the food, concealed
so near the farmer that they could hear him speak
and hear the click of the hoes as the people worked
in their drills. If you raised your head cautiously
and looked through between the branches of a shrub,
you could see him, and Bauldie actually covered him
with his rifle. The unconscious farmer knew not
that his life hung upon a thread, or, rather, upon
Bauldie's trigger. Bauldie looked inquiringly to his
chief, for he would dearly have loved to fire a cap,

but Speug shook his head so fiercely that the trapper
dropped down in his lair, and Speug afterwards
explained that the renegade had certainly deserved
death, but that it was dangerous to fire with so many
of his gang present, and the Seminoles on the other
side of the river. By and by the farmer and his
people had worked themselves to the other end of
the field, and the trappers, having ascertained that
there were no Indians watching them, prepared to
cross. Speug, who had reached the boat, spoke out
suddenly and unadvisedly, for the farmer had chained
and padlocked the boat. It would not have mattered
much to the boys in ordinary circumstances, for they
would have stripped and swum across, and back
again when they were tired of the other side, for
every one of them could swim like an otter ; but that
day they were trappers, with arms, and food, and a
tent, and powder which must be kept dry, to say
nothing of the kettle. There was a brief consultation, and Bauldie regretted that he did not shoot
the farmer dead on the spot, and as many of his
people as they could. Speug, who had been prowling
around—though cautiously, mind you, and ever
watching for a sign of the Seminoles—gave a low,
mysterious whistle, which was one of the signs
among the trappers ; and when the others joined
him he pointed and whispered, " A Seminole canoe."
It was an ancient boat which the farmer's father had
used, and which had lain for years upon the bank,

unused. Its seats were gone, its planks were leaking, it had two holes at least in it, and there were no oars. It was a thing which, in the farmer's hand, would have sunk six yards from the shore, but it had the semblance of a boat, and it was enough for the hardy trappers. Very carefully did they work it to the bank, lest it should slip a whole plank on the road, and very gently did they drop it in, lest the Seminoles should hear. " Piggie " stuffed one hole with his bonnet, and Bauldie the second with his ; Jock spread his jacket over an oozy part. They shipped all their stores, and one of them got in to bale, and the others, stripping off their clothes and adding them to the cargo of the boat, pushed out the boat before them, swimming by its side. It was a mere question of time whether the boat would go down in mid-channel ; but so splendidly did " Piggie " bale, ready at any moment to swim for his life, and so powerfully did the others push, swimming with their feet and one hand, and with the other hand guiding the boat, that they brought it over safely to the other side ; and the fact that half their clothes were wet through mattered little to men who had often hidden from the Indians in the water, with nothing but their eyes and nose out ; and, at any rate, the food was safe. The matches and the percussion caps also were dry, for " Piggie " had taken care of that, and, in the worst emergency, they would have been carried on the top of his head if he also had been obliged to swim. They brought the boat into a little creek, and, communicating by signs to one another—for they were too old hunters to be speaking now, when there might be a party of Seminoles in that very wood— Speug and Jock hid themselves, each behind a tree with rifle in hand, to cover the others, while " Piggie " and Bauldie drew the boat up under cover of the bushes, and hid it out of sight, so that even a Seminole's keen eyes would not have been able to detect it. The trappers made another hiding-place, and left there the superfluous garments of civilisation, confining themselves to a shirt and trousers, and a belt which holds the pistol and tomahawk. Speug and Jock, as the two veterans who could discover the trail of the Seminoles by a twisted leaf on a branch, or a broken stick on the ground, warned their friends to lie low, and they themselves disappeared into the brushwood. They had gone to scout, and to make sure that no wandering party of Indians was in the vicinity. By and by a wood-pigeon cooed three times, " Piggie " nodded to Bauldie, and Bauldie hooted like an owl, then they knew that it was safe to advance. The two rejoined the scouts, whom they found on the edge of a clearing, leaning on their rifles in a picturesque attitude. " Bull's-eye Charlie " led, and the others followed, pausing now and again at a sound in the woods, and once at a signal from " Bull's-eye " they separated swiftly, and each took up his position behind a tree.

But it was a false alarm. Then they went on as before, till they came to a pretty spot on the other side of the island, where they made their camp, cutting a pole for the tent, lighting a fire, which they did with immense success, and proceeding to cook dinner. As they had been afraid to fire, for fear of attracting any wandering Indian's notice, they had no deer nor wild turkey, which, in other circumstances, would have been their food ; but they made tea (very badly, and largely because they wished to use the kettle), and they had bread and butter, which had turned into oil through the warmth of Bauldie's person, a half ham which Speug contributed, a pot of jam for which " Piggie " will have to account some day, and six jam tarts which Howieson bought with his last farthing, and which had been reduced practically to one in Jock's pocket. Speug had managed two bottles of stone ginger-beer, which were deeply valued, and afforded them a big mouthful each, as they drank without any cup, and shared honestly by calculation of time.

What a day they had! They fought Indians from one end of the island to the other, killing and scalping twenty-nine. They bathed in the quieter current on the other side, and they dried themselves in the sun, and in the sun they slept till they were burned red ; and then just as they were thinking that it was time to go back to the camp and gather together their belongings and set off for home, Speug gave a whistle that had in it this time no pretence of danger, and bolted into the wood, followed by the other three. Whether he had heard the firing, or the Seminoles had sent a message, they never knew, but the farmer was on the island and proceeding in their direction through the brushwood. Speug did not think that he had seen them, and he would not quite know where they were, and in an instant that leader of men had formed what he thought the best of all his plans. He gave his directions to the other three, who executed a war-dance at the mere thought of the strategy, and then departed hurriedly for the camp ; but Speug, who was naked, and not ashamed, started rapidly in an opposite direction, and just gave the farmer a glimpse of him as he hurried up the island.

"Ye're there, are ye, ye young blackguards ! Wait till I catch ye ; trespassin' and lightin' fires, I'll be bound ; it's Perth gaol ye'll be in the nicht, or I'm no farmer of Middleton. Ye may hide if ye please, but I'll find ye, and ye'll no get the old boat to go back in, for I've found that, clever as ye thought yourselves, and knocked the bottom oot o' it."

It was twenty minutes before he discovered Speug, and then Speug was standing on the edge of the water at the top of the island, where the current runs swift and strong towards the other side.

"Was it me ye were seekin' ? " said Speug, rosy red all over, but not with modesty. "I thought I heard somebody crying. We're glad to see ye on the island. Have ye come to bathe?"

"Wait till I get a grip of ye, ye impident little deevil, and, my word, I'll bathe ye," and the farmer made for Speug.

"I'll bathe mysel," said Speug, when the enemy almost had his hands on him, and dived into the river, coming up nearly opposite the horrified man ; and then, as he went down with the current which took him over to the opposite side, he invited the farmer to come in. When he landed Speug bade the farmer good-bye with much courtesy, and hoped he would enjoy himself among his Indian friends.

"Wait till I cross," shouted the farmer, "and I'll be after ye, and though I ransack Muirtown I'll find ye out. Ye're a gey like spectacle to go back to the town. Ye'll no escape me this time, whoever ye be," and the farmer hurried down the island to his boat, which he had loosely fastened to one of the trees. When he reached the spot it was not to be found, but he could see his boat lying in its accustomed place on the other side, chained and padlocked. For the other three trappers had gathered all their possessions and clothed themselves like gentlemen, and taking Speug's clothes with them, ferried themselves across with rapidity and dignity. Once more Speug bade the farmer good-night, extending both hands to him in farewell, but now the one hand was in front of the other, and the thumb of the inner hand attached to Speug's nose. He thoughtfully offered to take any message to Muirtown Gaol or to the Provost that the farmer desired, and departed, wishing him a pleasant night and telling him where he would find the shank of a ham. As Peter dressed himself, his friends could only look at him in silent admiration, till at the thought of the renegade trapped so neatly and confined for at least a night on his own island, Howieson slapped his legs and triumphed aloud. And the four returned to Muirtown and to civilization full of joy.

XII

GUERILLA WARFARE

THERE is no person in a Scots country town to be compared with a Bailie for authority and dignity, and Bailie MacConachie, of Muirtown, was a glory to his order. Provosts might come and go— creatures of three years—but this man remained in office for ever, and so towered above his brethren of the same kind, that the definite article was attached to his title, and to quote " the Bailie " without his name was the recognized form and an end to all controversy. Nature had been kind to him, and, entering into the designs of Providence, had given him a bodily appearance corresponding to his judicial position. He stood six feet in his boots, and his erect carriage conveyed the impression of six inches more. His waistband passed forty-eight inches ; but, to do the great man justice, his chest measure was forty-two. His chin rested in folds upon his stock, and his broad, clean-shaven, solemn, immovable countenance suggested unfathomable depths of wisdom. His voice was deep and husky, and the clearance of his throat with which he emphasized his deliverances could be heard half a street away and was like the sealing of a legal deed. Never since he became a Bailie had he seen his boots—at least upon his feet—and his gait, as became his elevation, was a stately amble, as when a huge merchant-man puts out to sea, driving the water before her bow and yet swaying gently from side to side in her progress. Sunday and Saturday—except when officiating at the Sacrament, and of course he was then in full blacks—the Bailie wore exactly the same kind of dress—a black frock-coat, close buttoned, and grey trousers, with a dark blue stock his one concession to colour. As his position was quite assured, being, in the opinion of many, second only to that of the Sheriff and the Fiscal, he could afford to wear his clothes to the bone, and even to carry one or two stains upon his paunch as a means of identification. Walking through the town, he stood at his full height, with his hands folded upon the third button of his coat; but when he reached the North Meadow, on his way home, and passed the Seminary, he allowed his head to droop, and clasped his hands behind after the manner of the great Napoleon, and then it was understood that the Bailie's mind was wrestling with the affairs of State. People made way for him upon the street as he sailed along, and were pleased with a recognition, which always took the form of a judgement from the Bench, even though it dealt only with the weather or the crops.

There was no occasion, either in the Council or in the Presbytery, when the Bailie did not impress ; but every one agreed that he rose to his height on the Bench. No surprise, either of evidence or of law, could be sprung on him, no sensational incident ever stirred him, no excitement of the people ever carried him away. He was the terror of the publicans, and would refuse a licence if he saw fit without any fear ; but if the teetotalers tried to dictate to him, he would turn upon them and rend his own friends without mercy. When any Muirtown sinner was convicted in his court he would preface his sentence with a ponderous exhortation, and if the evidence were not sufficient he would allow the accused to go as an act of grace, but warn him never to appear again, lest a worse thing should befall him. There are profane people in every community, and there were those in Muirtown who used to say in private places that the Bailie was only a big drum, full of emptiness and sound ; but the local lawyers found it best to treat him with respect, and until the Seminary boys took his Majesty in hand he had never been worsted. No doubt an Edinburgh advocate, who had been imported into a petty case to browbeat the local Bench, thought he had the Bailie on the hip when that eminent man, growing weary of continual allusions to " the defunct," said that if he heard any-

thing more about "the defunct" he would adjourn
the case for a week, and allow him to appear in his
own interests. Then the advocate explained with
elaborate politeness that he was afraid that even the
summons of the Muirtown Bench could not produce
this party, and that his appearance, if he came, might
secure the court to himself.

"You mean," said the Bailie, eyeing the advocate
with unmoved dignity, "that the man is dead. Quite
so! Quite so! But let me tell you that if you had
been a Muirtown solicitor you would have had your
case better prepared, and not wasted our time with
the talk of dead people. You are still young, and
when you have had more experience you will know
that it is only the evidence of living witnesses that
can be received in a court of justice. Proceed with
your case and confine yourself to revelant evidence—
yes, sir, revelant evidence."

It only shows the inherent greatness of the man,
that in private life the Bailie followed the calling
of an Italian warehouseman, which really, in plain
words, was the same thing as a superior grocer, nor
was he above his trade for eight hours of the day.
When not engaged in official work, he could be found
behind his counter, and yet even there he seemed to
be upon the Bench. His white apron he wore as a
robe of office, he heard what the ladies had to say
with a judicial air, correcting them if they hinted at
any tea costing less than four and sixpence per

pound, commanding a cheese to be brought forward for inspection, as if it had been a prisoner in the dock, probing it with searching severity and giving a judgement upon it from which there was no appeal. He distinguished between customers, assigning to each such provisions as were suitable for their several homes, inquiring in a paternal manner after the welfare of their children, and when the case was concluded—that is to say, the tea and the sugar bought—even condescending to a certain high level of local gossip. When the customer left the shop it was with a sense of privilege, as if one had been called up for a little to sit with the judge. It was understood that only people of a certain standing were included among the Bailie's customers, and the sight of the Countess of Kilspindie's carriage at his door marked out his province of business. Yet if a little lassie stumbled into the shop and asked for a pennyworth of peppermints, he would order her to be served, adding a peppermint or two more, and some good advice which sent away the little woman much impressed; for though the Bailie committed one big, blazing indiscretion, and suffered terribly in consequence thereof, he was a good and honest man.

The Bailie made only one public mistake in his life, but it was on the largest scale, and every one wondered that a man so sagacious should have deliberately entered into a feud with the boys of the Seminary. The Bailie had battled in turn with the Licensed Victuallers, who as a fighting body are not to be despised, and with the Teetotalers, whom every wise man who loves peace of mind leaves alone; with the Tories, who were his opponents, and with the Liberals, his own party, when he happened to disagree with them; with the Town Council, whom he vanquished, and with the Salmon Fishery Board, whom he brought to terms; but all those battles were as nothing to a campaign with the boys. There is all the difference in the world between a war with regulars, conducted according to the rules of military science, and a series of guerilla skirmishes, wherein all the chances are with the alert and light-armed enemy. Any personage who goes to war with boys is bound to be beaten, for he may threaten and attack, but he can hardly ever hurt them, and never possibly can conquer them; and they will buzz round him like wasps, will sting him and then be off, will put him to shame before the public, will tease him on his most sensitive side, will lie in wait for him in unexpected places with an ingenuity and a perseverance and a mercilessness which are born of the Devil, who in such matters is the unfailing ally of all genuine boys.

It was no doubt annoying to a person of the Bailie's dignity and orderliness to see the terrace in which the Seminary stood, and which had the honour of containing his residence, turned into a playground, and outrageous that Jock Howieson, playing rounders in front of a magistrate's residence, should send the ball crack through the plate-glass window of a magistrate's dining-room. It was fearsome conduct on the part of Jock, and even the ball itself should have known better; but the Bailie might have been certain that Jock did not intend to lose his ball and his game also, and the maddest thing the magistrate could do was to make that ball a cause of war. It was easy enough to go to Bulldog's class-room and lodge a complaint, but as he could not identify the culprit, and no one would tell on Jock, the Bailie departed worsted, and the address which he gave the boys was received with derision. When he turned from the boys to the master, he fared no better, for Bulldog who hated tell-tales and had no particular respect for Bailies, told the great man plainly that his (Bulldog's) jurisdiction ceased at the outer door of the Seminary, and that it was not his business to keep order in the Terrace. Even the sergeant, when the Bailie commanded him to herd the boys in the courtyard, forgot the respect due to a magistrate, and refused point-blank, besides adding a gratuitous warning, which the Bailie deeply resented, to let the matter drop, or else he'd repent the day when he interfered with the laddies.

" I was a sergeant in the Black Watch, Bailie, and I was through the Crimean war—ye can see my medals ; but it takes me all my time to keep the pack in hand within my ain jurisdiction ; and if ye meddle wi' them outside yir jurisdiction, I tell ye, Bailie, they'll mak a fool o' ye afore they're done w' ye in face o' all Muirtown. There's a way o' managin' them, but peety ye if ye 'counter them. Noo, when they broke the glass in the Count's windows, if he didna pretend that he couldna identify them and paid the cost himself ! He may be French, but he's long-headed, for him and the laddies are that friendly there's naething they wouldna do for him. As ye value yir peace o' mind, Bailie, and yir poseetion in Muirtown, dinna quarrel wi' the Seminary. They're fine laddies as laddies go ; but for mischief, they're juist born deevils."

There is a foolish streak in every man, and the Bailie went on to his doom. As the authorities of the Seminary refused to do their duty—for which he would remember them in the Council when questions of salary and holidays came up—the Bailie fell back on the police, who had their own thoughts of his policy, but dared not argue with a magistrate ; and one morning an able-bodied constable appeared on the scene and informed the amazed school that he was there to prevent them playing on the Terrace. No doubt he did his duty according to his light, but neither he nor six constables could have quelled the Seminary any more than you can hold quicksilver in your hand.

When he walked with stately step up and down the broad pavement before Bulldog's windows, the Seminary went up and played opposite the Bailie's house, introducing his name into conversation, with opprobrious remarks regarding the stoutness of his person and the emptiness of his head, and finally weaving the story of his life into a verse of poetry which was composed by Speug, but is not suitable for a book of family reading. If the constable, with the fear of the magistrate before his eyes, went up to stand as a guard of honour before the Bailie's house, the school went down then to the Russian guns and held a meeting of triumph, challenging the constable to come back to the Seminary, and telling him what they would do to him. They formed a bodyguard round him some days, keeping just out of reach, and marched along with him, backward and forward ; other days they chaffed and teased him till his life was a burden to him, for he had no power to arrest them, and in his heart he sympathized with them. And then, at last, being weary of the constable, the school turned its attention to the Bailie.

One afternoon a meeting of choice spirits was held in the North Meadow, beyond the supervision of the constable, and after the Bailie had been called every name of abuse known to the Seminary, and Speug had ransacked the resources of the stable yard in profanity, he declared that the time had now come for active operation, and that the war must be

carried into the enemy's country. Speug declared
his conviction in the vernacular of the school, which
is here translated into respectable language, that the
Bailie was a gentleman of doubtful birth and dis-
creditable pedigree, that his conduct as a boy was
beyond description, and that his private life was
stained with every vice; that his intellect would
give him a right to be confined in the county
asylum, and that he had also qualified by his way
of living for the county gaol; that he didn't wash
more than once a year, and that the smell of him
was like to that from a badger's hole; that it was a
pity he didn't attend to his own business, and that he
had very little business to do; that he would soon
be bankrupt, and that if he wasn't bankrupt already
it was only because he cheated with his change;
that he sanded his sugar, and that his weights and
measures were a scandal; but that the Seminary
must do what they could to lead him to honest
ways and teach him industry, and that he (Speug)
with the aid of one or two friends would do his best
for the reformation of Bailie MacConachie, and in
this way return good for evil, as Mr. Byles, assistant
in the department of mathematics, used to teach.
And the school waited with expectation for the missionary effort upon which Speug with the assistance of
Howieson and Bauldie was understood to be engaged.

Next Friday evening an art committee met in a
stable-loft on the premises of Mr. McGuffie senior,

and devoted their skill—which was greater than they ever showed in their work—to the elaboration of a high-class advertisement which was to be shown round a certain district in Muirtown, and which they hoped would stimulate the custom at Bailie MacConachie's shop. Howieson had provided two large boards such as might be hung one on the breast and one on the back of a man, and those Speug had cut to the proper size and pasted over with thick white paper. Upon them Bauldie, who had quite a talent for drawing, wrought diligently for a space of two hours, with the assistance and encouragement of his friends, and when they set the boards up against the wall the committee was greatly pleased. Speug read aloud the advertisement with much unction—

CHEAP TEA! CHEAP TEA! CHEAP TEA!

SALE OF BANKRUPT STOCK

AT

BAILIE MACCONACHIE'S
THE FAMOUS ITALIAN WAREHOUSEMAN,
49, ST. ANDREW STREET.

ELEVENPENCE-HALFPENNY PER POUND.

Sale Begins at One o'clock on Saturday.
GLASS OF WHISKY FREE TO ALL PURCHASERS.
Poor People Specially Invited.
Be early. *Be early.*
BAILIE MACCONACHIE'S
CHEAP TEA! CHEAP TEA! CHEAP TEA!

The three artists contained themselves till they came to the last "Cheap Tea!" then Jock knocked Bauldie down among the hay, and Speug fell on the top of them, and they rolled in one bundle of delight, arising from time to time to study the advertisement and taste its humour.

"'Bankrupt stock!'" cried Bauldie, "and him an Elder of the Kirk! That'll learn him to be complaining of his windows."

"'Poor people specially invited,' and calls himself an Italian warehouseman. I would give half a dozen ginger-beer to see Lady Kilspindie there," stammered Jock with delight.

"'Glass of whisky free!'"—and Speug took a fresh turn in the hay—"it's against law to drink whisky in a grocer's shop—and him a magistrate! He'll no meddle wi' the Seminary again."

"'Be early!'" chanted Jock, "'be early!' My word! They'll be there, all the waufies of Muirtown; there'll no be room in the street. 'Glass of whisky free!'" and Jock wiped his eyes with his knuckles.

Upon Saturday, at noon, just as the Bailie was going along the Terrace to his house and congratulating himself that on that day at least he was free from all annoyance by the way, another character of Muirtown had started out through a very different part of the fair city. London John was as well known in Muirtown as the Bailie himself, and in his way was quite as imposing. Tall and gaunt, without an ounce of superfluous flesh, and with an inscrutable countenance, dressed in a long frock-coat which he had worn for at least a quarter of a century, and a tall hat which he had rescued·from an ashpit, with the remains of a pair of trousers, and something in the form of a shirt which was only seen when he laid aside the outer garment for active service, London John stalked with majesty through the streets of Muirtown. He earned his living as a sandwich man, or by carrying in coals, or by going errands, or by emptying ashpits. He could neither read nor write, but he remembered a number and never forgot what was due to him, and the solitary subject on which he spoke was the wonders of London, where it was supposed he had lost such reason as he had at once possessed. His coming was always welcome in the poorer parts of the town, for the sake of his discourse on London, but never had he received such an ovation before in the Vennel, which was largely inhabited by tramps and tinkers, unskilled labourers and casuals of all kinds. The cheap tea might not have aroused their enthusiasm, but at the mention of a free glass of whisky the deepest emotions of the Vennel were stirred.

"Tea at elevenpence halfpenny," cried Tinkler Tam, who jogged round the country with petty wares, which he sold in exchange for rabbit-skins, old clothes, and other *débris* of a house, "and a glass of whisky free! Ma certes! let me get a sight o' that," and London John was brought to a standstill while Tam read aloud the advertisement to a crowd who could appreciate the cheapness of the tea, and whose tongues began to hang out at the very thought of the whisky.

" A lee ! " cried the travelling merchant, touched at the suggestion of such deceit. " He daurna do sic a thing, else his shop would be gutted. Na, na, it reads plain as a pikestaff; ye pay elevenpence half-penny and ye get a pound of tea and a glass of whisky. I count it handsome o' the Bailie ; and if they didna say he was a teetotaler ! It's awfu' how a man is abused."

" He gave me six days in the court," said Jess Mitchell, who had had a difference of opinion with another lady in the Vennel and received the Bailie's best attention from the Bench, " and if I hadna to hear him preach a sermon as long as my leg besides —confound him for a smooth-tongued, psalm-singin', bletherin' old idiot! But I bear him no grudge ; I'll hae a taste o' that whisky, though I'm no mindin' so much about the tea. The sooner we're at the place the better, for I'll be bound there'll be more tea bought this day in Muirtown than a' the last year." And there was a general feeling that the Vennel had better make no delay, lest some other locality should obtain the first call.

As London John went on his way the news spread through the back streets and closes, and the Bailie's generous invitation fell on responsive ears. And if any person was inclined to doubt, there was the advertisement in plain terms, and over the board with its engaging news the austere and unmoved countenance of London John. That worthy could give no information about the remarkable placard, not even from whom he received it; but he was quite sure that he was to take it through the Vennel and neighbouring streets for two hours, and that he had received a shilling for his labour, which he proposed to spend at Bailie MacConachie's when his task was done. He also explained that in London, where he used to reside, whisky ran like water, and tea could be had for the asking. But his hearers had no interest that day in London.

It struck the Bailie as he returned from midday dinner, and long before he reached St. Andrew's Street, that something was happening, and he wondered whether they were changing the cavalry at the barracks. People looked curiously at him, and having made as though they would have spoken, passed on, shaking their heads. When he turned into the familiar street, down which he was accustomed to parade with a double weight of dignity, an enlivening spectacle met his eyes. Every shopkeeper was out at his door, and would indeed have been along the street, had he not judged it wiser to protect his property, and the windows above the shop were full of faces. Opposite his own most respectable place of business the street was crammed from side to side with a seething mob, through which Mr. McGuffie senior was striving to drive a dogcart with slender success and complaining loudly of obstruction. Respectable working women were there, together with their husbands, having finished the day's work; country folk who dropped into town on the Saturday had been attracted to the scene; the riff-raff of Muirtown had come out from their dens and lodging-houses, together with that casual population which has nothing particular to do and is glad of any excitement. They were of various kinds and different degrees of respectability, but they were all collected in answer to Bailie MacConachie's generous offer; they were also all ready to buy the tea, and a large number of them particularly ready for the whisky. The first to arrive on the scene had been Tinkler Tam, who put down elevenpence-halfpenny in copper money upon the counter with a crash, and informed the Bailie's senior assistant that to save time he would just take the whisky while they were making up the tea, and was promptly ordered out of the shop for an impudent, drunken blackguard. Thomas, in the course of a varied life, was not un-accustomed to be called disrespectful names, and it was not the first time he had been requested to leave high-class premises; but for once, at least, he had a perfectly good conscience and a strong ground of complaint.

"Impident, am I, and drunken, did ye say, ye meeserable, white-faced effeegy of a counter-jumper? If I werena present on business I would put such a face on you that yir mother wouldna know you; but I'm here wi' my friends" (great applause from the doorway, where the crowd was listening to the interview) "for a commercial transaction. Div ye no ken, ye misshapen object, that we're here on a special invitation of yir master, sent this mornin' to the Vennel?" (strong confirmation given under oath by Jess Mitchell), "and I'll juist give you the terms thereof, ye two-faced, leein', unprincipled wratch" (enthusiastic support from the street).

The ambassador of the proletariat—whose constituency filled the outer part of the shop, pressed their faces against the window and swayed with impatience across the street, and also seized a lamp-post for purposes of observation—rehearsed the terms of the advertisement with considerable accuracy and expounded them with various figures of speech, and then issued his ultimatum.

"Ye have heard the invitation sent oot by a magistrate o' Perth, and a man whom I've met on public occasions" (Tam had been prosecuted before the Bailie under the Game Acts): "we're here in response to a public advertisement in terms thereof, and my money is on the counter. I call these persons present to witness that I've fulfilled my side of the covenant, and I here and now before these witnesses demand the tea and the whisky as above stated" (howls from the crowd, who were greatly impressed by this judicial effort, and were getting every minute more thirsty).

"It's maist extraordinary that the Bailie is no here himsel' to receive his friends; but what is done by the servant is done by the master—that's good law" (vehement support from Jess Mitchell, who at the smell of the shop was getting beyond control); "and I give ye two meenuts, my dainty young friend, and if the material be not forthcoming at the end of that time, the law will allow us to help ourselves, and gin ye offer ony resistance I'll pit ye and yir neebour inside the sugar-cask." And it was fortunate for every person concerned that the police, who had been somewhat perplexed by the circumstances, arrived at the scene, and turned Tinkler Tam and his friends into the street and themselves stood guard over the shop. It was at this point that the Bailie arrived and was received with frantic applause and a Babel of appeal.

"Hurrah for the Bailie! Come awa', man, quick, else yir shop will be wreckit. Where ha' ye been? The folk are cryin' oot for ye. It's time ye started on the tea and the whisky. Make way for the Bailie. He's coming to start the auction. Three cheers for Bailie MacConachie!" And the Bailie, limp and dishevelled, amazed and furious, was hustled through the crowd to see the Italian warehouse guarded by the police, and the mob of Muirtown clamouring for tea and whisky at his hand, while face to face with him stood London John, who had now been produced for the occasion, bearing on his back and breast the seductive advertisement.

"It's a brazen lie!" And the enraged Bailie lost all self-control as he read the legend on the board. "A low, mean, dirty trick, a deliberately planned fraud. It's perfectly iniquitous, in fact, juist—juist damnable! Bankrupt—who is bankrupt? Is't me?" And the veins on the Bailie's neck swelled visibly. "Tea at elevenpence-halfpenny! I never had such trash in my shop. Three shillings is the lowest, and I never recommended it. Whisky!—there is not a drop in the shop. Who dare say I would turn this shop into a public-house? I'll be at the bottom of this, though it cost me a thousand pounds. Who hired ye to carry round the board, ye peetiful creature? If ye don't tell the truth I'll commit ye to gaol this very meenut." And the Bailie turned the battery of his wrath upon London John, who was greatly flattered by his own prominent position and not at all concerned about the Bailie's threat.

"It was," replied the Mercury of the Vennel, with great composure, "a big, stout man like yirsel', Bailie, that gied me the boards and a shillin'; or, noo that I think about it, he wasna so big, he was a little man, and gey shilpit (thin) about the neck. Dod! I'm no very sure, though, but that it was a woman wi' a red face and a shepherd's tartan plaid ; at ony rate, if it wasna her it micht be a bit lassie wi' bare head and feet ; and I'm thinkin' noo, Bailie, it was a bit lassi-kie, for she said to me, 'Have ye ever been in London ?' Noo, Bailie, I would like to tell you about London." And if the police had not silenced London John, the Bailie at that moment would have had a fit of apoplexy, for it was evident that the trail was blind and there was no getting to the real person behind London John.

The crowd had listened with considerable patience and self-restraint to this conversation, but as soon as the hope of tea and refreshment died away, and they realized that some one had fooled them, they looked out for a victim, and settled upon the Bailie.

"Ye should be ashamed of yourself," and Tinkler Tam, standing out from the midst of the crowd, and sitting as it were upon the bench sentenced the Bailie in the dock. "It's a fine business to be playing tricks on the poor folk o' Muirtown, wilin' them from their work to waste their time at your shop-door and sendin' them awa' empty-handed. If it had been the first o' April, and ye had been a laddie, I wouldna hev said much aboot it ; but at your age, and you a magistrate, to play sic a trick, it's perfectly disgraceful. Ye ought to get a month's hard labour, but aye thing's sure, ye'll no long be a Bailie o' Muirtown. It was fearsome to hear ye askin' London John who gave him the shillin' when he describit ye

juist as ye are standing; then the puir body, when
ye threatened him, brought in the lassie. Man,
though ye're a Bailie and I'm naething but Tinkler
Tam, I would scorn to mak use of a poor natural
that hasna his wits, juist to feed my vanity and
gither a crowd round my shop." Then the crowd
united in three long groans, and possibly might have
shown their indignation in a still more pronounced
form, but the police, being still further reinforced,
drove them along the streets, while the Bailie hid
himself in the recesses of his shop.

Three minutes later Speug sauntered into the shop
with Howieson and Bauldie, and demanded a pennyworth of peppermint drops. He also remarked to
Jock, as they were being folded up, "If there be as
mony o' the Bailie's friends callin' at the shop on
Monday, I doubt the police will no be able to spare
a constable to keep order on the Terrace." And as a
matter of fact the offensive patrol was withdrawn,
and the Seminary resumed possession of the deba-
table ground.

XIII

THE FALL OF GOLIATH

BAILIE MACCONACHIE made a mistake when he risked a war with the boys of the Seminary, and it was colossal folly on his part to continue the war after his first defeat in the affair of the advertisement. No doubt it was humiliating to have his respectable place of business filled with the mob of Muirtown demanding whisky as a right, and threatening him with penalties as a covenant-breaker when they did not get it; he had also very good reasons for believing that the unholy inspiration which gathered the vagrants to his shop came from the Seminary. His best policy, however, would have been to treat the matter as a joke; and if the Bailie had stopped on his way to dinner, and told the boys plainly that he knew quite well they were at the bottom of the affair, that they were a set of confounded young rascals, that he had intended to hang six of them and send the rest to penal servitude, that he was going to forgive them for the sake of their unhappy parents, and because it had not been half

bad fun after all, that there would be no more police-
men before the Seminary, and there must be no
more windows smashed in his (the Bailie's) house—
the Seminary, which always respected a fellow who
took his licking with good humour and didn't squeal,
would have given the Bailie the best cheer he ever
got in his public career, and a covenant of peace
would have been made between him and the boys
which would never have been forgotten. Had
another pane of glass been broken by a Seminary
ball, the value thereof in a packet of halfpence, with
an expression of regret, would have been handed in
before evening. The honorary freedom of the school
would have been conferred on the Bailie, without any
public ceremony, but with immense practical advantage, and although the Bailie was surfeited with civic
honours, yet even he might have tasted a new pleasure as he passed along the terrace to see the boys
suspend a game for an instant to let him pass in
stately walk, and to hear Speug cry, "Oot o' the
Bailie's road," and to receive a salute from tailless
Highland bonnets that were touched to none outside
the school, except to the Count and Dr. Manley. If
Providence had given a touch of imagination to the
Bailie, and his head had not been swollen by a position approaching that of the angels, he would have
come to terms at once with the boys, in which case
bygones would have been bygones, and he would
have been spared much humiliation.

Unfortunately the Bailie allowed his temper to get the better of him, raging furiously in public places, and breathing forth threatenings about what he would do to the plotter, till all Muirtown, which otherwise might have pitied him, held its sides. He kept our single detective at work for a fortnight, who finally extracted from London John that the "boardies" containing the shameful advertisement had been given him by a man uncommonly like the detective himself, and that the said "boardies" were not to be compared with those he used to carry in London. The detective also learned, on a somewhat risky visit to Mr. McGuffie's stables, that the Speug had spent the whole of that historical Saturday till the hour of two—when he called for peppermints at the Bailie's shop—in cleaning out his rabbit-hutch and other domestic duties—this on the testimony of three of Mr. McGuffie's grooms, each of whom was willing to swear the same anywhere, or fight the detective, with gloves or without gloves, in the stable-yard or any other place which might be agreed upon. The Bailie also, going from bad to worse, offered a reward of £5 for any information which would lead to the conviction of the offender, and received thirty letters —so many anonymous, attacking his character, public and private, and so many signed, from various cranks in Muirtown, in which the crime was assigned to Irish Roman Catholics, to the Publicans, to the Morisonians, and to a tribe of gipsies camped outside the city. They were all annoying, but there were two which cut the Bailie to the quick. One was written from the security of Glasgow, in which the writer promised, on receipt of the reward, to send a full account of the conspiracy, and, having got the money, replied briefly that he left the matter to the Bailie's own conscience; and the second, which asked for no reward except the writer's sense of having done his duty, and which hinted that if the Bailie put the question straight to his senior assistant, he might find he had been nourishing a viper in his bosom, and that a young man with such a smug appearance could be little else than a rascal. This letter, which was written in a schoolboy hand, and had five words misspelt, was signed, "An Elder of the Free Kirk." None of the letters seemed to help the matter forward, and life at the Bailie's residence was very troubled during those weeks.

When news of the Bailie's vindictive spirit spread through the Seminary, the boys were much pained, for it was sad to see an old man forgetting himself and harbouring a spirit of revenge. It seemed, indeed, as if all they had done for the Bailie was simply love's labour lost, and that they must begin again to bring him to a proper state of mind. The Seminary loved peace and hated war, being a body of quiet, well-behaved, hard-working lads. Still, if war was forced upon them, and detectives set upon their track, it was a duty to themselves and their families

to meet the situation bravely. Nothing could have
been more successful than the last campaign ; and,
although Speug had never boasted, and none dared
say that he had anything to do with it, there was a
feeling in the Seminary that the conduct of the next
campaign was safe in his hands. As it turned out, it
was certainly safe, and one ought not to detract from
genius, but there can be no doubt that Fortune
played into the hands of Speug.

Much may be allowed to a broad sense of humour,
and the walk of the Bailie was marvellous to behold ;
but it was rather poor business for Speug to walk
half the length of the Terrace a yard behind the
Bailie in an exact imitation of the magistrate's
manner, although the school was hugely delighted.
If the Bailie had taken no notice, the score had
been on his side ; but when he turned round and
gave Speug a sound box on the side of the head, he
lost himself, and out of that single mistake, by a
chain of consequences, arose the scandal which
almost drove the Bailie from Muirtown. Speug
could not have hoped for anything so good as that
foolish blow, and the moment that it came he saw
his opportunity. Many a stroke had he endured in
his day, from his father and from the grooms, when
his mischief was beyond endurance, and from Bulldog
when he caught him red-handed, and from the boys
in a fight, and there was no one of his age so indifferent to such afflictions. Had the hand been any

other than that of Bailie MacConachie, Speug would
have made derisive gestures and invited the second
stroke. As it was, he staggered across the pavement
and fell with a heavy thud upon the street, where,
after one sharp, piercing cry of pain, he lay motionless, but his moans could be heard along the Terrace.
His one hope was that, when he had seized the
occasion with such dramatic success, the Seminary
would not fail to play up and support his *rôle*, and,
although they were cleverer at reality than acting,
they entered heartily into their opportunity.

"Are ye conscious, Peter?" inquired Howieson
tenderly, as he stooped over the prostrate figure.
"Div ye hear us speakin' to ye? Dinna moan like
that, but tell us where ye're hurt. What are ye
gatherin' round like that for and keepin' away the
air? Hold up his head, Bauldie. Some o' ye lift
his feet out o' the gutter. Run to the lade, for
ony's sake, and bring some water in yir bonnets."

It was pretty to see Jock and Bauldie lifting the
unconscious form of their beloved friend, and carrying
him carefully across the pavement, and placing Speug
in a sitting position against the railing, and then
rendering what would now be called first aid to the
wounded, while that ingenuous youth kept his eyes
tightly closed and moaned occasionally, to show that
he was still living. Never in his life had Providence
given him a chance of playing so much mischief, and
he was not going to be disobedient. They opened

his shirt at the breast to give him air, they anxiously
searched the side of his head for the wound, and
washed away imaginary blood with very dirty
pocket-handkerchiefs. They bathed his forehead with
such profuseness that the water ran down his chest,
whereat Speug expressed himself in low but stern
tones, so Nestie advised them to stick to his head;
and some of the smaller boys were only prevented
from taking off his boots by a seasonable warning
from Bauldie and a reasonable fear of consequences.
The Seminary circle was reinforced by all the message-
boys within sight, and several ladies who were coming
home from the shops. Two maiden ladies, against
whose railings Peter had been propped in the hour
of his distress, came out—their hearts full of compassion and their hands of remedies. As Jock and
Bauldie did not consider it safe that Peter should be
moved at once, one maiden lady placed a cushion
between his head and the railings, while the other
chafed his forehead with scent, and both insisted
that Dr. Manley should be sent for at once. This
was the first suggestion which seemed to have any
effect on Peter, for it would not at all have suited
his plans that that matter-of-fact physician should
have arrived on the spot. And when a bottle of
ferocious smelling-salts was held to the patient's nose,
Speug showed signs of returning consciousness.

" Poor dear ! " said one lady ; " what a mercy he
wasn't killed ! A blow behind the ear is often fatal.

He's coming round nicely. The colour is returning
to his cheeks. Bailie MacConachie, did you say?"
as Jock Howieson unfolded to the ladies in simple,
straightforward, truthful words the story of the
murderous attack. "I can't believe that any man
would so abuse a poor helpless child." (At this
moment Peter, who had been reconnoitring the whole
scene through his half-closed eyes, seized the opportunity to wink to the mourners with such irresistible
effect as to prove once again the close connexion
between tears and laughter.) "And him a magistrate," concluded the sympathetic female. "He ought
to be ashamed of himself; but if I were the laddie's
friends, I would make the Bailie hear about it on the
deaf side of his head."

Upon a sign from Speug, who was getting a little
weary of inaction, he was helped to his feet, and after
one or two staggers seemed to come to himself, and
submitted with agreeable humour to the attention of
his friends, who dusted him from head to foot, under
the superintendence of the ladies and to the huge
delight of the message-boys, who were now entering
into the meaning of the scene. His bonnet, which
had been thoughtfully used as a water-can, was placed
wrong end foremost upon his head, but Peter resisted
the proposal to tie up his head in Bauldie's handkerchief, partly because there was a limit even to his
endurance, and because Bauldie's handkerchief served
many a purpose in the course of the day. The

maiden ladies were anxious that he should rest in their house, but Speug indicated that he preferred to be taken home, where he could break the news himself to his anxious father. And so an impressive procession was formed, with so many boys in front to clear the way, and then Speug, upheld on the one hand by Nestie, and on the other by Jock, while Bauldie commanded the rearguard and kept the message-boys at a distance, in order to secure due respect for the sufferer. It was with difficulty that Speug could sustain his *rôle* until he and his friends got safely within the shelter of the stable-yard, when they plunged into a straw-shed and rolled together in one heap of triumphant mischief.

"You're a g-genius, Peter," said Nestie, "and it would be pure waste for you to be a h-horse-dealer. You must go on the st-stage. The way you came whack on the pavement was j-just immense; and do you know, Peter, you looked quite nice when you lay f-fainting. One lady called you a pretty boy, and I was quite sorry you were unconscious."

"Ye're a disgustin' liar, Nestie, besides being an impident young brat. I heard every word, and she never said 'pretty'; but," and Speug looked round thoughtfully, "if I knew which o' ye emptied the water down my breast, I'd give him something to remember. I'm wet to the skin," and Speug made a drive at Bauldie, who caught Howieson by the leg, who pulled down Nestie by the hair of the head, and they all fought together in high glee. Speug extricated himself and demanded news of the Bailie. Then the three told Speug the story together in bits, one beginning where another left off.

"He was that astonished when ye coupit over that he couldna speak, and Jock cried, 'The Bailie has killed Speug.'" "He was wantin' to lift ye up, but Bauldie gets in afore him and dares him to strike ye a second time." "It would have done you good, Peter, to see the Bailie walking along to his house, just like an ordinary man, all the s-starch out of him, and taking a look back to see what was h-happening." "Aye, and he stoppit opposite the lade to get another look, and if Cosh didna empty a cupful of water on his legs by mistake! I didna think Cosh had the spirit." "He was ashamed to stand at the w-window, but I saw him p-peeping out behind the curtains, just to find out whether you were living." "If his servant lass didna follow us across the meadow, and, my word, she's back to the Bailie with a fine story." "He's sweatin' the now for fear he be taken up for assault, and maybe manslaughter." "What w-would you say, Peter, just to die altogether, and we would gi-give you an A1 funeral? If you'll just be g-good-natured and do it, I'll write your l-life myself. It's perfectly sc-scrummageous." And then Peter fell on Nestie, and Howieson on Bauldie, and they rejoiced together once more in the straw.

"You're 'avin' an 'igh 'ole time in 'ere, young

gentlemen," and Mr. McGuffie's English groom
looked down on the boys; "but you're missin' the
Derby, that's what you are. Hold Pompous has
come 'isself, and if he ain't been hexplainin' to the
master 'ow he 'appened to knock Speug down. He's
out o' breath now, and the master he's took up the
runnin', and—my eye and Betty Martin—ain't he
talkin'! Not cussin'—no, not one swear word has
he let go. Young gentlemen, upon my Alfred David,
if the master ain't preachin' for all the world as if he
was a blessed beak on the Bench and old Pompous
was a 'habit and repute.' It's as good as a circus;
you just go and 'ear 'im," and in exactly one and a
quarter seconds the boys were an unseen audience
when Mr. Peter McGuffie senior gave his opinion of
the conduct of Bailie MacConachie, which he had been
doing already for some time with much effect.

"Imitatin' ye, was he, and followin' ye along the
street, walkin' as ye walk, and so ye knocked him
down in open day? Why should he not be doing as
ye did? Is yir walk protected by law, that nobody
dare step the same way on the streets of Muirtown?
Answer me that, if ye please. Bailies are pretty
high and mighty in this town, they are; but I never
heard yet that the street belonged to them, and that a
laddie was in a danger of death if he followed in their
steps. That would be a fine pass. Aren't boys
always imitatin' somebody? Why, you stupid old
fool, half the laddies in this district try to imitate me;

and, as sure as ye're standing there, I've seen half a dozen of them, each one with a straw in his mouth, and the bit legs of him straddled, and his bonnet on the side of his head, and the belly of him stuck out like a pillow, just the eemage of myself. What would ye think of me if I knockit one of them down, ye double-distilled old fool?

"I'm astonished at ye, for ye might be pleased to think that the laddies, instead of copying a horse-dealer, are trying to be magistrates. Didna the Provost tell the laddies the last time he gave the prizes to 'take notice of my freend Bailie Mac-Conachie, and try to be like him'? And now, when one of them has taken his advice, if ye dinna turn round on the street and half kill him, till he had to be brought home half faintin' to his father's house! Fine-like conduct for a magistrate! Ye blood-thirsty old ruffian!

"Came to make inquiries, did ye? Ye made enough inquiries, by all accounts, on the Terrace. Expression of regret, was it? We dont want yir regret, ye hypocritical Pharisee! Present of a top? I wonder ye have the face! Ye break a laddie's head and then offer him a top! I can buy tops my-self for my family. Confound ye! to think ye're standing there after manglin' a poor, defenceless, harmless, motherless laddie! Ye should be ashamed to show yir face in Muirtown; and if there was any public spirit in this town, ye would be drummed out o' the place!

"Look ye here, Bailie MacConachie"—and Mr. McGuffie adopted a conciliatory tone—"the best of us will make mistakes, and ye've made a particularly big one when ye knockit down Peter McGuffie in the face of the public of Muirtown. Ye may bet on that and take my tip for it. Let's settle this matter fair and sure as between man and man. Ye say ye're sorry, and ye don't want any noise made about it. Well, now, I've lived here man and boy for fifty years, and any man in Muirtown will tell you I'm straight. If I give a warranty with any horse, ye needn't be afraid to buy that horse, and I'll deal with ye on the square.

"You and me are about an age off and on, and we ought to be pretty even as fighting men. Ye have the pull of me in height, but I would say that I am nimbler on my legs. Ye might be called a heavy weight, and I am a middle weight, but there isn't much in that. We could meet pretty level with the gloves.

"Suppose, now, we just went into the straw-shed here, and stripped and fought the matter of six rounds, easy and quiet? There would be no mischief done, and no bad blood left, and that would be the end of the matter.

"Magistrate, did ye say, and elder in the Kirk? What do ye take me for? Do ye mean to say I'd split on ye, and go round Muirtown saying that Bailie MacConachie and me had a friendly turn with the gloves! Ye don't do me justice. Why, there's nobody outside this stable-yard would ever hear tell of it; and if they did, they would respect ye, and count ye an able-bodied man, which is more than a Bailie any day. Is it a deal, Bailie? Ye won't, won't ye, and I ought to be ashamed of myself, ought I? And a prizefight would be a disgrace to Muirtown, would it? Muirtown is pretty easy disgraced, then. Who's speaking about a prizefight, ye haverin' old body? But I see how the wind blows. If the other man stands a bare five feet, and ye can get at him before he's ready, ye're mighty handy with yir fists. Ye cowardly old sneak. But when ye're offered the chance of facing a man about yir own size, ye count it a disgrace. My opinion is, ye havna the spirit of a mouse in yir big body! I'm ashamed to think ye're a magistrate of Muirtown! Dinna speak to me, MacConachie, for I might lose control and send ye out of the stable-yard, with my foot followin'! My advice is to be off as quick as ye can, for if some of the grooms got hold of ye they would make an awful mess o' ye— they're not just particularly fond of magistrates, and they've a great notion of Peter.

"One word before we part, Bailie," and the Bailie took that word walking, "So far as I understand, ye might be arrested for assault, and I might prosecute ye for damages; but I will let ye off just this once with a word of solemn advice. Ye're a Bailie of Muirtown, and ye're an elder in the Kirk, and ye're an Italian warehouseman; but for all that, Mac-Conachie, remember ye're just a man. Ye're swollen up and fozzy with pride and vanity, and ye pace down the streets like an elephant let loose from a menagerie; but, MacConachie, consider ye're just a man, ye're wily and cunning and pawky and long-headed, and ye've got yir own way in this town for many a year; but lay it to heart, ye're just a man. Ye've sat on the Bench and laid down the law, and when ye wagged yir head everybody kept quiet, and when ye've scrapit yir throat they thought it was Gospel; but, MacConachie, dinna forget it, ye're just a man. Ye needna hurry," and Mr. McGuffie, standing in the gateway of the stable-yard, pursued the Bailie along the street with exhortations. " I've said all I wanted to say, and I've just one word more. Ye've fought with the Tories and ye've fought with the Publicans, ye've fought with this body and with that body and ye've beaten them, and ye thought ye were cock of the roost in Muirtown; but ye meddled with the laddies, and they've licket ye once, Bailie, and they've licket ye twice, Bailie, and if ye dinna cry ' Peace,' they'll lick ye again, and that'll be the end of ye, Bailie MacConachie."

When Mr. McGuffie returned to the stable-yard he called for his son, and passed a careful hand over Peter's head, and then he declared that Speug was a chip of the old block and prophesied aloud that there lay before him a long and useful life.

XIV

THE BAILIE'S DOUBLE

MUIRTOWN is not a large city, and schoolboys of high principle and domestic habits used to go home in the dinner-hour and take the meal with their anxious mothers, who seized the opportunity of repairing the rents made in their clothes since morning, and giving them good advice on their behaviour. Thoroughly good boys, who had been tossed to and fro, much against their will, in the tempest of morning play, were glad to go into harbour and come back at two o'clock, not only re-victualled, but also re-fitted and re-painted for the troubled voyage of the afternoon; and boys not so entirely good as the Dowbiggins, and other models of propriety, still appreciated the home trip, because, although there might be an embarrassing review of garments, and awkward questions might be asked about a mark on the face, there was always a toothsome dainty for a growing laddie, weary with intellectual work and the toils of a snow-fight. As the business of a horsedealer took Mr. McGuffie senior in various directions, and as in no case were the arrangements of his house since Mrs. McGuffie's death of an extremely regular character, there was no meal to which his promising son—Speug—could return with any confidence; and therefore Peter did not make a practice of going home at one o'clock, unless there was a special event at the stables such as the arrival of a new horse, in which case he invited a few friends to an inspection, with light refreshments; or unless, having racked his brain to the utmost for four hours, he was still in sheer despair of mischief. With one or two other young friends of a like mind, he was accustomed to spend the dinner-hour in what might be called extramural studies—rowing over to the island below the bridge against the tide and coming back gloriously with the current; assisting the salmon-fishers to draw their nets and gather the silver spoil; in the happy snow-time raiding the playground of a rival school when the boys were away, and leaving insulting remarks wrought in snow; or attending the drill of the cavalry on the South Meadow. Like other guerillas, he carried his biltong and mealies with him, and took his meal anywhere and by preference when on the run. Perhaps that was one reason why Speug in after years made one of the best of South African fighters.

When Speug was disinclined for active occupation, and desired to improve his mind by contact with the greater world, he took a cab, or hotel 'bus (the box-seat of every one in Muirtown was at Speug's disposal, and his edifying conversation was much enjoyed by the driver), and went to spend his hour at Muirtown Station, which, as everybody knows, is at the shooting season a spectacle to be classed with Niagara or the Jungfrau for interest, and at any time is worth seeing. It pleased Speug, whose interests were varied and human rather than classical and literary, to receive the English express, or even one from Edinburgh, as it swept into the station ; or to see the Aberdeen fast train fairly off; to watch a horse safely entrained, and if necessary to give understanding assistance ; and to pass the time of day with the guards, ticket-collectors, and carriage-cleaners, the last of whom would allow him as a favour to see the inside of the huge mail-carriage, with its pigeon-holes and its ingenious apparatus for delivering letters at roadside stations while the train passed at full speed. It was an hour of what might be called irregular study, but one never knows what he may pick up if he only keeps his eyes open (and the eyes of Speug were as open as a savage's), and it was on a visit to Muirtown railway station that Peter found the opportunity for what he ever considered his most successful achievement at the Seminary, and one on which the recollection of his companions still fondly dwells.

When a cab passed the *Muirtown Arms* 'bus at the entrance to the station, and the cabman signalled to Peter on the box-seat, and referred to the contents with an excited thumb and great joy on his face, Peter knew that there would be something worth seeing when the cab emptied at the ticket-office ; but he could not have imagined anything so entirely satisfying. First, Bailie MacConachie emerged, dressed in the famous frock-coat and grey trousers, in the high collar and magisterial stock, but without his usual calm and dignity. His coat was only half buttoned, his tie was slightly awry, and although his hat had been distinctly tilted to the side on getting out of the cab, he was too much occupied to set it right. Instead of clearing his throat as he alighted among the waiting porters, and giving them, as it were, the chance of honouring a live Bailie going forth upon his journey, he did not seem to wish for any public reception, or, indeed, for any spectators, and in fact had every sign of a man who desired to be *incognito*.

" No, no, I've no luggage today," the Bailie hastily explained to an obliging porter, and he stood between the man and the cab so as to block all vision. " Just running down to Dundee on business and . . . seeing a friend off."

As the embarrassed magistrate endeavoured to disperse the porters, the driver, leaning over the roof of the cab, winked with much unction to Peter, and indicated to that ingenuous youth that it would be worth while for him to wait and see the mysterious friend. Speug, in fact, understood from all this tele-graphic communication that there were going to be circumstances of a quite remarkable character, and in which he—Peter McGuffie—was expected to be per-sonally interested. He dragged Jock Howieson, who was spending the hour with him, behind a pile of luggage, and from their hiding-place they saw, to their utter amazement, a second Bailie come slowly and gingerly, but yet withal triumphantly, out of the cab. The same height as the great man himself, and built after the same pattern; a perfect reproduction also in dress, except that the trousers were baggier, and the coat shabbier, and the collar frayed at the edges, and the hat had the appearance of having been used either as a seat or as a pillow, or perhaps for both purposes, at different times; and the air of this second, but by no means ghostly, Bailie was like that of the first, as confident, as mighty, as knowing, with the addition of a certain joviality of expression and benignant humanity, and a certain indifference to all the trials and difficulties of life which is characteristic of a man who has been "tasting," not wisely, but too well.

"Lean on me, James," said the Bailie nervously, as the figure came with a heavy lurch on the pavement. "The faintness may pass off. Take care of your feet," and the Bailie shouldered his double to the ticket-office and propped it against the wall while he went to take the tickets.

It might have been ill, and the remarkable walk might have been due to weakness of the heart, for you never can tell, and one ought to be charitable ; but there was no sign of an invalid about this new Bailie, nor was he at all too exhausted for genial conversation. He explained during the other Bailie's brief absence, to all who were willing to listen, in a style that was rather suggestive than exhaustive, that he had been paying a visit to Muirtown for the good of his health, and that he felt better—in fact, very much better ; that where he lived the supply of liquid refreshment was limited, and that in consequence he had suffered through weakness of the heart ; that he had intended to stay longer in a place where there was every comfort of life, and that nothing would have induced him to leave but the immoral conduct of his twin brother ; that Bailie MacConachie, he was sorry to say, being his brother, was fearfully given to drink, and that he, James MacConachie, could no longer stay with him ; that he, his brother, was not fit to be a Bailie, and that he was a hypocrite whose judgement would not tarry, and indeed, according to his language, was already pronounced. He also gave a certificate of character to the refreshment to be obtained at the *Black Bull*, Muirtown, and cheerfully invited any person who had a friendly heart to go with him there and then to drink the Queen's health. On seeing his brother returning, the figure concluded his address—which had been mightily enjoyed by three porters, a couple of Highland drovers, a Perth loafer, who had once passed through the police-court when the Bailie was on the Bench, and an elderly lady, who was anxious that a doctor should be sent for—by explaining once more that his brother was a gentleman beside whom the Pharisees were straightforward and honourable members of society.

As the procession was again re-formed, and the two Bailies left the ticket-office together, one of them waving a regretful farewell to his sympathetic congregation, the boys executed a war-dance of triumph; for the contrast between the twin brethren afforded just that kind of comedy which appeals to a boy's heart, and because they had an instinct that the incident would be of service in the war between the Bailie and the Seminary, which had gone on for a year and showed no signs of closing.

" The Bailie keeps him oot o' sight somewhere in the country, I'll warrant," said Speug to Jock, in great spirits, " and there's naebody in Muirtown kens he's got a twin brother. Dod, Jock, he's juist the very eemage of him, and he's got a suit o' his auld clothes on. It would take Dr. Manley himself or the Chief Constable to tell the one from the ither. Jock Howieson, if you and me could get the use o' that lad, we would have a michty time. I would give my four rabbits and . . . and my Skye terrier pup just for an hour of him." And although they had no hope that circumstances would deal so kindly with

them, yet they went on to the platform to see the last
of the two Bailies.

Under the influence of the senior Bailie's chasten-
ing conversation, who at first reminded his brother of
a drunkard's end, which had no effect, and then
threatened to cut off his modest weekly allowance,
which had an immediate effect, the figure consented
to be taken along the platform, and might even
have been safely deposited in its carriage, had not
the word " Refreshment-room," printed in absurdly
large type, attracted his attention.

" Div ye see that, man? " said the figure, pointing
jubilantly to the board. " I declare it juist a Providence. It's no that I'm thirsty, Bailie, and I canna
bear drinkin'; that's never been a fault of mine,
though I doubt ye're failin' into the habit yirsel'.
No, I'm no thirsty, but I've a sinkin' at the heart.
Ye'll come in, and we'll taste together afore we part.
I forgive ye onything ye said. I bear no grudge,
and I'll let ye pay, Bailie." And the figure had the
Bailie almost at the door of the refreshment-room
before he could make a stand.

" Mair than I can carry already, Bailie, did ye say?
Gude forgie ye. I wonder ye're not black ashamed
to say sic a word, and me draggin' ye along the platform and holdin' ye up, juist to cover yir character.
Well, well, I canna fecht wi' ye, for I'm no the man I
was once. The fact is, I havna strength to go
another step, and if ye'll no let me get a cordial, I'll

juist have to sit down on the platform." And the horrified Bailie had to accept the assistance of a porter to support his exhausted brother and to guide him to his carriage.

From an adjacent third-class compartment, where Speug and Jock promptly secreted themselves, they heard the senior Bailie's exhortation to his frail kinsman—that he must on no account come out of the carriage; that he must hold his tongue and not talk nonsense to his fellow travellers; that he must not mention his—the Bailie's—name, nor claim to be connected with him; and that he must not come back to Muirtown again until the Bailie sent for him; and all this he must lay to heart as he valued his weekly allowance. The Bailie also expressed his deep regret, which, indeed, seemed to be very sincere, that he had to leave by the Dundee train before the departure of the slow Fife train by which his double travelled. And when this fact emerged—that the other Bailie was to be left even for five minutes at their disposal—Speug threw Howieson's bonnet to the end of the compartment, with his own following in a rapture of joy.

" Dinna be afraid," said the figure in the compartment to the Bailie on the platform, who was torn between his profitable business engagement at Dundee and the fear of leaving his brother to his own devices. " After the way ye've treated me and put me to shame afore the platform, I wouldna stay another day in Muirtown for a thousand pounds. I am no angry, Bailie," the figure continued with mournful dignity, "for that's no my speerit, but I'm hurt at yir conduct. Weel, if ye maun go, ye maun, and I heard the Dundee engine whistlin'; but for ony sake dinna be tastin' in Dundee and disgracin' the family. Drink is an awfu' failin', but ye canna say I havna warned ye." And as the Bailie hurried to catch the Dundee train the figure shook its head mournfully, with the air of one who hopes for the best, but who has had too good reason to expect the worst.

"Bailie," said Speug, presenting himself with a fine mixture of haste and importance before the figure which was still moralising to itself on the evils of drink, "div ye no mind that the Rector o' the Seminary is expectin' ye to address the laddies this afternoon, and they'll be waitin' this very meenut in the Latin class-room?" and Speug made signs that he should come at once, and offered to secure a cab. The figure could only shake its head and explain that on account of the disgraceful conduct of a relative, who had given way to drink, it had no heart for public appearances; but the idea of a return to the enjoyment of Muirtown was evidently filtering in.

"Are ye no Bailie MacConachie?" demanded Speug. "A porter threipit (insisted) that he had seen the Bailie in the Dundee train, but naebody can mistake Bailie MacConachie. The school will be terrible pleased to see ye, Bailie."

"Who said I wasna Bailie MacConachie?" and the figure was plainly roused. "Him in the Dundee train? Laddies, there's a black sheep in every family and that man is a poor, helpless brother o' mine that's taken to bad habits, and I've juist to support him and keep him oot o' sicht. It's an awfu' trial," and the figure wept, but immediately brisked itself up again. "Of course I'm Bailie MacConachie. Laddies, was't at the *Black Bull* they're expectin' me?"

"The very place, Bailie; but ye maun say juist a word at the Seminary in passin'," and Speug signalled to a ticket-collector who had just come upon the scene.

"Would ye mind helpin' Bailie MacConachie oot o' the carriage, for he's forgotten an engagement at the Seminary, and he's juist a wee thingie faint with the heat?"

"It's no the heat, man," as the amazed collector helped the magistrate on to the platform, "it's family trouble. Are ye connected with the *Black Bull*? Well, at any rate, ye seem a well-behaved young man, and these are twa fine laddies." And outside the station, surrounded by a sympathising circle of drivers, who were entering into the spirit of Speug's campaign, this astonishing Bailie warned every one to beware of strong drink, and urged them to take the pledge without delay. He also inquired anxiously whether there was a cab there from the *Black Bull* and explained that the Rector of the Seminary, with his laddies, was waiting for him in that place of

hospitality. He added that he had been on his way
to the General Assembly of the Kirk, where he sat
as a ruling elder, and he warmly denounced the spread
of false doctrine. But at last they got him into the
cab, where, after a pathetic appeal to Speug and his
companion to learn the Catechism and sing the
Psalms of David, he fell fast asleep.

By a happy stroke of strategy, Howieson engaged
the attention of the sergeant in the back-yard, who
considered that Jock was playing truant and was
anxious to arrest him, while the cabman, fortunately
an able-bodied fellow, with Speug's assistance induced the Bailie to leave the cab and convoyed him
upstairs and to the door of the Rector's class-room.
At this point the great man fell into low spirits, and
bemoaned the failure of a strenuous life, in which he
had vainly fought the immorality of Muirtown, and
declared, unless he obtained an immediate tonic, he
would succumb to a broken heart. He also charged
Speug with treachery in having brought him to the
County Gaol instead of to the *Black Bull.* It
was painfully explained him that he was now in the
Seminary, and within that door an anxious school
was waiting for him—Bailie MacConachie—and his
address.

" Who said I wasna Bailie MacConachie, and that I
was a drunken body? I'll teach them to smuggle me
oot o' Muirtown as if I was a waufie (disreputable
character). He thinks I'm at Leuchars, but I'm here "

(with much triumph), "and I'm Bailie MacConachie" (with much dignity). And the Bailie was evidently full awake.

"Losh keeps, laddies, what am I saying? Family trouble shakes the mind. Take the pledge when ye're young, laddie, and ye'll no regret it when ye're old. I've been an abstainer since the age of ten. Noo, laddie" (with much cunning), "if I am to address the school, what think ye would be a fine subject, apairt from the Catechism? for it's a responsibility, especially me being a Bailie. If ye can mind onything, laddie, I'll give ye sixpence next time we meet."

Although Speug was reticent in the class, for reasons that commended themselves to his practical judgement, he had a rich wealth of speech upon occasion, and he fairly drilled into the head of Bailie MacConachie's double that it had been a very foolish thing for him—the Bailie—to quarrel with the Seminary about their playground upon the Meadow, and an act of an unchristian bitterness to strike him —the Speug—upon the head and nearly injure him for life, but that he—the Bailie—was sorry for all his bad conduct, and that he would never do the like again as long as he was Bailie of Muirtown; and Speug concluded, while the cabman stood open-mouthed with admiration, "Ye micht juist say that ye have an awfu' respect for me—Speug—ye know."

"I'll be sure to do that," said the delighted Bailie,

"for it's a fact. Ye're a fine laddie and have a fearsome power o' the gab (mouth) ; I expect to see ye in
the pulpit yet ; but keeps a' it's time I was at the
Black Bull, so ye micht juist slip in and tell the
Rector I'm at the door—Bailie MacConachie of Muirtown."

Had it been the class-room of Bulldog, master of
mathematics, arithmetic, and writing, and, it might
also be added, master of discipline, Speug would as
soon have ventured into his presence on such an
errand as into the lion's den of the travelling
menagerie which had recently visited Muirtown, and
at which he had spent many an unlicensed hour.
But the Rector was that dear delight of boys, a short-
sighted, absent-minded, unsuspicious scholar, who
lived in a world of his own with Homer and Horace,
and could only be fairly roused (to sorrow) by a false
quantity or (to joy) by a happy translation.

Muirtown Seminary had an inexhaustible confidence in Speug's genius for mischief and effrontery
of manner, but the Rector's class sat breathless when
Peter came in with an unshaken countenance, and
politely intimated to the Rector that a magistrate of
Muirtown had come and desired to speak to the
school.   Before the Rector could fairly withdraw
himself from a cunning phrase of Horace's, or the
school had energy to cheer, the wonderful Bailie was
launched into the room with almost too much vigour
by the cabman, who remained in the shadow and

whispered a last direction to "hold up your head and keep to the right." They had forgotten—Speug's only oversight—to take off the Bailie's hat, which was set jauntily on the side of his head, and the course which he took through the room was devious, and mainly regulated by the furniture, while his expression was a fine blend of affable dignity and genial good humour. "Gosh!" exclaimed Bauldie, and he liberated the feeling of the class, who understood that their enemy had been delivered into their hands, and that Peter McGuffie—their own Speug— had been the means thereof. Yet could it be the case? Yes! It was the very countenance, line by line, and the very clothes, piece by piece, though looking a trifle shabby, of the premier Bailie of Muirtown, and it was evident that he had been "tasting," and that very freely.

"I am—er—proud to bid you welcome, Mr. Bailie," said the Rector, bowing with old-fashioned courtesy, and not having the faintest idea what like was the figure before him. "We are always delighted to receive a visit from any of the magistrates of the city, who are to our humble school" (and here the Rector was very gracious) "what Maecenas was to Horace, whose *curiosa felicitas* we are now studying. Is it your pleasure, Mr. Bailie, to examine the school?"

During this stately reception the Bailie came to rest upon a desk, and regarded the Rector's flowing gown with unconcealed admiration, which he indicated to the school by frank gestures.

"It would be a great satisfaction to hear the laddies answer 'The Chief End of Man,' and to say juist a word to them aboot good conduct; but you and me has an engagement, and ye ken where we're expected. I juist looked in to say——" And here the worthy man's thoughts began to wander, and he made an indistinct allusion to the *Black Bull*, so that Speug had to prompt him severely from behind. "Aye, aye! we're all poor, frail creatures, and I'm the last man to hurt the feelings of the Seminary. Seminary laddie mysel, prize medal Greek. Bygones be bygones!... No man in Muirtown I respect more than... Speug an honourable tradesman" (breaking away on his own account with much spirit), "a faithful husband, and an affectionate father. What? All a mistake from beginning to end. Family trouble did it—conduct of a relative," and the Bailie wept. Bailies and other municipal dignitaries were a species of human beings so strange and incalculable to the Rector, that he was hardly amazed at anything that they might say; and having some vague idea that there had been a quarrel between the Seminary and some Bailie or other, about something or other, some time or other, he concluded that this was an official intimation that the quarrel was over, and that it was in style and allusion according to the habits of municipal circles.

"It is," he responded, bowing again, "my grateful duty, as Rector of the Seminary, to thank you for your presence here to-day—the Mercury of the gods, if I may so say—and for your courteous intimation that the—er—controversy to which you—er—have delicately alluded is healed. Any dispute between the Council and the Seminary could only have a favourable issue. *Amantium irae amoris integratio* has had another illustration, Mr. Bailie; but it would please us that you should hear the class translate the Ode we have in hand, which happens to be '*Ad Sodales.*'" And a boy began to translate "*Nunc est bibendum.*"

"Time to drink, did ye say?" and the Bailie, who had been taking a brief nap, was immediately conscious. "Man, ye never said a truer word. Work hard at yir lessons, laddies, and for ony sake dinna forget the Catechism. Yir maister has an engagement wi' me, and he'll no be back for an hour. Come awa,' man" (in a loud whisper to the amazed Rector), "it's time we were off." And the Bailie, making a hurried rush for the door, found himself in the arms of the school sergeant, who had caught the sound of the uproar in the Rector's class-room, and suspected trouble.

"Preserve us a', body and soul!" cried the Crimean veteran, as he brought the Bailie to an equilibrium. "Could onybody have expected this?" And then, with much presence of mind, he closed the door of the Latin class-room and conducted the Bailie downstairs to his cab, while the magistrate remonstrated that the Rector was coming with him, and that both were going to discuss the higher education of youth at the *Black Bull*.

"Na, na, Bailie," said the sergeant. "It's no to the *Black Bull*, or ony other bull, ye're to go this afternoon, but back to yir ain hoose. If ye maun taste, would it no have been more respectable to keep indoors, instead of making an exhibeetion of yourself afore the Seminary? It's no becomin' in a magistrate, and it's michty bad for the laddies."

It was the sergeant who delivered the astonishing figure at the blameless home of Bailie MacConachie, although it is right to say that this visit was not at all in the plan, and called forth a vigorous protest from the Bailie's substitute. And to the day of his death, the real and proper Bailie spent odd moments of his spare time in explaining to an incredulous public that he had never "tasted" in his life, and that on the day in question he had been transacting private business in Dundee.

XV

THE TRIUMPH OF THE
SEMINARY

A S the East is distant from the West, so far
was Muirtown Seminary removed in its
manners and customs from an English public
school; but at one point they met on common
ground, and that was the "tuck-shop." It does not
matter that an English house master be careful to
provide an ample supply of wholesome food for
his boys, and even add, on occasion, toothsome
dainties, such as jam at Sunday tea, and sausages
for a Saturday supper, they will agree unanimously,
and declare aloud, that they can hardly recall such
a thing as breakfast, so ghostly has it grown, and
that they would be ashamed to offer their dinner
to the beasts which perish. They will write such
descriptions home, and hold such conferences with
friends spending the holidays with them, and
they will all vie with one another in applying such
weird and fearsome adjectives to the butter, milk,

coffee, meat, potatoes, and pudding—but at the mention of pudding they will simply look at one another and be silent, despairing of the English language—that their horrified parents will take counsel together by the hour whether their poor boy ought not to be taken from school and surrounded by home comforts. When the emaciated invalid hears of this drastic measure, he protests strongly, and insists that it would ruin him for life ; for, to do the ruffians justice, a boy may be half-starved and swished every second day, and bullied between times, till his life is hardly worth living, he will still stand by his school, and prefer it as a place of residence to his home. Neither ample meals, nor the pretty bedroom with white curtains, nor the long lie in the morning, nor a party in the evening, nor all his mother's petting, will make up to this savage for the racket of the dormitories, and the fight at the bathroom, and the babel at the dinner-table, and the recreations which enliven "prep," and the excitement of a house match, and the hazardous delights of football, and the tricks on a new boy, and the buttered eggs—a dozen at least between two at a study supper. It only remains therefore that his father should write a pathetic letter to the *Standard*, and that other parents should join in, for a fortnight, explaining to the English public that the manhood of the country is being destroyed in its early years, and the boys at school will read the letters aloud with much unction, and declare that "Pater has warmed up old Skinny properly," while their mother sends them generous remittances that they may obtain nourishing food to supplement their starvation rations. This money will be spent rapidly, but also shrewdly, at the "tuck-shop," where some old servant of the school is making a small fortune in providing for the boys such meat as their souls love, and for a fortnight Tom and his friends, for he is not a fellow to see his chums die before his eyes, will live on the fat of the land, which, upon the whole, means cocoa, sardines, sausages, and eggs.

Seminary boys had their meals at home, and were very soundly fed with porridge and milk in the morning, followed by tea and ham, if their conduct had been passably decent. Scots broth and meat for dinner, with an occasional pudding, and a tea in the evening which began with something solid and ended with jam, made fair rations, and, although such things may very likely be done now, when we are all screaming about our rights, no boy of the middle Victorian period wrote to the *Muirtown Advertiser* complaining of the home scale of diet. Yet, being boys, neither could they be satisfied with the ordinary and civilized means of living, but required certain extra delicacies to help them through the day. It was not often that a Seminary lad had a shilling in his pocket, and once only had gold been seen—when Dr. Manley paid Speug a medical fee for his advice in Bull-dog's sickness—but there were few in the Seminary who were not able to rattle some pennies together, and, in the end, every penny found its way to the till of that comprehensive merchant and remarkable woman, Mrs. McWhae. Her shop and the other old houses beside it have been pulled down long ago, to make room for a handsome block of buildings, and I think her exact site is occupied by the plate-glass windows and gorgeous display of the "Breadalbane Emporium," where you can buy everything from a frying pan to a draw-ing-room suite, but where you cannot get a certain delicacy called "gundy," which Mrs. McWhae alone could make as it ought to be made, and at the remembrance thereof the very teeth begin to water. Mrs. McWhae did not sell books, nor clothes, nor any other effeminate luxury of life, but she kept in stock everything that was really necessary to the life of a well-living and high-minded boy. There he could obtain marbles from the common clay, six for a halfpenny, on to the finer "streakies," six for penny, till you came to large marbles with a red and blue pattern on a white ground, which were a halfpenny each, and climbed to "glassies" at a penny each; and there was one glass levia-thian which contained all colours within its sphere,

and which was kept only to be handled and admired. Tops were there, too, from polished little
beauties with shining steel tips, which were intended
only for amusement, and were spun with fine white
cord, to unadorned, massive, vicious-looking warriors
with sharpened projecting points, which were intended for the battlefield, and were spun with
rough, strong twine, and which, dexterously used,
would split another top from head to foot as when
you slice butter with a knife. Her stock of kites
in the season was something to see, and although
she did not venture upon cricket-bats, which were
sold by the hairdresser, nor cricket-balls, she had
every other kind of ball—solid gutta-percha balls,
for hasty games in the "breaks," white skin-covered
rounder balls, and hollow india-rubber balls, which
you could fill with water at the lade, and then use
with much success as a squirt. Girls, we noticed,
employed this "softie" in silly games of their own,
trying whether they could make it rebound a
hundred times from the ground, but we had no
doubt about its proper use in the purposes of
Creation. And Mrs. McWhae—peace to her ashes!
—provided all things in meat and drink which a
boy could desire; unless, of course, on some great
occasion he wished to revel imperially—then he
went to Fenwick's rock-shop, where generations
have turned their eager feet, and beyond which
nothing is left to desire. Fenwick's, however, was

rather for our fathers than for ourselves, and we were almost content with Mrs. McWhae, where you could get ginger-beer of her own making at a penny a bottle, better than that which they sold at the *Muirtown Arms* at sixpence ; and treacle-beer also at a penny, but in this case the bottle was double the size and was enough for two fellows ; and halfpenny rolls, if you were fiercely hungry and could not get home to dinner, so tough that only a boy's teeth could tear them to pieces ; and tarts, so full that it required long skill to secure every drop of the jam, and your fingers were well worth licking afterwards ; and pepper-mint balls of black and white, one of which would keep your mouth sweet for an hour of Latin—that is, if you only sucked gently and didn't crunch. But the glory of the establishment was the "gundy." There was a room behind the shop where Mrs. McWhae, who was a widow, elderly and not pre-possessing, lived and slept, and dressed herself, and cooked her food, and, perhaps, on rare occa-sions, washed, and there she prepared her tempting meats and drinks for the Seminary. We lived in a pre-scientific age, and did not go curiously into the origin of things, being content to take the Creation as it stood, and to use the gifts of the gods in their finished form. But I believe that "gundy" was made of the coarsest and cheapest sugar, which our hostess boiled to a certain point, and then with her own fair hands, which it was said she wetted with her lips, drew out and out, till at last, by the constant drawing, it came to a light brown colour; after which she cut the finished product into sticks of a foot long, and wrapped it up in evil-looking brown paper, twisting the two ends. And, wonders of wonders! all within that paper, and the paper itself, you could have for one halfpenny! Good! There is no word for it, as the preachers say, "humanly speaking." The flavour thereof so rich, so satisfying, so stimulating, and the amount thereof so full and so tenacious. Why, that "gundy" would so cling to your teeth and hide itself about your mouth, and spread itself out, that he was a clever fellow who had drained its last resources within an hour. Mrs. McWhae was a widow of a military gentleman, who, it was understood, had performed prodigies of valour in the Black Watch, and she was a woman of masculine vigour, who only dealt upon a cash basis, and in any case of dispute was able to use her hands effectively. Like most women she was open to blandishments, and Nestie Molyneux, with his English tongue and pretty ways, could get round the old lady, and she had profound though inexpressed respect for Speug, whom she regarded as a straightforward fighter, and the two friends would sometimes be allowed the highest privilege in her power, to see her make a brew of "gundy." And it is from hints dropped by those two favoured customers that the above theory of the making of this delectable sweet has been formed.

It was possible, with a proper celerity, to visit Mrs. McWhae's during the " breaks," and to spend three minutes in those happy precincts and not be absolutely late for the next class ; and during the dinner-hour her shop was crowded, and the steps outside and the very pavement were blocked by the Seminary, waiting for their " gundy " and ginger-beer.   Little boys who had been fortunate enough to get their provisions early, and were coming out to enjoy the " gundy " in some secret place, hid their treasure within their waistcoats, lest a bigger fellow should supply himself without the trouble of waiting his turn, and defer payment to the end of the year.   And one of the lords of the school would on occasion clear out a dozen of the small fry, in order that he might select his refreshments comfortably.   It was indeed the Seminary Club, with its bow-window like other clubs, and the steps on which the members could stand, and from the steps you commanded three streets, so that there were many things to see, and in snowball time many things to do.   McWhae's had only one inconvenience, and that was that the line of communication could be cut off by raiding parties from the " Pennies " and other rival schools. When the snow was deep on the ground, and the enemy was strong on the field, it was necessary to bring down supplies under charge of a convoy, and if anything could have added to the flavour of the "gundy," it was that you had fought your way up Breadalbane Street to get it, and your way back to enjoy it, that you had lost your bonnet in a scrimmage, and that the remains of a snowball were trickling down your back. Precious then was the dainty sweet as the water which the mighty men brought to David from the well of Bethlehem.

"My word!" cried Speug, who was winding up the dinner-hour with Nestie Molyneux, on the upper step of the club-house, "if there isn't the 'Bumbees' driving in a four-in-hand!" and the brake of the *Muirtown Arms* passed, with a dozen smart and well-set-up lads rejoicing openly, and, wheeling round by the corner of the Cathedral, disappeared up the road which ran to Drumtochty. "And where think ye have their royal highnesses been?"

If the name of a school be St. Columba's, and the boys call themselves Columbians, it is very profane to an absolutely respectable Scots saint, and very rude to a number of well-behaved lads, to call them "Bumbees"; but Speug was neither reverent nor polite, and the Seminary, although mainly occupied with local quarrels, yet harboured a distant grudge against the new public school of St. Columba's, which had been recently started in a romantic part

of Perthshire. Its founders were a number of excellent and perhaps slightly superior persons, who
were justly aghast at the somewhat rough life and
unfinished scholarship of the Scots grammar schools,
and who did not desire that Scots lads of the better
class should be sent of necessity to the English
public schools. Their idea was to establish a public
school after the English method in Scotland, and so
St. Columba's kept terms, and had dormitories, and
a chapel, and playing-fields, and did everything on a
smaller scale which was done at Rugby and Harrow.
The masters of St. Columba's would have nothing to
do with such modest men as the staff of the Seminary.
The Columbians occasionally came down to Muirtown and sniffed through the town. Two or three
boys had been taken from the Seminary, because it
was vulgar, and sent to St. Columba's, in order to
get into genteel society. And those things had
gradually filtered into the mind of the Seminary,
which was certainly a rough school, but at the same
time very proud and patriotic, and there was a
latent desire in the mind of the Seminary that the
Columbians should come down in snow-time and
show their contempt for the Muirtown grammar
school, when that school would explain to the
Columbians what it thought of them and all their
works. As this pleasure was denied the Seminary,
and the sight of the brake was too much for Speug's
uncultured nature, he forgot himself, and yelled

opprobrious names, in which the word "Bumbee" was distinct and prominent.

"Your m-manners are very b-bad, Speug, and I am a-ashamed of you. D-don't you know that the 'B-bumbees' have been p-playing in England and w-won their match? Twenty-two runs and s-seven wickets to fall. G-good s-sport, my Speug; read it in the newspaper."

"It wasna bad. I didna think the 'Bumbees' had as muckle spunk in them; seven wickets, did ye say, against the English? If I had kenned that, Nestie, ye little scoundrel, I would have given them a cheer. Seven wickets—they did the job properly." And Speug took his "gundy" with relish.

"Speug!"—and Nestie spoke with much impressiveness—"I have an idea. Why shouldn't the Seminary challenge the 'Bumbees' to a match next s-summer? We could p-practice hard all this summer, and begin s-soon next year and t-try them in July."

"It would be juist michty," said Speug, who was cheered at the thought of any battle, and he regarded Nestie with admiration, and then his face fell and he declared it of no use.

"They wouldna come, dash them for their cheek! and if they came they'd lick us clean. They have a professional and they play from morning till night. We're light-weights, Nestie. If they went in first, we'd never get them oot; and if we went in, they'd have us oot in half an 'oor."

"For shame, Speug, to run down the Seminary as if you were a 'Penny'! Didn't the county professional say that Robertson was the b-best young player he'd seen for t-ten years? And Bauldie hits a good b-ball, and no b-bowler can get you out, Speug, and there are other chaps just want p-practice. We might be b-beaten, but we'd make a stiff fight for the old Seminary."

"Ye can bowl, Nestie," said Speug generously, as they went back to school at the trot; "ye're the trickiest overhand I ever saw; and Jock Howieson is a fearsome quick and straight bowler; and for a wicket-keeper Dunc Robertson is no easy to beat. Gosh!" exclaimed Speug, as they wheeled into the back-yard, "we'll try it."

The Seminary were slow to move, but once they took fire they burned gloriously; and when Dunc Robertson and Nestie Molyneux, who had been sent up to St. Columba's as the most presentable deputation, returned and informed the school assembled round the Russian guns that the "Bumbees" would send down their second eleven, since the first was too old for the Seminary, and play a single innings match on a Saturday afternoon in the end of July, next year, the Seminary lifted up their voice in joyful anticipation.

It did not matter that the "Bumbees" had only consented in terms of condescension by way of encouraging local sport, as they had tried to organise a Drumtochty eleven, or that it was quite understood that the result would be a hopeless defeat for the Seminary. They were coming, and the Seminary had a year to make ready; and if they were beaten in cricket, well, it couldn't be helped, but it was the first time Bulldog's boys had been beaten in any-thing, and they would know the reason why.

Special practice began that evening and continued that evening, and every other evening except Sundays as long as light lasted and on till the middle of October, when football could no longer be delayed. Practice began again a month before the proper season and continued on the same lines till the great day in July. The spirit of the Seminary was fairly up, and from the Rector who began freely to refer to the Olympian games, to the little chaps who had just come from a dame's school and were proud to field balls at bowling practice, the whole school was swept into the excitement of the coming event, and it is said that Bulldog stumped over every evening after dinner to watch the play and was the last to leave.

"B-Bully's fairly on the job, Speug, and he's j-just itching to have a bat himself. Say, Speug, if we get badly licked, he'll be ill again; but if we p-pull it off, I bet he'll give a rippin' old supper."

News spread through the town that the Seminary was to fight the "Bumbees" for the glory of the Fair City, and enthusiasm began to kindle in all directions. Our cricket club had played upon the Meadow as best it could; but now the Council of the city set apart a piece of ground, and six of the leading dignitaries paid to have it cut and rolled, so that there might be a good pitch for playing and something worth seeing on the day of battle. There were half a dozen good players in Muirtown in those days, two of whom were in the All Scotland eleven, and they used to come along in spare evenings and coach the boys, while the county professional now and again dropped in, just to see whether he could bowl Speug out, and after half an hour's hopeless attack upon that imperturbable youth, the professional declared the Seminary had a chance. But the word was passed round that there should be no boasting, and that Muirtown must be prepared for a hopeless and honourable defeat. Mr. McGuffie senior was the only man on the morning of the match who was prepared to bet on even terms, and his offers were refused by the citizens, first because betting was sinful, and, second, it was possible, though not likely, they might lose.

The Columbians came down as usual in a brake, with only two horses this time, and made a pretty show when they were dressed in their white flannels and school colours, and every one admitted that they were a good-looking and well-set-up eleven; they brought half a dozen other fellows with them, to help to cheer their victory and to keep their score, and a master to be umpire. The Seminary eleven were in all colours and such dress as commended itself to their taste. Robertson and Molyneux and one or two others in full flannels, but Speug in a grey shirt and a pair of tight tweed trousers of preposterous pattern, which were greatly admired by his father's grooms—and, for that matter, by the whole school; and although Jock Howieson had been persuaded into flannel bags, as we called them then, he stuck to a red shirt of outrageous appearance, which was enough to frighten any bowler. Jack Moncrieffe, the Muirtown cricket crack and bowler of the All Scotland, was umpire for the Seminary, and the very sight of him taught the first lesson of respect to the "Bumbees"; and when they learned that Jim Fleming, the other Muirtown crack, had been coaching the Seminary all the summer, they began to feel that it might be a real match, not merely a few lessons in the manly game of cricket given to encourage a common school, don't you know.

There was a representative turn-out of Muirtown men, together with a goodly sprinkling of Muirtown mothers and sisters. Bulldog took up his position early, just in front of the tent, and never moved till the match was over; nor did he speak, save once; but the Seminary knew that he was thinking plenty, and that the master of mathematics had his eye upon them. Some distance off, the Count—that faithful friend of his Seminary "dogs"—promenaded up and down a beat of some dozen yards, and spent the time in one long excitement, cheering with weird foreign accent when a good hit was made, swearing in French when anything went wrong, bewailing almost unto tears the loss of a Seminary wicket, and hurrying to shake hands with every one of his eleven, whether he had done well or ill, when he came in from the wicket. Mr. McGuffie moved through the crowd from time to time, and finally succeeded in making a bet on the most advantageous terms with that eminent dignitary, the Earl of Kilspindie's coachman, who was so contemptuous of the Seminary from the Castle point of view that he took the odds of five to one in sovereigns that they would be beaten. And on the outskirts of the crowd, half ashamed to be there and doubtful of his reception, hovered Bailie MacConachie.

The Seminary won the toss, and by the advice of Jim Fleming sent the Columbians in, and there was no Seminary lad nor any Muirtown man, for the Frenchman did not count—who denied that the strangers played a good, clean game—pretty form, and brave scoring ; and on their part the Columbians were not slow to acknowledge that the Seminary knew how to field, wherever they had learned it. No ball sliding off the bat, could pass Dunc Robertson, and as for byes they were impossible with Speug as long-stop, for those were the days when there were long-stops. Cosh had his faults, and they were not few, but the Seminary thought more of him after a miraculous catch which he made at long-off; and Bauldie, at square-leg, might not be able to prevent a two occasionally, but he refused to allow fours. Jock Howieson was a graceless bowler and an offence to the eye, but his balls were always in the line of the middle stump, and their rate that of an express train; and Nestie not only had a pretty style, but a way of insinuating himself among the wickets which four Columbians had not the power to refuse. There was a bit of work at long-field, which even the Columbians could not help cheering, though it lost them a wicket, and the way in which a ball was sent up from cover-point to Dunc Robertson, and so took another wicket, wrung a word of private praise from the Columbian umpire. Still, the Seminary was fighting against heavy odds, an uphill, hopeless battle, and when the visitors went out with a hundred and one to their score, Mr. McGuffie senior was doubtful of his sovereign; and only the Count prophesied triumph, going round and shaking hands individually with every one of his "dogs," and magnifying their doings unto the sky. Bailie MacConachie, by this time was lost in the crowd, working his way gradually to the front, and looking as if he would have liked to cheer, but thinking it better not to call attention to his presence. Then the Seminary went in, and there is no question but that they had hard times at the hands of the Columbians, who were well trained and played all together. Robertson, who was the hope of the Seminary, went out for twenty, and Bauldie for ten ; Nestie played carefully, but only managed twelve, and the other fellows were too easily bowled or caught out, each adding something, but none doing much, till at last the score stood at sixty-nine, with the last two of the Seminary in.   Things were looking very black, and even the Count was dashed, while Bulldog's face suggested that next Monday the whole school would be thrashed, and that a special treat would be reserved for the eleven.   Mr. McGuffie, however, with a sportsman's instinct, seized the opportunity to make another bet with his lordship's coachman, and increased the odds from five to ten, and the dignitary declared it was simply robbing McGuffie of his money.

" We'll see aboot that, my man, when the horses pass the line.   I've seen many a race changed before the finish," and Mr. McGuffie took his position in the front row to see the end.

Thirty-three runs to make to win the match, and only one wicket to fall, and the Columbians discounted their victory in a gentlemanly fashion, while Jim Fleming looked very grave.   " Give them no chances," he said to Howieson, as that stolid youth went in to join Speug, who had been at the wicket for some time, but had only scored ten.   Any over might close the match, and perhaps the Columbians' bowlers grew careless, for three overs passed and the

two friends of many a scrimmage were still in, and
neither of them had shown any intention of going
out. Quite the contrary, for Speug had broken into
fours, and Howieson, who played with the graceful-
ness of a cow, would allow no ball to interfere with
his wickets, and had run up a couple of twos on his
own account.

"Juist beginnin'," said Speug's father. "Him oot
sune? I tell you he's settlin' down for the afternoon
and that laddie Howieson is a dour deevil. The fact
is "—Mr. McGuffie took a circle of spectators into
his confidence—" they're juist gettin' into the stride."
The Count preened his plumage and plucked up
heart again, while the Seminary lads, gathered in a
solid mass to the left of the tent, were afraid to
cheer lest they should invite defeat, and, while they
pretended unconcern, could feel their hearts beating.
"They couldn't be better matched," said Nestie.
"Speug and Jock—they've had l-lots of things in
hand together, and they'll d-do it yet. See!" and at
that moment Speug sent a ball to the boundary.
Now there were only seventeen, instead of thirty-three
runs to make.

They were playing a game of the utmost carefulness,
blocking the balls which were dangerous and could
not be played; declining to give the faintest chance
of a catch, and taking a run short rather than be run
out, and so the score crept up with a two from
Howieson, who had got into a habit of twos, and

being a phlegmatic youth, kept to it, and a three and a four from Speug, and another two from Howieson, and a three from Speug.

Across the heads of the people McGuffie shouted to the coachman, " Take you again, Petrie—ten to one, five to one, three to one against the Seminary ? " And when there was no answer, Mr. McGuffie offered to take it even from anybody, and finally appealed to the man, next him. It was Bailie MacConachie, who forgetful of the past and everything except the glory of Muirtown, was now standing beside Speug's father and did not care. " Speug's no dead yet Bailie"; and then, catching the look in MacConachie's face, " bygones are bygones, we're a' Muirtown men the day " ; and then his voice rose again across the crowd, " I'll give ye odds, coachman—two to one against the ' Bumbees,' " for Howieson had scored another two, and two more runs would win the match for the Seminary.

Then a terrible thing happened, for Howieson, instead of stopping the ball with his bat, must needs stop it with his leg. " How's that ? " cried the Columbian wicket-keeper, " how's that, umpire ? " Was his leg before wicket or not ? And for the moment every one, Seminary and Columbian, Bulldog, McGuffie, Bailie, men, women and children, held their breath. It would have been maddening to have been beaten only by one run, and after such a gallant fight.

"Not out!" replied the umpire in two seconds; but it seemed ten minutes, and a yell went up from the throats of the Seminary, and Bailie MacConachie took off his hat and wiped his forehead, which Mr. McGuffie noted with sympathy and laid up to the Bailie's credit. There was another crisis at hand which had been forgotten by Muirtown, but it was very keenly present to the minds of the Columbians. One over more and the time limit would be reached and the game closed. If the Seminary could make two runs, they would win; if the Columbians could get Speug's wicket, they would win. They put on their most dangerous man, whose ball had a trick of coming down just six inches in front of the block, and then, having escaped the attention of the batsman, of coming perilously near the wicket. His attack compelled the most watchful defence, and hardly allowed the chance of a run. Two balls Speug blocked, but could do no more with them; the third got past and shaved the wicket; the fourth Speug sent to slip but the fielding allowed no run; the fifth, full of cunning, he stopped with difficulty, and fear seized the heart of Muirtown that the last would capture the wickets and give the victory to the visitors. And it was the cleverest of all the balls, for it was sent to land inside the block, just so much nearer as might deceive the batsman accustomed to the former distance. No sooner had it left the bowler's hand than Fleming saw the risk and gnawed his moustache. Every eye followed the ball through the air on what seemed, for the anxiety of it, a course of miles. The Columbians drew together unconsciously in common hope. Robertson, the Seminary captain, dug his right heel into the ground, and opposite, between the field and the river, the leader of that rapscallion school, the " Pennies," stood erect, intent, open-mouthed with his crew around, for once silent and motionless. Speug took a swift stride forward and met the ball nearly three feet from the ground, and, gathering up all the strength in his tough little body, he caught that ball on the middle of the bat and sent it over square-leg's head, who had come in too near and made one hopeless clutch at it, and through the ranks of the " Pennies," who cleared out on every side to let it pass as they had never yielded to Speug himself; and ere Muirtown had found voice to cheer, the red-haired varlet who ruled the "Pennies" had flung his bonnet, such as it was, into the air, for, the ball was in the river, and the Seminary had won by three runs and one wicket.

Things happened then which are beyond the pen of man, but it was freely said that the " Hurrah " of Bull-dog, master of mathematics, drowned the hunting-cry of Mr. McGuffie, and that when the Count, in his joy over the victory of his " jolly dogs," knocked off Bailie MacConachie's hat, and would have apologised, the Bailie kicked his own hat in triumph. This is certain, that the Seminary carried Speug and Howieson, both protesting, from the North Meadow, in through the big school door ; that Bulldog walked at the head of the procession, like a general coming home in his glory ; that he insisted on the Bailie walking with him ; that, after all the cheering was over, Speug proposed one cheer more for Bailie MacConachie, and that when the eleven departed for Bulldog's house for supper half the Seminary escorted the Bailie home.

XVI

BULLDOG'S RECOMPENSE

WHEN the rumour flew through Muirtown in spring that Bulldog was to resign at the close of the summer term it was laughed to scorn, and treated as an agreeable jest. Had it been the rector who was more a learned ghost than a human being, or the English master who had grown stout and pursy, or some of the other masters who came and went like shadows, Muirtown had not given another thought to the matter, but Bulldog retiring, it was a very facetious idea, and Muirtown held its sides. Perhaps it was delicate health was the cause; and then Dr. Manley stormed through half Muirtown, declaring that he had never known Dugald MacKinnon have an hour's sickness except once when that little scoundrel Speug, or rather he should say Sir Peter McGuffie, consulting physician, brought his master through triumphantly with a trifle of assistance from himself as a general practitioner. Was it old age that ailed Bulldog? Then Bailie MacConachie was constrained to testify in public places, and was supported by all the other Bailies except MacFarlane, who got his education at Drumtochty, that the mathematical master of Muirtown Academy had thrashed them all as boys, every man jack of them, being then not much older than themselves, and that he was now—barring his white hair—rather fresher than in the days of their youth? Had success departed at last from the mathematical class-room, after resting there as in a temple of wingless victory for three generations? Was it not known everywhere that William Pirie, whose grandfather was a senior pupil when Bulldog took the reins fifty-eight years ago, had simply romped through Edinburgh University gathering medals, prizes, bursaries, fellowships, and everything else that a mathematician could lay his hands on, and then had won a scholarship at Trinity College, Cambridge, with papers that were talked about in the College for fourteen days, and were laid past by one examiner as a treasure of achievement. May be, and this was no doubt the very heart of the jest, Bulldog had lost control of the boys, and his right hand had forgotten its cunning! So the boys were insulted in their homes by sympathetic inquiries as to when they had their last interview with the tawse and whether the canings were as nippy as ever, for Muirtown was proud to think that its favourite master was an expert in every branch of his calling and dealt with the grandchildren as thoroughly as

he had done with the grandfathers. And Bailie
MacFarlane meeting Bulldog crossing the bridge
one morning as alert in step and austere in countenance as ever, asked him how he was keeping with
affected sympathy, and allowed himself the luxury
of a chuckle as one who has made a jocose
remark.

It came therefore with a shock to Muirtown when
the following letter was read in the Town Council
and was known next morning to every citizen from
the Procurator Fiscal to London John.

*To the Lord Provost, the Bailies, and the Council of
Muirtown.*

"GENTLEMEN,—I beg to resign, as from the
close of the present term, the position of Master
of Mathematics, Arithmetic and Writing, in Muirtown Seminary, and to thank the council for the
trust which they have placed in me for fifty-eight
years.

"I am, my Lord Provost and Gentlemen,
"Your obedient servant,
"DUGALD MACKINNON."

When Muirtown recovered itself a conflict began
between Bulldog and the citizens which lasted for
four intense weeks in which the town was at fever
heat and Bulldog was outwardly colder and calmer
than ever. And he won all along the line. The
Council passed a resolution of respectful admiration,

studded with stately adjectives, and for such a document almost heated in feeling, to which Mr. MacKinnon sent a courteous but guarded reply. The Council intimated that they would consider his letter to be non-existent, and not even put him to the trouble of withdrawing, and Mr. MacKinnon intimated to the Town Clerk that in that case he must trouble the Council with an exact copy. The Council then appointed a deputation to wait on him, and Mr. MacKinnon declared himself unworthy of such an unprecedented honour, and declined to see them. And then the Council, in despair, and with a sad sense of the inevitable, strained their powers to the utmost with immense unanimity, and voted a handsome pension to " Dugald MacKinnon, Esq., Master of Arts, in grateful, although unworthy recognition of the unbroken, unwearied, and invaluable service he has rendered to the education of this ancient city for a period of more than half a century, during which time nearly two thousand lads have been sent forth equipped for the practical business of life in Muirtown, in the great cities of our land and unto the ends of the earth." Mr. MacKinnon explained in a letter of perfect handwriting that he was quite undeserving of such a resolution, as he had done nothing more than his duty, and that he could not accept any retiring allowance—first, because he was not sure that it was strictly legal, and, secondly, because he had made provision for

his last years, but on this occasion he signed himself
"Your most obliged servant." It was then deter-
mined to entertain this obdurate man at a banquet,
and to make a presentation of plate to him. And
Mr. MacKinnon was again most grateful for the
kindness of his fellow citizens and the honour they
proposed to do him, but he clearly indicated he
would neither accept the banquet nor a piece of
plate. It dawned gradually upon Muirtown, a city
slow but sure of understanding, and with a silent
sense of the fitness of things, that Mr. Dugald
MacKinnon, having reigned like Cæsar Augustus for
fifty-eight years without contradiction and without
conciliation, giving no favours and receiving none,
but doing his part by the laddies of Muirtown with
all his strength of mind and conscience and right
arm, was not going to weaken at the end of his
career. For him to rise at the close of a dinner
and return thanks for a piece of plate would have
been out of keeping with his severe and lonely past,
and for him to be a pensioner, even of the Town
Council, would have been an indignity. He had
reigned longer and more absolutely than any master
in the annals of the Seminary, and to the last day
he had held the sceptre without flinching. As a
king, strong, uncompromising and invincible, he
would lay aside the purple, and disappear into private
life. And Muirtown was proud of Bulldog.

Bulldog had beaten the magistrates of Muirtown

in all their glory, and his fellow citizens united in
one enthusiastic body, but he had not yet settled
with the boys. They had not expressed in resolu-
tions or any other way their appreciation of their
master, and they had followed the futile attempts
of their parents with silent contempt. It was
wonderful that grown up people should be so far
left to themselves as to suppose that Bulldog, their
own Bulldog, would ever condescend to be dined
by Bailies and stand at the close of dinner like a
dithering idiot with a silver jug in his hands, or
some such trash, while his hands were itching to
thrash every one of his hosts as he had thrashed
them long ago. When the boys heard their fathers
raging at Bulldog's proud obstinacy they offered no
remark, but when they got together they chortled
with glee, and felt that there was comfort and
compensation for many an honest thrashing, in the
fact that Bulldog was as much ruler of Muirtown
as he had been of the Seminary. No rebellion
against him had ever had the faintest gleam of
hope, and no rebel had ever escaped without his
just punishment, but the boys, rascals to the last
and full of devilry, agreed together by an instinct
rather than a conference that they would close
Bulldog's last term with a royal insurrection. He
had governed them with an iron hand, and they
had been proud to be governed, considering the
wounds of Bulldog ten thousand times more de-

sirable than the kisses of McIntyres', but they would
have one big revenge and then Bulldog and his
"fiddlers" would part for ever. They held long
confabulations together in the Rector's class-room
while that learned man was reading aloud some new
and specially ingenious translation of an ode, and
in the class-room of modern languages, while Moossy's
successor was trying to teach Jock Howieson how
to pronounce a modified U, in the German tongue,
in Mrs. McWhae's tuck-shop when the "gundy"
allowed them to speak at all, and at the Russian
guns where they gathered in the break instead of
playing rounders. The junior boys were not admitted to those mysterious meetings, but were told
to wait and see what they would see, and whatever
plan the seniors formed not a word of it oozed out
in the town. But the Seminary was going to do
something mighty, and Bulldog would repent the
years of his tyranny.

Funds were necessary for the campaign, since it
was going to be a big affair, and Speug directed
that a war chest should at once be established. No
one outside the secret junta knew what was going
to be done with the money, but orders were issued
that by hook or crook every boy in school except
the merest kids should pay sixpence a week to
Jock Howieson, who was not an accomplished
classical scholar nor specially versed in geometry,
but who could keep the most intricate accounts in

his head with unerring accuracy, and knew every
boy in the Seminary by head mark. And although
he was not a fluent speaker, he was richly endowed
with other powers of persuasion, and he would be
a very daring young gentleman indeed, and almost
indifferent to circumstances, who did not pay his
sixpence to Jock before set of sun each Monday.
Jock made no demands, and gave no receipts; he
engaged in no conversation whatever, but simply
waited and took. If any one tried to compound
with Jock for threepence, one look at the miserable
produced the sixpence; and when little Cosh following in the devious steps of his elder brother in-
sinuated that he had paid already, Jock dropped
him into the lade to refresh his memory. No one
directly inquired what was to be done with the
money, for every one knew it was safe with Jock,
and that it would be well spent by the mighty four
who now ruled the school : Jock, Bauldie, Nestie,
and Speug—Dunc Robertson after a brief course at
Sandhurst having got his commission in his father's
regiment. And it was also known that every halfpenny was going to give a big surprise to Bulldog,
so the boys, during those weeks treated their fathers
with obsequious respect for commercial reasons, and
coaxed additional pennies out of their mothers on
every false pretence, and paid endearing visits to
maiden aunts, and passed Mrs. McWhae's shop,
turning away their eyes and noses from vanity, and

sold to grinding capitalists their tops, marbles, young
rabbits, and kites ; and "as sure as death" every
Monday the silent but observant treasurer received
for eight weeks £5 4s., at the rate of sixpence a
head, from 208 boys.   They kept their secret like
an oyster, and there was not one informer among
the 208 ; but curiosity grew hot, and there were many
speculations, and it was widely believed that the
money would be used in sending a cane of the
most magnificent proportions to Bulldog, as a remembrance of his teaching days, and a mark of
respect from his pupils.   One boy, being left to
himself, dared to suggest this to Speug ; and when
he looked round at some distance off, Speug's eye
was still upon him, and he declared from his experience that it was not healthy to question Speug.
Two hundred and four boys, however, with the
observant faculties of Indian scouts, and intent upon
discovery could not be altogether baffled, and various
bits of reliable information were passed round the
school.   That the four had gone one evening into
Bailie MacConachie's, who was now on terms of high
popularity with the school ; that the Count who was
even then sickening for his death, and Mr. McGuffie
whom nothing but an accident could kill, had also
been present ; that at different times the Count
had been seen examining the gold watches in
Gillespie's shop, whose watches were carried by every
man of standing in the Scots Midlands, and pro-

nouncing his judgement on their appearance with
vivacious gestures ; that the Bailie had been seen
examining the interior of a watch with awful
solemnity while Councillor Gillespie hung upon his
decision ; and, to crown all, that Mr. McGuffie senior,
after a lengthy interview with the head of the firm,
during which he had given him gratuitous advice
on three coming races, had left Gillespie's, declaring
with pronounced language that if certain persons did
not obtain certain things for £40 he, Mr. McGuffie,
although not a person given to betting, would wager
ten to one that the place of business would close
in a year. It was whispered therefore in the corridors, with some show of truth, that the Seminary
was going to take vengeance on Bulldog with a gift,
and that the gift, whatever it might be, was lying
in Gillespie's shop. And the school speculated
whether there was any one of their number, even
Speug himself, who would dare to face Bulldog with
a gift ; and whether, if he did, that uncompromising
man might not occupy his last week of mastership
in thrashing the school one by one, from the oldest
unto the youngest, for their blazing impertinence.

The closing day was a Thursday that year, and
it was characteristic of Bulldog that he met his
classes as usual on Wednesday, and when Howieson
disgraced himself beyond usual in Euclid, having
disgraced himself more moderately on four preceding
days that he administered discipline on Jock with

conscientious severity. Jock was the last boy Bulldog thrashed, and he was so lifted up as to be
absolutely unendurable for the rest of the day, and
boasted of the distinction for many a year. As four
o'clock approached, the boys began to grow restless,
and Bulldog's own voice was not perfectly steady
when he closed the last problem with Q. E. D.

"Q. E. D.; yes, Q. E. D., laddies, we have carried
the argument to its conclusion according to the
principles of things, and the book is finished. There
is still seven minutes of the hour remaining, we will
spend it in revising the work of the Senior Algebra
Class."

Their work has not been revised unto this day, for
at that moment the door opened without any one
knocking, and without any one offering an apology,
and William Pirie, Master of Arts of Edinburgh,
and scholar of Trinity College, Cambridge, and
Duncan Robertson, 2nd Lieutenant in the Perthshire
Buffs, made their appearance, accompanied by Bailie
MacConachie, whose dignity was fearsome ; the Count,
who waved his hand gracefully to the school, and
Mr. McGuffie, who included everybody in an affable
nod ; and behind this imposing deputation every boy
of Muirtown Seminary who was not already in the
mathematical class-room. Bulldog turned upon them
like a lion caught in a snare, and if he had had only
thirty seconds preparation, it is firmly believed he
would have driven the whole deputation, old and

young, out of the class-room and dealt with the conspirators who remained unto the setting of the sun. But it was a cunning plot, arranged and timed with minute care, and before Bulldog could say a word Pirie had begun, and he knew better than to say much.

"If we have offended you, sir, you will pardon us for it is our last offence, and we have this time a fair excuse. Your laddies could not let you leave that desk and go out of this room for the last time without telling you that they are grateful, because you have tried to make them scholars, and to make them men. If any of us be able in after years to do our part well, we shall owe it more than anything else to your teaching and your discipline."

Then Robertson, who was the other spokesman the four had chosen, began.

"Can't make a speech, sir, it is not in my line, but everything Pirie said is true, and we are proud of our chief."

"This," said Pirie, turning to the boys, "is the watch and chain which we ask the master to do us the honour of wearing through the days to come, and the inscription, sir," and now Pirie turned to the desk, "crowns our offence, but you will know how to read it!"

"TO BULLDOG,

WITH THE RESPECT AND AFFECTION

OF

HIS LADDIES."

It was Bailie MacConachie—may everything be pardoned to him—who started the cheer; but it was Mr. McGuffie who led it over hedge and ditch, and it was of such a kind that the mathematical class-room had to be repaired before the beginning of the next term. During the storm Bulldog stood with the watch in his hand, and his cheeks as white as his hair, and when at last there was silence he tried to speak, but the tender heart had broken the iron mask, and all he could say was "laddies."

The Count, with quick tact, led off the second cheer, and the boys filed out of the class-room. Bulldog sat down at the desk, the watch before him, and covered his face with his hands. When an hour later he walked across the North Meadow there was not a boy to be seen but Bailie MacFarlane, who met him on the bridge (and passed without speaking), noticed that Bulldog was wearing his laddies' gift.

Sitting in his garden that evening and looking down upon the plain, Bulldog called Nestie to his side, and pointed to the river. The evening sun was shining on the fields, ripening for harvest, and on the orchards, laden with fruit; and in the soft light, a rough weather-beaten coaster, which had fought her way through many a gale in the North Sea, and could not hold together much longer, was dropping down with the tide. Newer and swifter vessels would take her place in the days to come, but the old craft had done her work well and faithfully, and now the cleanest and kindest of Scots rivers was carrying her gently to the eternal ocean.